PLAYING
LOVE'S REFRAIN

What Reviewers Say About Lesley Davis's Work

Playing With Fire

"Strong, mature characters embracing their feelings (good, bad and indifferent). An awfully attractive African-American MC, Takira Lathan. Dealing head-on with stereotypes. Good chemistry. A lovely relationship wherein the MCs talk to each other about themselves, their insecurities, their feelings and even what they like sexually. This book has a lot going for it."—*Reviewer@large*

"First of all, this book is a total geek dream. …This book was packed with tropes, like seriously all the best ones, and had everything from references, to cute moments inspired by making sure we all believe in a little bit of magic. It was uplifting and just added a little something extra to this story, like the right ingredients in a secret sauce."—*LESBIreviewed*

Raging at the Stars

"*Raging at the Stars* is a very entertaining and engaging read. The alien invasion storyline—with a twist—is very original and the plot is very well developed. The two leads are very likeable and the supporting characters are equally interesting. The author's style of writing is very engaging, especially the witty dialogue."
—Melina Bickard, Librarian, Waterloo Library (London)

"A sci-fi book with a side of romance and a hint of aliens (Or is there really a hint? What else could be going on?). Anyway, it's basically my perfect book, and I thought it was totally awesome."
—Danielle Kimerer, Librarian, Nevins Memorial Public Library (MA)

"I am 800% here for this book. It reminded me of a fun mashup of *X-Files* and *Independence Day*, with lesbians, and honestly, I can't think of anything cooler at this moment. ...I'll definitely track down more of Davis's titles. Definitely recommend."—*Kissing Backwards: Lesbian Book Reviews*

Playing in Shadow

"*Playing in Shadow* is different from my typical romance reading, but at the same time exactly the same. I loved the two main characters and the secondary characters. The issues they all face were realistic and handled really well. ...I do not often read LGBT romance, but thus far every time I have I have been thrilled with how fantastic the writing is. I guess I need to read more!"—Sharon Tyler, Librarian, Cheshire Public Library (CT)

"Overall this was an amazing read, great and engaging story, and as it progresses adding layers to the characters and the complexity of their struggles it starts to consume a little bit of your heart making you wish this was a Saga and not just one story."—*Collector of Book Boyfriends*

"The story is emotional and feels very honest. You won't miss out on the romance either, with equal parts of 'Awe, that's so sweet!' and 'Whoa, Steamy!'"—Katie Larson, Librarian, Tooele City Public Library (Utah)

Starstruck

"Both leads were well developed with believable backgrounds and Mischa was a delight. It was nice to 'run into' Trent and Elton from the author's previous book."—Melina Bickard, Librarian, Waterloo Library (London)

"Away with the Faeries" in *Women of the Dark Streets*

"Wondrous three-way duel between vampires, werewolves and faeries. The ending had me bowled over and howling with laughter. Grandiose!"—*Rainbow Book Reviews*

Truth Behind the Mask

"It is rare to find good lesbian science fantasy. It is also rare to have a deaf lesbian heroine. Davis has given readers both in *Truth Behind the Mask*. In her tightly wrapped novel, Davis vividly describes the feeling of the night wind and the heat of the fires. She is just as deft at describing the blossoming love between Pagan and Erith, two of her main characters. *Truth Behind the Mask* has enough intriguing twists and turns to keep the pages flying right to the exciting conclusion."—*Just About Write*

Playing Passion's Game

"*Playing Passion's Game* is a delightful read with lots of twists, turns, and good laughs. Davis has provided a varied and interesting supportive cast. Those who enjoy computer games will recognize some familiar scenes, and those new to the topic get to learn about a whole new world."—*Just About Write*

Pale Wings Protecting

"*Pale Wings Protecting* is a provocative paranormal mystery; it's an otherworldly thriller couched inside a tale of budding romance. The novel contains an absorbing narrative, full of thrilling revelations, that skillfully leads the reader into the uncanny dimensions of the supernatural."—*Lambda Literary Review*

"[*Pale Wings Protecting*] was just a delicious delight with so many levels of intrigue on the case level and the personal level. Plus, the celestial and diabolical beings were incredibly intriguing. ...I was riveted from beginning to end and I certainly will look forward to additional books by Lesley Davis. By all means, give this story a total once-over!"—*Rainbow Book Reviews*

Dark Wings Descending—*Lambda Literary Award Finalist*

"[*Dark Wings Descending*] is an intriguing story that presents a vision of life after death many will find challenging. It also gives the reader some wonderful sex scenes, humor, and a great read!" —*Reviewer RLynne*

Visit us at www.boldstrokesbooks.com

By the Author

Truth Behind the Mask

Playing Passion's Game

Playing In Shadow

Starstruck

Raging at the Stars

Playing With Fire

In The Spotlight

Playing Love's Refrain

The Wings Series

Dark Wings Descending

Pale Wings Protecting

White Wings Weeping

PLAYING LOVE'S REFRAIN

by

Lesley Davis

2022

PLAYING LOVE'S REFRAIN
© 2022 By Lesley Davis. All Rights Reserved.

ISBN 13: 978-1-63679-286-6

This Trade Paperback Original Is Published By
Bold Strokes Books, Inc.
P.O. Box 249
Valley Falls, NY 12185

First Edition: December 2022

Credits
Editor: Cindy Cresap
Production Design: Susan Ramundo
Cover Design By Tammy Seidick

Acknowledgments

Radclyffe, I'm so happy my writing journey is with BSB. This will be my eleventh book with you. Here's to many more.

Sandy Lowe, thank you for all your help, guidance, and endless enthusiasm.

Cindy Cresap, thank you for always making the editing process a wonderful learning experience and not leaving me feeling like Grogu, in the Razor Crest's crawl space, armed with red and blue wires and no clue where they go!

Tammy Seidick, thank you for a most striking cover!! It totally rocks!

Always, always, a huge thank you to my readers who keep messaging me for more of Trent and her clan! (Yes, she's in this one!!) And to my friends whose support keeps me sitting at my laptop telling these tales.

Jane Morrison
Pam Goodwin and Gina Paroline
Kim and Tracy Palmer-Bell (Kim, there's a store in here we'd
    happily spend all day in!)
Cheryl and Anne Hunter
Annie Ellis and Julia Lowndes (Congrats on your wedding!! xx)
Donna and Jools Chidley-Gosling (for your constant support
    and geeky chats!)
Kerry Pfadenhauer (I told you I'd give us a Whovian!)

And to Cindy Pfannenstiel, thank you for supporting every story that I write. I couldn't ask for a better beta reader or best friend. xx

Dedication

To those amazing people who weave words to beautiful melodies. (Something I am in total awe of, being someone who could only play one piece on the violin because I learnt it by heart as the music sheet may as well have been in hieroglyphics)

To my musical trinity—Kate Bush, my one and always

Taylor Swift—who makes me wish I were younger so I could dance to every bop without fear of putting my back out

And in loving memory of Olivia Newton-John who made me believe that we could be magic.

CHAPTER ONE

Drew Dawes loved the smell of new comic books. A delivery had arrived and, like a child at Christmas, Drew was poring over each new box with barely restrained excitement. She found the treasure she was looking for when she opened the last box. She ran her fingers reverently over the latest *Doctor Who* comic book. She quickly laid one aside for herself then placed the rest on the shelf showcasing the new arrivals. It didn't take long for her to have everything displayed and the boxes ready for recycling.

Drew checked her watch; it was nearly time for opening. She cast an exacting gaze around her store. Rows of comic books filled a sizable portion of the store floor. Glass cases lined the walls, housing expensive statues of superheroes and fantasy characters. Highly collectible Funko Pops took up a whole wall of their own. Posters decorated the entire store. Captain America stood alongside Black Panther, Captain Marvel with Wonder Woman, and Black Widow beside the garishly visaged Harley Quinn. Spaceships and a large Superman in flight hung from the ceiling. The combined power on display gave Drew comfort and a sense of peace. This store was her dream, her safe place, her life. Every morning she had the same routine in preparation for receiving her steady stream of customers. Others, like her, who were fascinated by the stories told in the comic books and graphic novels that lined the shelves. Ones who loved the worlds of science fiction, fantasy, and the fantastic heroes and heroines who inhabited those worlds. Drew ate, slept, and breathed the worlds of fantasy. She had long acknowledged they played a large part in keeping her sane.

"Is this music from that Michelle Pfeiffer movie you love so much? The one where she's just a young thing and that skinny guy from *Blade Runner* is with her?"

Drew looked over at the counter where her grandma, Mae Dawes, stood, head cocked as she listened to the strains of the *Ladyhawke* soundtrack playing softly through the speakers.

"Yes, Grandma. The one where she's a hawk and he's a wolf because an evil priest has cursed them never to be together." Drew had a soft spot for the old eighties film, and not just for how beautiful Michelle Pfeiffer was in it.

"You're such a romantic," her grandma said with a fond smile. "You get that from your grandpa. Arthur always knew how to romance a girl."

Drew gave her grandma a rueful smile. "Sadly, it's not a trait I've had much use for."

"Well, you just need to step outside this store more often. You can't expect the love of your life to come walking through that door to find you. Especially as the majority of your customers are teenage boys, which has never been your thing." Her grandma chuckled to herself. "And that, I think, you get from me. But like I was saying, sometimes you have to take that first step and put yourself out there."

Drew straightened a comic book in its pile. She'd heard this conversation a million times. "I don't have the time. This store won't run itself."

"Just one night a week, then. One night where you go out and show the world how cool you are."

Drew bit back a grin at the word "cool." That was the last thing she'd ever be. "And who'd look after you while I was out?"

"I don't need a babysitter. You can leave me in front of the TV with a beer and a bag of Lay's. I'd be no trouble. I've got that grabby thing you brought me in case I drop the remote on the floor." Her grandma held Drew's gaze. "Think about it, please. Make this old woman happy."

"I hate it when you play the age card."

"I'm seventy-four years old, Drew, when else am I going to use it to my advantage?"

Drew shook her head at her. "And I'm thirty-one. I've still got time to settle down should I choose to. I've got that convention coming up soon. I'll be out all weekend with a whole ton of people. Will that satisfy your need for me to socialize?"

"Only if you come home with a pretty lass and not one dressed as Harley Quinn with shorts so tight they show off her unmentionables!"

Drew laughed at her grandma's scandalized face. "I'll bear that in mind."

"You need to get out and dance a little, flirt a little, romance the ladies, and find your dream girl."

Drew narrowed her eyes at her grandma as she started rummaging under the counter. The music stopped abruptly. "Grandma...." she warned her.

"Don't make me have to bring out the big guns." Her grandma grinned as she held a CD up as if it were a lethal weapon.

"Don't you dare..." Drew regretted the day she'd shown her grandma how to work the stereo equipment for the store.

"Oh, my goodness, this disc just popped out of the player. I guess I need to put it back in," her grandma said, her innocent tone ruined by a wicked grin she did little to disguise.

Drew braced herself for what was coming. Her grandma had little regard for routine and structure. She loved spontaneity and loud music. Drew closed her eyes in defeat as the familiar intro to a boisterous pop song began.

"Goddammit, Grandma. I'm going to have that damn song in my head all day now!" Drew whined as the joyous strains of Olivia Newton-John singing "Xanadu" pounded out around the store.

"There's nothing like a bit of Olivia to start your day off right." Her grandma busted out a little shimmy as best she could while holding herself up with her ever-present walking stick. She sang along with Olivia for a while, blew Drew a kiss, then ambled out to go back to the apartment they lived in above the store. The sounds of "Xanadu" drowned out the sound of the stair lift taking her grandma back upstairs.

Drew sighed but let the music play on. She made sure her grandma was out of hearing range and only then did she begin to sing quietly to the lyrics she knew by heart. This was her grandma's favorite song from her favorite movie. Drew had watched it with her as a child more times than she could remember. It was a movie with a positive message, a rarity in the cinematic world. The movie suited her grandma to a T, especially the theme song. It was loud, boisterous, colorful, and hard to forget. It was an anthem, a call to believers to take the hand of their muse and follow their dreams.

Drew wandered back to the stereo as the song played out its glorious conclusion in a mass of synthesizers, strings, and the unmatchable sweet voice of Olivia. Shaking her head, Drew carefully put the CD back in its case and tried to hide it again behind the stack of CDs that were under the desk. She knew her grandma would still find it.

Drew slipped in a new CD to play. She cast one last look around the store, satisfying herself everything was in place, and only then did she look outside. There was already a line forming of her regular customers. New comic book day was the best day *ever*.

She opened the door to usher them in. "Greetings, fellow geeks. Welcome to Dawes & Destiny Comics."

Florencia "Wren" Banderas loved the sound of a busy kitchen. The steady thrum of burners firing under pans, the sound of utensils tapping out their own rhythm against steel pans. It was all music to her ears. She'd been working all day to the sound of this symphony. The loud clang of a metal tray tossed haphazardly on top of another, however, jarred her out of her zen-like mood. She leveled narrowed eyes at the culprit.

Zenya grinned at her unrepentantly. "Wakey wakey, Chef. Your shift is over. Get out of here before you're sucked in with the barbeque crowd."

Wren's boss, Takira Lathan, popped her head around the back door. Her face lit up when she saw Wren was still in the kitchen. "Perfect. Wren, before you head off home, can you do me a favor?"

Zenya smirked and sidled past Wren to go back to her own worktable. "I told you to skedaddle while you had the chance," she said for Wren's ears alone.

Wren gathered up her bag and slipped her jacket on before hastening to see what Takira needed. She found her outside tending to the barbeque with a few of the other staff helping out. The smell of meat cooking and the rich tang of the barbeque sauce made her mouth water. The harsh growl from her stomach reminded her she hadn't stopped for lunch again. With cheery hellos to everyone, Wren eased her way around the customers waiting in line.

Takira was packing up a box of ribs. She placed it into a paper bag and handed it to Wren. "Would you be an angel and slip this next door for Mae? She's not feeling too good today and she never misses out on BBQ Friday."

Wren took the box. "That's the old lady with the wheelchair, right?" Wren had only been working at Takira's for two months, but she was pretty good at remembering faces.

Takira nodded. "She lives above the comic book store." She loaded another box and bagged it for Wren. "And this is for you. I am well aware you worked through lunch again to help us cope with the office party that came in, celebrating their new client."

Wren recognized Takira's tone of voice. It was the chastising one she used on her little son, Finn. It was the tone that said she wasn't exactly mad, more exasperated.

Wren felt her shoulders rise up to her ears with embarrassment. "I just want to do a good job."

"You're doing an excellent job. I couldn't have picked anyone better to take my place in the restaurant. I'd just rather you took time to grab a break when you can so you don't pass out from exhaustion and I have to step over your body in the kitchen." Takira wagged a finger at her. "Don't make me sic Dante on you."

Dante Groves was the manager of Takira's and Takira's devoted partner in romance. She was the butchest woman Wren had ever seen and she'd been a little intimidated by her at first. She quickly came to realize Dante was a first-class manager, very easy to talk to, and an absolute teddy bear when it came to her love for Takira and Finn.

Wren didn't want to disappoint either of her employers when they were so good to her. "I'll try and get more of a routine in place for self-care." She held up her bag of food. "These will help immensely. Thank you."

Takira pointed over the fence to the left. "Say hi to Mae for me. Tell her we miss her."

Wren took a leisurely walk around the large restaurant and headed next door. She stopped for a moment to actually pay attention to the store's frontage and see what the windows were displaying. She was usually too busy heading into work to pay any notice to the buildings surrounding the restaurant.

"Dawes & Destiny Comics." She read the sign out loud to herself and was admiring the *Star Wars* display in the window when the front door swung open, nearly hitting her. Wren jumped back just in time to avoid a collision. The teenager who stepped out had his head down in his comic bag, too busy looking at his purchases to have noticed Wren standing on the other side of the glass. His eyes widened when he realized what had nearly happened and his face turned bright red. He mumbled apologies in a puberty-laden voice. His gaze lifted to stray over Wren and stalled at her chest before darting back to her face. Wren was surprised to see he could turn even redder. She watched him trip over his own feet at the sight of her.

"Sorry, miss, so sorry…" he muttered, clasping his comic bag to him and, head down, eyes averted, he quickly got out of her way.

Wren rolled her eyes. "Nerd," she muttered. Anyone would think he'd never seen a woman before. She pulled the door open and entered the store. The inside was a mass of bold colors and posters of men striking muscle poses.

Welcome to Nerd Central, she thought.

CHAPTER TWO

The store wasn't as huge as Takira's restaurant, but it was big enough to house more comic books than Wren had ever seen. She peered at the statues placed behind glass and barely recognized half of the characters on display. Wren didn't really have time for movies. For years she'd been too busy working her way through school, then training in a multitude of restaurants until, at the age of thirty, she'd reached her goal of working at one with a stellar reputation. One day Wren would strike out for a restaurant bearing her own name over the door, but for now she was happy earning her own reputation. Under Takira's guidance, as Wren took over the head chef's role. Takira had stepped down to devote more time to her family and her own projects and Wren had jumped at the chance to step into her shoes.

Wren leaned on the counter and rang the bell to get someone's attention. The hideously loud thud of someone's head connecting with the underside of the counter told her she'd achieved her objective. Wren grimaced in sympathy with the muffled groan and curse word that escaped from whoever was underneath. Wren wasn't sure who was going to surface from behind the counter, but the woman who stood up, gingerly rubbing at her head, wasn't at all what she expected. She was tall. She had at least four inches over Wren's more modest five foot four, causing Wren to tilt her head back a little to see her. She was blond, with her hair shaved in a fashionable fade with the top left just a little longer and tousled. It didn't help that she was rubbing at her scalp and messing up her hair even more as she tried to soothe the bump she'd received. Blue eyes looked at Wren and the smile was genuine, if a little pained.

"Sorry I startled you." Wren couldn't get over how handsome this woman was. Her face was slender, with a strong jawline, and a masculine air that Wren found very attractive. Her smile was beautiful, leaving Wren spellbound for a moment. She couldn't help but return it with one of her own. She just stared at this woman, tall and lean, wearing a black T-shirt emblazoned with a shiny gold Wonder Woman shield.

Oh boy, who knew geeks could be so damn gorgeous?

"Can I help you?"

Wren nearly swooned on the spot. Her voice, with just the hint of a drawl, did curious things to Wren's insides. She tried to tamp down the butterflies that were threatening to break free at just those four simple words. This woman was really too gorgeous to be real. Wren was smitten, and it took her a long moment to remember why she was in the store. She held up the bag of fragrant ribs.

"I have a delivery from Takira's for Mae."

The woman wrinkled her nose. "Ahh, that's what the smell is. Yeah, I don't usually allow food in the store. You guys usually bring Grandma's food to the back door, the one for the apartment upstairs." She reached over the counter for the bag. "But thank you. I'll go take these up for her."

"I didn't mean to stink up your store with barbeque ribs." Wren felt terrible and was only just realizing how strong the smell was coming from the two bags.

"Living next door to Takira's when it's barbeque night? There's no escaping it." The woman laughed then asked, "So are you the new delivery girl or something?"

"I am tonight, but I'm actually the new head chef." Wren stuck her hand out. "I'm Wren Banderas."

The woman took her hand and shook it. "Wow, definitely not a delivery girl. Sorry for demoting you. Hi, Chef Wren. I'm Drew Dawes. Welcome to my store."

Wren looked around her. She was impressed, even if this wasn't something she had much interest in. "I don't really know much about anything that's going on in here." She spotted a familiar face. "Him, I do know. That's Captain America. My ten-year-old niece has a massive crush on him. She's way too young to be eyeing men with that many muscles objectively." Wren leaned forward a bit as if imparting a secret. "When I was her age all I wanted to do was sit on a stool and watch my muffins rise through the oven door as they baked."

"So, you knew from an early age what you wanted to be?"

Wren nodded. "I was always destined to be a chef. My parents encouraged it because my papa was Spanish and my mama is Italian. Our world revolves around food. What about you? Were your parents prepared for you to own your own comic book store?"

Wren caught the brief glimpse of something flash in Drew's eyes. Pain? Anger? *Grief?* Wren wasn't sure and Drew had quickly lowered her eyes back to the food she held in her hands, effectively stopping Wren from seeing anything else.

"No, my parents had other plans for me, but when they died my grandma let me pick my own path to make." She shifted her shoulders a little as if ridding herself of something heavy. "So, if she wants to indulge in sticky sweet ribs every single Friday night, then she gets them." Drew stepped away from the counter. "I'd better go take these up to her. I don't want her yelling at me for letting them go cold."

Wren rattled her own bag. "I've got my own supper waiting. It's always nicer when it's food I didn't have to cook myself."

"It was nice to meet you, Wren." The smile Drew gave her made Wren's chest ache. It was so damn sweet.

"Maybe I'll see you next door," Wren said, knowing she had to leave but reluctant all the same to move away from Drew's presence.

"Maybe." Drew nodded. "Grandma sometimes sends me out with her menu choices for the day. Perhaps I'll see you living *your* dream."

"Maybe I'll slip you a piece of Takira's famous fruit pie." Her heart wept at the shy look of delight Drew gave her.

"I do have a sweet tooth, but don't let Dante catch you."

"I'll be extra sneaky and bring it to your back door so I don't get in trouble with the store owner again."

Drew laughed. "Or you could come in through the store. I'm sure she'd make an exception for you and pie."

"I'll remember that." Wren forced her feet to move. Her food was cooling rapidly and she was tired after a long day working but, suddenly, she didn't want to go home. She wanted to learn more about this woman and her fascination with comic books and superheroes. She wanted another moment to commit to memory the exact color of Drew's eyes, the cut of her jaw, and the shape of her lips. She wanted to see more of the large blue tattoo that covered Drew's forearm. She had no clue what it was, but the object floated in a starfield that looked almost real on Drew's skin.

In the end, she made herself leave, almost tripping as she turned abruptly on her heel. She chided herself. She was no better than the pimply adolescent who had left the store earlier. She said her good-byes and walked back to the restaurant parking lot to find her car. She blew out a deep breath when she finally sat down in her seat. It did little to calm her. It had been a long time since she'd reacted so fast and been so flustered over a woman. Working full-time at the restaurant left her very little time for socializing with even friends, let alone in searching for romance.

Maybe she should listen to what Takira had said about taking breaks and put it to good use. She wondered if she could tempt Drew into joining her on one. Nothing serious, just making new friends. Wren was new to the area, after all. And a friendly comic book store owner, who was too handsome for her own good, seemed like the perfect friend to get to know.

Wren caught sight of herself in the rearview mirror and made a face at herself. She quickly started the engine before someone she worked with reported to Takira that Wren was arguing with herself in the parking lot like a madwoman.

❖

Drew had already lowered the shutters outside and was giving the store inside one last check to make sure everything was secure. She turned out the lights and headed upstairs to her apartment. Drew let herself in and toe-heeled her Nikes off, leaving them by the door. She wrinkled her nose at the faint aroma of barbeque sauce still hanging in the air. Drew picked up the offending box and tiptoed past her grandma who was fast asleep on the sofa. Her glasses were slightly askew as she had half her face buried in a cushion. Her gentle snores made Drew smile. She loved the soft rasping noise. It meant her grandma was still with her.

Drew knew her grandma hated how much Drew worried about her. Her grandma's mobility was a great deal of trouble for her. She had a walking stick for around the apartment and a motorized mobility scooter to give her freedom and some semblance of independence outside. Drew had a stairlift installed so that her grandma could come and go as she wished. Her grandma had a busier social life than Drew had ever had. Once they'd moved into the store, Grandma had immediately taken herself around to their neighbors and introduced herself. She'd become a firm fixture at Takira's and had a weekly meetup with a group of other widows who loved good food and talkative company. Drew called them the Old Biddy Brigade, much to her grandma's amusement and promises to get them all sweatshirts with that emblazoned on them.

Her grandparents, Mae and Arthur Dawes, raised Drew after her parents died. Drew had been just twelve years old. A car accident had almost taken her grandma from her too. Her broken bones had finally mended, but the damage sustained had left her grandma permanently disabled. Her grandpa looked after Drew while Grandma was in the hospital, and then both he and Drew had cared for her once she was home. Drew missed her grandpa. He'd lived long enough to watch her graduate from high school. Then it had just been Drew and her grandma. Drew had been caring for her ever since. She never saw it as a chore. She held down a steady job and was a full-time care giver. She'd managed to make it work. Her grandma was the kindest, sweetest, most loving person Drew had ever known. Grandma's tenacity, cutting wit, and sheer determination not to let anything stop her from enjoying life made it easy.

"That cat of yours snores," her grandma grumbled into the cushion.

"We don't have a cat yet, Grandma. It's next on my to-do list."

"Well, I know for a fact it wasn't me snoring because I am way too ladylike for that." Grandma shifted to sit up a little and wiped at her face.

Drew snorted. Grandma totally outdid Drew in the flannel department. There wasn't a color she wouldn't wear, but it had to be flannel. Her flannel shirt was always tucked into her jeans so that her big belt buckle was on show. Drew always felt her grandma would have been more at home on a cattle farm than the wheat and vegetable one she and Grandpa had owned. Her hair was pure white now, cut short for convenience but still holding her natural curl. She was a handsome woman, and Drew knew she took more after her in looks than she had her parents. When Drew had told her she was a lesbian, her grandma had researched everything she could to make sure Drew felt supported. It was through learning the LGBTQ acronym that her grandma realized she had been bi all her life. She'd made a cake for them to share, decorated with rainbow candles, to celebrate both of them coming out.

Drew didn't know what she'd do without her.

"Did you enjoy your ribs?"

Grandma sighed and patted her stomach. "They were delicious as always. Wasn't it kind of Takira to send them tonight? I'd seen that Dante of hers this afternoon and told her I was having to miss a night because of my damned hip giving me hell."

"I swear, Grandma, you're the only one who gets food delivered without paying online or at the door for it. They just let you take your money round when you can. That's so unusual."

"They know I'm a good customer and, besides, it's not like they don't know where I live. Who brought them over?"

"Someone I hadn't seen before. She said she was new."

"A new girl?" Her grandma perked up at this. "They've taken on a few new staff. Was it a redhead?"

Drew shook her head. No, Wren had long brown hair, subtly layered throughout its length. The center parting framed her beautiful face and her hair had a subtle curl to it that made Drew want to wrap her fingers around it to see if it was as soft as it looked. Her eyes were dark brown too and shone when Wren smiled.

"The blonde then? She's quite pretty in her own way." Her grandma pondered for a moment. "But if you want a truly stunning blonde, you won't find nicer than your friend Trent's wife."

Drew had to agree. Juliet Sullivan-Williams was beautiful and had left Drew completely tongue-tied on their first meeting, just like most femmes did. Juliet was also head over heels in love with Trent Williams, who was only out-butched by Dante. Trent was a regular at the store. She usually brought their daughter in to pick up the comic books Drew ordered in especially for the little girl. She and Drew had become good friends over the years.

"The other blonde is a server at the restaurant, the tall one. Could that be her?"

Drew shook her head. Wren was short in comparison to the extra inches Drew had over her. Blessed with curves in all the right places, she was small but perfectly packaged. Drew wondered if she'd gotten her brown skin tone from her Italian father. She was curious to know what she'd gotten from her mother's side. She suspected a feisty temperament if the twinkle in her eyes was anything to go by.

And her smile. Wren had a smile that could light up a room. Drew had found it enchanting.

Drew watched her grandma wracking her brain trying to guess. She decided to put her out of her misery. "She's a chef, not a server. Said her name was Wren."

Her grandma shot her a glare. "Damn it, child. Why didn't you just lead with that? Why'd you have me playing a guessing game?"

"Just keeping your mind active, Grandma." Drew grinned at her grandma's exasperation. She opened the fridge door only to hear a soft thud as something hit it. She peered around to see a cushion on the floor. "Hey! No throwing in the kitchen! I've already had one bang to the head today."

"What happened?" Her grandma was instantly concerned.

"Wren kind of snuck up on me while I was under the counter and made me jump. I think I left a dent in the wood." She rubbed at her head ruefully.

"You can still sass your grandma so I'd say you're not too badly hurt." Her grandma's eyes got a faraway look. "Wren, the pretty dark-haired girl. She's taken Takira's job in the kitchen while Takira goes back to doing what she does best, creating award-winning food. I remember now. Sooooo," her grandma drawled, "is she single?"

Drew pulled a salad she'd prepared earlier from the fridge and sniffed at it. "How should I know?"

"You didn't ask?"

"I was more concerned with the smell of your barbeque ribs permeating the comic books than asking personal questions."

"I think you should take my money to the restaurant for me tomorrow. Go thank Wren for me."

"You could just go yourself," Drew said. "Like you usually do."

"I might be tired tomorrow. I know you'll be a sweetheart and go pay my debt."

Drew looked over at her and wasn't surprised to see her smiling like she'd had the best idea ever. "Stop trying to matchmake, Grandma."

"She makes a lasagna that's to die for. I've had it at least nine times now."

"Oh, well, that settles it then. I'll be front of the line at opening time and rush right in to propose." Drew sat down at the kitchen table and began to eat.

"I wish you didn't get your sarcasm from me."

"You raised me well."

Her grandma smiled proudly at her. "Yes, I believe I did." She settled back into the sofa. "By the way, you need ice cream."

Drew looked up at the swift change of topic. "Did you eat my Ben & Jerry's *again*?"

Her grandma sighed. "I didn't have my glasses on. I was halfway down the tub before I realized it wasn't my probiotic yogurt."

Drew shook her head. She'd lost so much ice cream to the "no glasses" excuse. "I'll pick some up tomorrow."

"And?"

"And I'll go pay your ribs bill at Takira's." Drew knew she was a sucker. Her grandma was nothing if not relentless in getting what she wanted. Drew had learned it was easier to just give in.

"Good girl." Her grandma got up slowly from the sofa. She ambled over to Drew to plant a kiss on her head before heading off to the bathroom. "I'm sure Wren will think you're a good girl too once she gets to know you."

Drew sighed. *Damned old woman always has to have the last word.*

CHAPTER THREE

The lunch crowd was thinning when Wren finally allowed herself a chance to breathe.

"Who'd have thought all these old ladies would descend on us every lunchtime and eat all our cake?" Zenya expertly dodged a server who hurried in to pick up her order. She sidled up to Kae who was stocking the bar and placed a swift kiss on her cheek. Kae grinned at her but didn't break her rhythm of filling the fridge.

Wren smiled at them; they made a sweet couple. She tried not to let a sigh escape as she witnessed their happiness. She was doing fine on her own. She had her dream job; she was earning a comfortable wage. She was one step higher on the career plan set out for herself. Wren heard Zenya giggling behind her as she and Kae shared a cute moment. Wren wasn't jealous. So, she didn't have much of a life outside of the restaurant. That was okay. She could try for that later when her star had risen a little higher and her future was more set.

Jackson, a young male server, attracted her attention as he headed for the kitchen. "A customer would like a word with you, Chef."

Wren tried not to look startled. "Me?" She ran through her list of meals that morning and wondered which one warranted a customer asking for her directly.

"Yes, it's the old lady with the wheelchair, over by the window? The one who sits with Mrs. Daniels."

Wren looked over and, sure enough, Mrs. Dawes, "Mae to my friends," was sitting with the restaurant's favorite customer, Mrs. Daniels. Wren had no idea if anyone knew Mrs. Daniels's first name. If they did, it was a well-kept secret. The two women were leaning over the table, looking like they were conspiring. That didn't bode well.

Wren straightened her white coat and made sure her Takira's apron was spotless. She quickly checked that her hair was still secure in the severe bun she fashioned to keep it out of the way. Zenya nudged her forward to stop her stalling any further. As she walked around the tables, Wren enjoyed the customers greeting her. In her final interview with Takira and Dante, both had described the restaurant, its staff, and the customers as a family. Wren had seen how true that was right from the start. She was proud to be a part of it.

Mrs. Daniels and Mae met Wren with smiles.

"Good afternoon, ladies. I trust everything was to your satisfaction today?" Wren employed her most professional tone.

Mae nodded. "Everything was beautiful as always. I just wanted to thank you for delivering my ribs last night. It was so kind of you."

"You live right next door; I didn't have to go far. It was my pleasure."

Mrs. Daniels leaned in. "So, you met Drew. Was that your first time?"

Wren nodded. "Yes."

"Such a good girl. Always looks out for her grandma," Mrs. Daniels said. "Hard working too."

"She has a marvelous store," Wren agreed, not quite sure where this conversation was going.

"Are you into comic books?" Mae asked.

Wren shook her head. "I don't have much time for anything outside of work, to be honest. I can't remember the last time I read a book that wasn't a recipe one."

"That's a shame. A lovely young girl like you should be out there, exploring the world, meeting new people..." Mae trailed off. "I tell my granddaughter the same thing, but she's got her head buried in those comic books. That store is a testament of her dedication to her dreams." Mae looked at Wren. "That's an admirable quality, isn't it? Someone who's devoted to what they love? Just like you are to your job. I think it shows stability and commitment."

Wren nodded warily. She spotted the twinkle in Mae's eye and finally got a clue as to what they were up to.

"And she's a handsome gal," Mrs. Daniels added, driving their less than subtle point home.

Mae nodded. "She gets that from me."

Wren had to admit, as sales pitches went, this was a good one. She deliberately leaned on the table to draw the two women in. Wren kept her voice low. "Does Drew know you two are the human equivalent of Tinder where she's concerned?"

Both of them frowned at her. "What's that?" Mae asked, genuinely baffled.

"It means, does Drew know you're trying to find her a romantic partner while you're dining over fried chicken and fudge brownies?" Wren was satisfied to see them share a guilty look, caught out in their intentions. "I've only met Drew once, but I don't think she's the kind of 'gal' to take kindly to her grandma and her..." Wren looked at Mrs. Daniels, "grandma's partner in crime, asking strange women out on a date with her."

"You're not strange, you're Chef Wren," Mae argued.

"Did you consider the fact I might not even be gay?"

"You wear a rainbow pin on your uniform," Mae pointed out.

"I could be an ally." Wren kept her face as expressionless as she could.

"I hadn't thought of that." Mae looked so crestfallen Wren almost felt sorry for her.

"That would be disappointing," Mrs. Daniels muttered. She gave Wren a steely look. "But you're not, are you?"

Wren tried not to roll her eyes at these two. She didn't expect to be discussing her lesbian status with two of the oldest customers to frequent the restaurant.

"No, I'm gay. And your granddaughter should ask out who she wants to without your interference." Wren gave them a look that made them shrink a little. "Drew probably wouldn't be happy to know you're doing this, right?"

Mae sighed. "She'd probably threaten to let the air out of my tires. Forgive us, it was just the dying wish of an old lady to see her only granddaughter happy."

Wren couldn't hold back her laughter at the frail tone Mae used. "Something tells me a woman as ornery as yourself isn't dying anytime soon." Wren huffed at her. "*Dying wish.* I'll let the air out of your tires myself for that." She looked at them both. "Are you done pimping out Drew so that I can go back to the kitchen?"

They nodded, not in the least bit chastened. Wren shook her head at them and walked away.

"She's feisty. I like that!" Mae said just loud enough that Wren caught it.

Wren rolled her eyes. She'd have to watch out for those two troublemakers. She didn't turn back around to them, instead she headed to the kitchen. She passed the front counter and spied the cakes and pies Takira had freshly made that were on display. Wren helped herself to two large pieces of the strawberry and caramel cheesecake and placed them carefully into a box. Then she grabbed a bottle of water and a sandwich to finish her lunch. Everyone who worked at Takira's got a free meal every day. The money Wren saved on that alone was building her a nice little nest egg.

"Chef Takira, I'm going on my lunch break if that's okay?"

Takira looked up from her cooking. "Chef Wren, the kitchen is yours now. You don't need my permission. But yes! Go! And don't you dare come back in under an hour!"

Wren laughed as Takira shooed her out and she left the restaurant instead of sitting inside somewhere like usual. She deliberately made sure not to pass by the window where Mrs. Daniels and Mae were sitting. Wren felt like a teenager sneaking out after hours as she cut across the parking lot and walked straight into Dawes & Destiny Comics as if she were a regular customer. She caught sight of Drew across the store and held up her food.

"I come bearing cheesecake. Am I allowed to come in farther or should I use the tradesmen's entrance?"

❖

Drew smiled at Wren's cheeky comment. She pretended to consider her choices until Wren gave her a menacing stare. "I think for cheesecake I can offer you a seat behind the counter where only the best people get to sit." Drew weaved her way through the comic book aisles and met Wren at the counter. She looked at the food in Wren's hands, puzzled. "You staying today?"

"I brought my lunch with me, if you don't mind. Takira is making me take breaks because I keep working through them. I thought I'd share some cake with you and maybe half of a cheese sandwich? I purposely picked out the least smelly of the sandwiches so I wouldn't incur your wrath."

Drew wrinkled her nose at the offer of the sandwich. "I'll skip on the sandwich, but I will never say no to any baked goods." Her gaze fixed on the box. "What kind of cheesecake you got in there?"

"I have a strawberry and caramel one that I watched Takira make this morning and have been desperate to taste. There were only three pieces left so I was quick to grab these." Wren put down the rest of her meal and opened the cake box for Drew to look inside.

Drew felt her mouth begin to water at the rich-looking cheesecake decorated with swirls of cream, huge strawberries, and enough caramel drizzled over it all that even Drew's sweet tooth would cry uncle at.

"Wow, you look like you've just entered cake nirvana." Wren slipped the box's sides out flat so that Drew could reach in. "Sorry, I didn't bring any plates, but I did snag you a fork." She held out a small plastic one that usually accompanied the restaurant's salads to-go. Drew took it without fuss and settled herself on a stool to start tucking in. The moan she let out would have been embarrassing, but Drew didn't care. She was in cake heaven.

"Oh my God, this is the best cheesecake I have ever tasted." She took another mouthful and savored the explosion of strawberry to cream to caramel ratio on her tongue. Drew closed her eyes and just let the flavors overwhelm her.

Wren settled on a stool beside her. "I can honestly say I have never witnessed orgasm by cheesecake before."

Drew nearly choked. She quickly swallowed before she dared to look over at Wren who was grinning at her while eating her sandwich. Drew knew her face was bright red at the comment. She hesitated to take another bite. Wren put her hand on top of Drew's and squeezed.

"No, don't be embarrassed. As a chef, to see someone enjoy the food prepared for them is the greatest high you can get. I'll admit, I make worse noises than that with Black Forest truffles. I only ever make them for Christmas, otherwise I'd gorge myself silly on them. But the mixture of dark chocolate with cherry liquor and the heavy cream…" Wren closed her eyes and groaned.

It was the sexiest sound Drew had ever heard.

Wren opened her eyes again and looked at her sandwich. "Cheese and salad just doesn't cut it. Give me rich chocolate fondants and mousses any day."

Drew swallowed hard at the yearning in Wren's eyes. She felt bereft when Wren removed her hand to clasp onto her sandwich again.

"Please stop. I've gained three pounds just imagining what you're describing." Drew took another bite of the cheesecake. "Damn, I can't believe these cakes have been next door all the time I've been here. It's just as well. I'd be spending more time at your restaurant than in my own store."

"How long has your store been here?"

"I think it's been nearly four years. They built the restaurant first, then my store, and the sports one."

Drew marveled at how at ease she was just chatting with a woman she'd only met once before. She was curious though and wondered how she could politely ask why Wren had come back and was bearing gifts too. "So, to what do I owe the pleasure of your company, Chef Wren?" She took another bite of cake.

"Your grandma and her sidekick are trying to set me up on a date with you."

Drew swore with her mouth full but kept eating.

"You don't seem all that surprised," Wren said in amusement. "I should have seen it coming. I'm afraid you put yourself on her radar by coming over here last night. And it probably didn't help that I didn't throw you and the stinky ribs out of the store."

"Why didn't you?"

Drew didn't know. She had a strict no food or drink policy in the store that she strongly enforced. She looked down at the cake. "You were...nice," she said honestly, hating how weak that sounded. She cleared her throat, trying not to sound so self-conscious. "And then you come over today and bring me cake and I cave in again. You're all kinds of dangerous to this mild-mannered comic book dealer."

"Mild-mannered? You just said 'fuck fuck fuckity fuck' cussing out your grandma, albeit with a mouthful of cake."

"It's my grandma's mission in life to get me married off to a nice girl and furnish her with a lap full of grandbabies."

Wren grimaced. "I've not planned for children anywhere in my career path."

Drew finished her last bite of cake and wiped her mouth on a napkin. "That's okay, Grandma says furbabies count."

"Do you have a pet?"

"No, but maybe one day. That's a dream pinned on my to-do list."

"Cat or dog?"

"I'd really love a dog, but he'd probably bark his head off at the restaurant crowd so maybe a cat would be easier. A little orange one I could call Goose or Chewie."

"You've obviously put a lot of thought into this, though the weird choice of names puzzles me."

"Goose is Captain Marvel's cat in the movie, Chewie is its name in the comic books."

"And Captain Marvel is...?"

Drew dutifully pointed her out on the wall of heroes. Wren nodded as if she understood. Drew tried not to smile at how totally clueless Wren was to all things comic book related.

"Of course, being a huge *Doctor Who* fan," Drew continued, "if I had a dog, I'd probably have to call him K-9."

"And what's *Doctor Who*?"

Drew let her jaw drop. "You don't know who *Doctor Who* is?" She dragged the cake box over beside her. "Leave the cake, but you can go. Be gone, heathen! Never darken my door again!"

Wren laughed at her. "I'm guessing it's a movie or something?"

"It's a British TV show."

"Never heard of it, but I've seen all the episodes of *The Great British Baking Show*. Does that redeem me?

Drew sighed. "At least it shows you watch TV sometimes. I was beginning to think you lived in the restaurant, chained to the sink."

"I do occasionally watch movies, just not ones where everyone has superpowers."

"What is your favorite movie?" Drew was interested to see where Wren's interests lay.

"I love *Angels and Demons*, from the Dan Brown book? I love a good puzzle to work out." Wren rested her head on her palm, her gaze never leaving Drew's face. "What's yours, or are there too many to count?" She waved a hand in the direction of the wall covered in posters.

Drew pondered for a moment; there really were *too* many to choose from. "It would have to be *The Matrix*. You love puzzles and I love having my brain stretched by a movie with endless hidden meanings."

"And Carrie-Anne Moss looking super sexy all in black, with her hair slicked back."

Drew smiled. "Finally, something we have in common. An admiration for the amazing Trinity. Grandma will be so pleased. Should I start decorating for a nursery?"

Wren's delighted laughter warmed Drew's soul. They began a spirited conversation of the state of movies and women's roles in them, and before Drew knew it Wren had started to clear up her lunch. Where had the time gone? She hoped no customer had wandered in while Wren had proved to be a most fascinating distraction. They could have looted half of the store while Drew was arguing the merits of superpowers over the frills and flounces of period dramas.

"I have just enough time to get back to work after our delightful first date," Wren said, tossing her sandwich wrapper into a trash can under the counter.

Drew choked on thin air. "What?"

Wren's expression was mischievous as she slid off her stool. "You can tell Mae and Mrs. Daniels we had a lovely time. Maybe that will get them off your back for a while."

"But," Drew looked down at her T-shirt decorated with a bright yellow Flash symbol, "I never got to dress up. If I had known, I could at least have changed into something more suitable."

Wren looked at her. "Define first date *suitable* for you."

Drew just grinned. "I'd have worn my Punisher tee for the occasion." Wren gave her the blank look that Drew was beginning to recognize all too well. "It's a basic black T-shirt with a white skull on it. Oh, and the skull has elongated teeth. It's from the more *mature* side to Marvel."

Wren considered this, then nodded her approval. "Next time, then." She cocked her head to one side and studied Drew. "You're perfect just the way you are, Drew Dawes. Just don't let anyone bully you into something you don't want to do." Wren patted Drew's cheek. "Don't expect a kiss. I never put out on the first date."

Drew watched in stunned silence as Wren breezed out the door with a cheeky grin and a wave of her hand.

The door had barely shut behind her when Drew heard the familiar sound of her grandma's wheelchair beeping out its parking maneuvers in the hallway. Drew waited for her to come through into the store.

"Hi, sweetheart," Grandma called out to her. "Have you had something to eat?"

Drew nodded. "I had lunch with Wren. You remember Wren, don't you? She works at the restaurant you frequent." Drew was satisfied to watch her grandma's face turn crimson. It clashed hideously with the whiteness of her hair.

"We...I...she..."

"I don't want to hear your excuses, Grandma. You should know more than anyone not to force me into something I don't get to choose for myself."

"I'm sorry, Drew, I never thought of it like that. I won't do it again." Suitably chastened, her grandma waited a moment then said, "You've got to admit she's pretty though."

She's gorgeous. And funny and thoughtful and her fingers on my skin released a blast of electricity that's still coursing through my veins. "She's also busy, Grandma. She has a job that's very demanding. She doesn't have time for a geeky comic book store owner."

"But she made time for you today," her grandma pointed out, a smile starting to bloom on her face.

"That's because she was giving me a heads up about your and Mrs. Daniels's shenanigans."

"Have to admit, I never pegged her for a tattletale," her grandma muttered. She turned to head back out the door. "I'm going to take a nap to rest my meal."

"Press your button if you need me."

"I will, dear." Her grandma paused at the door. "You know, Wren would be lucky to have someone like you in her life."

"Yeah, yeah. I'm such a catch. Just stop throwing out lures to any lesbian that appears in your sights. I thought you'd learned your lesson with Kae."

Her grandma made a face. "That was…unfortunate."

Drew snorted at her. "She came storming around here when you'd asked Zenya out for me. Kae's fists were ready to defend her woman's honor on my clueless face. I didn't even know Zenya then!"

"She's a lovely girl."

"Who's all but married to Kae!"

"I just want you to be happy."

"I'm content, Grandma. Let that be enough for now, please?" Drew knew she was pleading. She didn't have the energy to keep fighting over this.

Her grandma nodded. "I love you, sweetheart."

"I love you too."

"So, how *was* your lunch...?"

"Go to bed, Grandma! Don't make me ground you!"

Her grandma beat a hasty retreat. Drew was sure she could hear her laughter over the sound of the stairlift.

"Crazy old woman," Drew grumbled. She began clearing up the counter when she realized Wren had left the second piece of cake in the box untouched. Drew had been so intent on her own cake and their conversation she hadn't noticed Wren not eating her share. Without hesitation, Drew picked up her fork and pulled the box closer to her as if afraid someone was going to snatch it away.

Finders keepers.

She sent out a silent thank you in Wren's direction and blissed out on every mouthful of cheesecake she ate. "Best first date in forever."

CHAPTER FOUR

The sound of someone cutting their grass finally roused Wren from a deep sleep. She stretched out like a lazy cat, then snuggled back down again under her sheet. Sunlight streamed through the window and bathed her in warmth. She was loathe to move. She told herself she'd have just a few more minutes before she had to greet the day.

The teeth-jarring sound of the mower roared closer as the guy who kept all the apartment buildings' greenery in check started cutting right underneath Wren's window. Wren screwed her eyes up tight, refusing to have the atrocious engine noise wake her up.

"It's Saturday! I have the day off. Let me, just once, sleep in!" She burrowed her face into her pillow. "Your damn grass will be ten feet tall again within a week with all the crap you sprinkle on it to encourage it to grow!" She knew that was an exaggeration but the mower wasn't stopping and now she could hear the radio the guy had playing. The thump thump thump from the radio accompanying the rowdy engine cruising back and forth across the lawn area got on Wren's last nerve. She fumbled for her phone to see what ungodly hour it was that the apartment handyman thought to disturb the peace. She sat up quickly.

"Shit! It's after twelve! I'm supposed to be going home for lunch today!" Wren scrambled out of bed, pulling her sleep shirt over her head as she made a beeline for the bathroom. She detoured only to switch her coffee maker on before shimmying out of her sleep shorts and leaving them in a heap on the floor. The sound of the coffee pot gurgling didn't deaden the noise outside, but it was a sweeter sound to Wren's ears. She showered quickly and congratulated herself for having the forethought of laying out her clean clothes last night. She wore her oldest, softest jeans and a light denim shirt. Out of habit she rolled the sleeves up to her elbows. Her feet celebrated being in memory foam Sketchers and not her serviceable kitchen shoes. She dried her hair with the dryer, leaving it loose to curl over her shoulders. She got through two cups of coffee and a bagel that ended up toasted a little too enthusiastically while she did three things at once. Finally, Wren brushed her teeth and set to putting on what little makeup she wore. She smiled as she could hear her father calling her a "natural beauty" and telling her not to waste time with powder and paint. Wren just added a touch of color to her lips and gave herself an exacting once-over in the mirror. Satisfied she could leave the apartment, she grabbed her car keys and was just shutting the door behind her when her phone pinged with a text message.

Your sister and niece will be joining us for lunch.

Wren groaned. Trust her mother to leave it until the last minute to warn her. It was too late for her to cancel. Her stomach clenched at the thought of having to see her sister today. Valentina Banderas-Russo was Wren's older sister. Val had dutifully followed in their father's footsteps and made quite the name for herself as a corporate lawyer. Wren had long since given up pretending she knew even a fraction of what Val's profession entailed, other than she dealt with large corporations and the multitude of legalities that came with the running of them. Since their father's death five years ago, Val had taken over his practice. She was now the Banderas who ran the firm, the head of the family business.

Wren had realized very early in her childhood that she and Val wouldn't be bosom buddies. With ten years separating them, Val had been dismissive and jealous of the baby born "too late" for her to play with. She'd clung to their father, becoming his "Mini-Me," and was soon starting her path in following in his footsteps. Things had been easier once Wren reached an age that Val could hold a conversation with her, but Wren had still felt like an only child for most of her life. Val had married another lawyer, an up-and-coming entertainment lawyer named Marco Russo. The marriage barely lasted nine years. Wren's beloved niece, Ana, was the best thing that came from their pairing. The subsequent divorce had been cool but amicable. Wren still remained on friendly terms with Marco. He'd always treated her like the little sister he'd never had. In fact, he'd been more of a brother to her than Val was ever a sister. He and Val shared joint custody and Ana seemed perfectly fine with ferrying back and forth between them. It must have been Val's weekend to have Ana if they were going home.

That meant she got to be Auntie Wren today. Wren would get to spend time with her niece whom she adored.

"Now, what kind of gift can I get her?" Wren pondered this predicament as she walked down the three flights of stairs in her apartment block. By the time she'd stepped off the last step she was smiling.

"Dawes & Destiny Comics, here I come!"

Saturday was always a busy day for the store. Drew was thankful she had a reliable staff who enjoyed the steady stream of customers in and out of the store as much as she did. Drew was currently replenishing the Funko wall and tidying them again. Nineteen-year-old Aaron was at the counter, manning the cash register. He was a quiet, soft-spoken guy, with an endless passion for *The Lord of the Rings*. He always dressed in a shirt and tie and wore his name tag displayed prominently on the breast pocket. He wore glasses, kept his short hair neat and tidy, and his father wanted him to become a banker. Aaron had other ambitions.

Beside him was eighteen-year-old Dakota. She was unmissable. Today she was sporting a bubblegum pink wig, cut short at the front but falling in a long braid down her back. She wore a white sailor suit with a pale pink collar, cuffs, and tie. A pale pink pleated skirt fell to mid-thigh. White stockings and black shoes finished the ensemble.

Her makeup highlighted her eyes deliberately, exaggerating them to look bigger.

Drew wasn't a fan of Anime, but she had to admire Dakota's take on the costumes and the dedication she had to her craft. She was super friendly and the customers loved her. The boys, and more than a few girls, fell over themselves to have her serve them. Dakota's devotion to Anime had inspired a modest Anime section in the store that always sold well when she was working. She and Aaron had been an item from the second Drew had hired them. It had been love at first sight for the couple and they'd been inseparable ever since. Dakota toned down her cosplay for the store, but both she and Aaron traveled to Comic Cons and showed off their magnificent costumes. Drew had seen the more revealing anime costumes Dakota wore at the cons. She'd also been amazed by Aaron's authentic-looking Legolas costume and his Gandalf robes, complete with the long white beard. When he dressed as Aragorn, Dakota often became the beautiful elf Arwen. They worked for hours together on their costumes; it was a true labor of love. Drew understood them completely. She derived a lot of pleasure from taking on another persona, if only for a weekend, and mixing among other likeminded people.

She watched Aaron and Dakota as they chatted with the customers. Drew wondered what she would have done had Wren come in when they had been in charge. Drew would never have met her. She wondered why that thought bothered her so much. No one had caught her attention in some time, but Wren had taken up residence in Drew's head and she couldn't stop thinking about the tiny chef who commanded her full attention just by stepping through the door.

As if on cue, the doorbell over the door jangled to let a new customer enter and Drew glanced over to see who it was. Drew felt pinned in place by Wren's gaze as she sought her out. For a crazy moment, Drew thought she was hallucinating, but Wren smiled and Drew instinctively began moving toward her. She saw Aaron begin to lean forward to ask if he could help, but Dakota wrenched him back behind the counter by his shirt collar. Dakota was too observant for her own good, Drew thought, before her whole attention narrowed in on Wren.

"What are you doing risking your life in here on a Saturday?" Drew asked, enjoying seeing Wren in her jeans and with her hair down. Drew nearly shoved her hands into her pockets to stop from reaching out to feel how soft the well-worn denim on Wren's hips was to the touch.

"I'm in need of your help."

Drew nodded, knowing whatever Wren wanted, she would move heaven and earth to do it. "Anything." She thought she heard Dakota giggle and shot her a withering look before turning her attention back to Wren.

"I need you to make me the coolest aunt on the planet."

Drew blinked in surprise. "You don't need me for that. You seem to have that all taken care of yourself." Drew waved her hands at her in a "look at you" gesture. She was surprised to see Wren's cheeks flush a little.

"Smooth, Drew Dawes, that was *real* smooth." Wren's smile was oddly shy. Drew realized she'd caught her off guard. She liked that she could do that.

Drew heard Dakota agree with Wren. She turned to her. "Shouldn't you be seeing to the customers?"

Dakota gave her a cheeky grin and a quirky V for Victory sign. "This is way more entertaining!"

Wren gaped at her. "I haven't seen you in here before. I'd remember you for sure. You look *amazing*."

Dakota preened at the praise. "Are you a friend of Drew's?"

Wren looked back at Drew appraisingly. "Yeah, I think we're getting there. I already know she's easily bribable with cake."

Drew chuckled. It was true. "You left your cake here yesterday. I may have eaten it. So, I definitely owe you one. What do you need?"

"I need a gift for a very geeky niece." She grimaced as she looked around the store. "Sorry, no offense."

Drew shook her head at Wren's chagrin. "None taken. Geeks are cool."

"Hell yes, we are!" A group of teenagers, hands full of comic books, grinned at them both before heading to the counter to pay.

"See?" Drew said. "Don't forget that the Bible says the geek shall inherit the earth."

Wren laughed. Drew, drawn by how genuine Wren's enjoyment was, had to laugh too. Wren's amusement deepened as Dakota made a comment that Drew didn't hear. Wren's eyes almost closed as her smile widened to light up her face.

She was so breathtakingly beautiful.

"I knew I'd come to the right place. What do you have that screams ten-year-old girl? I don't think she has a comic book collection, but I know she has a crush on the guy over there with the star shield."

"What size T-shirt is she?"

"Medium. Puberty is just starting to alter her shape. I know she's very self-conscious about it. She usually wears things a size bigger so she can hide in them."

Drew began flicking through the plastic wrapped T-shirts until she found a Chris Evans Captain America one, in the right size. She held it out to Wren.

"Will this be enough to earn you cool aunt brownie points?"

"I think she'll love it. I'm seeing her today so I want to take a gift. Now that she's sorted, I'll pop next door to get a cake for us all. Today is 'lunch with the family' day."

Drew noticed Wren didn't look too excited. "Is that not a 'yay, family' day?"

Wren's expression said it all. "My mother will keep asking me to move back home to live, even though I have lived on my own for the past ten years. My niece is the light of my life, but her mother can be a trial at times. She likes to tell me how to live my life." Wren lowered her voice to whisper, "It's a bit of a b-i-t-c-h."

Drew leaned in to whisper back. "Geeks can spell, you know." She felt sorry that Wren's lunch wasn't going to be fun. "Tell me about your niece while I take your money."

"Oh, she's an utter sweetheart. She'll probably spend lunch with her headphones on to drown out the adults. She's a massive Taylor Swift fan."

"She has excellent taste in music. I like to listen to her too."

"Yeah, Ana learned really early that the best way not to hear the inevitable 'discussions' over why I haven't got my own restaurant yet is to play her music loud."

"That doesn't sound like a fun way to spend a Saturday. Do you have to go? You could hang out here, with us cool kids." Drew loved how the kids in the store who were close enough to hear her all agreed. Wren laughed at their eagerness.

"I wish I could. I'd probably have a whole lot more fun. But I haven't seen my mother in a while because of taking up residence at the restaurant so I need to suck it up and go get through this." She shrugged ruefully. "You know what it's like, family obligation and all that."

Drew nodded. She knew that all too well. "At least you know your niece will be happy to see you. And you have a cool gift."

Wren nodded. "Do you think she'll like it?"

"I think she'll love that *you* bought it for her."

"Do *you* like this character?" Wren patted the bag Drew had given her.

Drew smiled and pointed to a poster on display. Gal Gadot stood, resplendent in her Amazon clothing. "I prefer my superheroes strong and smart and *female.*"

Wren studied the poster for a long moment. Her gaze then flicked back to Drew. "We can talk more about her on Monday over lunch. If you're free, that is?"

Drew tried not to look so surprised. "Yeah, I'll be here, as usual." She was thankful she didn't stutter.

"I'll be sure to bring cake," Wren added with a mischievous glint in her eye.

"Then I definitely won't leave the store," Drew promised. She watched Wren turn to leave. Drew really didn't want her to go. "Don't let your family wear you down," she called after her.

"I'll do my best, but if they drive me too crazy, I might have to go all Wonder Woman on them." Wren waved good-bye and left the store.

Drew's gaze followed her.

"Man, I'd pay to see that," Dakota said, leaning on the counter next to Drew as they both watched Wren walk across the parking lot.

"Me too," Drew said as she imagined Wren dressed as an Amazon princess. The image of her wielding the God Killer sword and tying Drew up in the Lasso of Truth took a hold in Drew's head. *Oh God, I'm totally screwed.*

"I think she likes you, boss," Dakota said.

"I think I like her too." Drew watched Wren disappear from sight and felt the loss deep within her.

"So, are you gonna do something about it?" Aaron joined them in leaning on the counter.

I have no idea. I have the store to run, I have Grandma to care for, I have no room in my life for someone as fine as Wren. Drew shrugged and decided to joke it off.

"What do ya think, do you think a chef and a gal like me...?"

Aaron snorted. "Tell me you did not just misquote Han Solo."

Dakota shook her head at her. "She always does when she's trying to deflect. Aaron, we have our work cut out for us if we're going to get Drew ready for her lunch date on Monday and not have her totally screw it up."

"Hey! I've already had a lunch date with her and I did just fine without you two meddling kids," Drew said, feeling defensive and ganged up on.

"You never told us about that." Aaron shared a significant look with Dakota.

Drew spotted it. She pushed away from the counter and retreated. "No! Don't you two get any ideas about helping me woo Wren."

"The fact you say 'woo' shows how much you need our help," Dakota said.

"I'm going back to the Funko Pops." Drew beat a hasty retreat across the store, as far as she could get away from them.

"You can run but you can't hide!" Dakota singsonged after her.

Drew ignored her and busied herself straightening the shelves again. Her mind wandered to what kind of afternoon Wren was walking into. Drew knew all too well what pain family could cause. She also knew what a joy family *could* be, thanks to her grandma. She hoped Wren's fears were unfounded and that her weekend would be a peaceful one.

She spotted Dakota purposely heading her way. She feared she wasn't going to be as fortunate.

CHAPTER FIVE

The Banderas family home never changed. It still bore the same brilliant white paint job with a subtle pale blue trim that Luca and Renata Banderas, Wren's parents, had picked out when they'd had the house designed. The huge Georgian-style home screamed elegance and prosperity. Wren found it overly large and ostentatious, but it was a sign of her father's success, and her mother wouldn't think of moving from it, even though she rattled around it alone now. Everything inside and out was exactly how her father had left it. Trapped in time, a monument to his hard work, and his family. There was a part of Wren that loved being back in the house she'd lived in all her life. The other part hated how empty it felt without her father's presence.

It's as if we're waiting for him to come home soon and if we dare to move just one thing out of place, he'll walk on by.

Wren choked back the familiar sting of tears that threatened to fall whenever she thought of her father. He'd been her champion, the one who urged her to follow her dreams. A massive heart attack had taken him from them. Val had dealt with all the legalities and funeral requirements. Wren had been grateful as she had to become the strong shoulder for her grieving mother. Her mother had spent every day of her adult life with him. His loss had been devastating and served to show Wren how much he held the family together.

Her mother had begged Wren to stay home with her, but Wren had been a chef at a restaurant in Chicago at that time, starting to make a name for herself. She hadn't been prepared to give up her job just as she was gathering some notoriety in the restaurant world. Besides, Val lived close enough to keep tabs on their mother. Wren knew it wasn't the same. Their personalities were such opposites. Val could be cool, standoffish even, with a fiery temper when roused. Wren was always the more cheerful and thoughtful daughter. The one who hid her crippling self-doubt and the constant need to prove herself from her family the best she could. She knew she had to stand on her own two feet to get the career she wanted. She didn't want to go back to living under her mother's roof. Lack of privacy and personal space was something Wren wasn't keen to give up once she'd tasted that freedom.

Today was not going to be the peaceful visit with just her mother like Wren had hoped. Taking a deep, cleansing breath to fortify herself, Wren used her key to let herself in.

"Hi, Mama!" she shouted out into the hallway. Her mother's voice came to her from the back of the house. Wren knew she'd find her in her usual spot, sitting at the window, looking out at the expansive gardens that were her pride and joy.

Wren didn't know one plant from another unless they were able to go into a cooking pot.

"There you are, Florencia."

Wren smiled at her mother's determination never to shorten her name. Wren gave her a kiss and joined her looking out the large window at the garden awash with greenery and an abundance of roses. Wren noticed something different immediately.

"You got the landscapers in?" Wren had recommended a firm who had been happy to make the long drive. Wren knew her mother would compensate them well for traveling.

"Yes. They're replacing the old seating area with a gazebo for me and changing some of the old worn paving. When it's complete, you can come join me for a glass of wine under the stars." Her mother eyed her hopefully. "Maybe bring a girlfriend home?"

Wren sighed. "Mama, I've barely been in the house two seconds. At the risk of repeating myself for the hundredth time, I am too busy working to find someone yet."

Her mother reached over to cup Wren's cheek in her hand. "But you're such a pretty girl. You deserve a love by your side."

"It's just not high on my list of priorities at the moment. But if I do manage to squeeze a romance into my busy schedule, I will be sure to bring her home so you can interrogate her."

Her mother looked mollified by that. "You bring home a nice girl." She paused for a moment. "Not one covered in tattoos."

For a moment, Wren thought about Drew and the curious blue tattoo that decorated her arm. "I can't promise anything, Mama. Some nice girls come with tattoos."

Her mother shook her head. "We never had those kinds of things in my day." She directed Wren's gaze back to the garden. "I have two ladies working on my garden. They're going to make it a vision."

"*You* made it a vision, Mama. It's just growing beyond what you can cope with." The *on your own* stayed silent, but Wren knew they both could hear it. "Especially as your regular gardener just retired."

"The blond one, Juliet? She says she'll find me a reputable, more local gardener to take over once they have everything done for me. They're very efficient. And she shows me pictures of her baby every day." Her mother clutched at her chest dramatically. "Oh, what a precious little blond girl. With striking eyes and such pale hair. She's the very image of Juliet, but she tells me this baby is very much her mama's child."

Wren nodded, knowing the family. "Little Harley Quinn. Yes, she comes into the restaurant regularly. I've gotten to know her and her mothers' well. She's a lovely little girl and quite the character. She plays with Finn, Takira's son, so I get to see her a lot."

"The other girl, the one who gets her hands dirty?" Her mother was searching for her name.

Wren liked that analogy. Monica Simons was the owner of the landscaping business who was very hands-on in it. Juliet was more finance and administration but liked to get out in the sun now and then. "Monica?"

"Yes, the dark-haired one. Light and dark, those two girls, but such a force together. Monica has a tattoo." Her mother touched a spot on her neck.

Wren fought against the grin desperate to escape at her mother's scandalous tone.

"She says she's a moth. I don't understand."

Wren couldn't stop her laughter at that. "A *goth*, Mama. It means she dresses very differently than what you see her in when she's gardening." Wren got out her phone and flicked through her photos. She held one up for her mother to see. Her mother's jaw dropped open.

"*This* is my gardener?" She gaped at the phone.

"This is how Monica usually looks." She watched as her mother stared at the phone in stunned silence.

"She is an amazing gardener, but this? She is *beautiful*."

Wren let out a small breath of relief. "She makes all her own clothes."

"She made *this* dress?"

"Yes." Wren knew the dress was fantastic. She'd seen it in person. It was a black crinoline with a high-necked bodice, resplendent with lace adornments. Worn, curiously, with black biker boots with silver buckles. Monica totally rocked the look.

"Why is she gardening when she can create an incredible dress like this?"

"Because gardening pays the bills and costume design on the side is a chance for her to let her creativity shine without starving. I'd asked her the very same question."

"She can design your wedding dress. A little less of the black lace perhaps. I would pay well for her eye for detail."

"Mama!" Wren huffed at her, but her ire calmed at the sight of her mother's sly smile. "Stop teasing."

"I'm just saying." Her mother shrugged. "Juliet is gay. *She* has a baby."

"Yes, and she's married to a woman who has *multiple* tattoos." Wren felt she needed to throw that in.

"Is she handsome? I feel someone as pretty as Juliet would have a handsome woman on her arm."

Wren thought about Trent and the androgenous look she embodied. There was something very magnetic about her and Wren would be lying if she didn't admit to feeling the pull on their first meeting. She liked women who were opposite to how she looked. Drew fit that bill admirably too. Wren shook off that thought as she checked through her photos to show her mother what Trent looked like. She shared a marvelous picture of the Sullivan-Williams family together in the restaurant at someone's party. Trent had one arm around Juliet and Harley held close in her other. They were all smiling for the camera.

Her mother whistled softly under her breath. She tapped the phone with her finger. "This. You need to bring home a girl just like this. My, my."

To Wren's amusement, her mother fanned herself.

"Handsome, sexy, yes *very* sexy. Good with babies too and it's plain to see she loves her wife. Yes, someone like this one. You need to bring home a girl like this. I will totally approve!"

Wren laughed at how flustered her mother was getting over the photo. "They broke the mold when they made Trent, Mama. But I'll be sure to take your preferences for a daughter-in-law on board. But again, don't pin any hopes and dreams on any more grandchildren. Not from me anyway. You know I've never wanted them. Ana growing up is more than enough adolescence angst for me to go through."

"You'd make pretty babies," her mother said, not letting go just yet.

"And I'll make an amazing chef running my own restaurant someday. My future never included children and family. Papa understood that. He encouraged me to put business first."

"Your papa didn't want any boys around you. No man was ever going to be good enough for his little Florencia."

"Well, we both agreed on that." Wren put away her phone. "Enough talk of a fictional marriage and babies. I have cake and a new coffee blend for you to try."

Her mother's eyes lit up. "Did your Takira make the cake?"

"Yes, she did."

"Use the bigger plates." Her mother shooed her away toward the kitchen.

"You and your sweet tooth. How you're not wearing a full set of dentures is beyond me."

"I have excellent genes and a very handsome dentist! I never miss an appointment!"

Scandalized, Wren stopped in her tracks. "Mama! You are shameless!"

Her mother bared her teeth at her in a shit-eating grin. "True, but I have perfect teeth because of it!"

Wren laughed as she hustled into the kitchen to prepare a generous slice of cake as hinted for with the mention of the bigger plates. She put the kettle on and went back to hand her mother her cake while they waited on the coffee.

"So, how is work?" her mother asked.

"No, no more about me. Let's hear about you."

"But you have a much more exciting life than me. I don't do anything but grocery shop for a few things and meet up with my friends for coffee and cake every week. It's very routine. I'm just rattling around this house all by myself."

Wren groaned silently. *Any minute now. Three..two..one…*

"I mean, if you were to come home…"

Then you'd never be out of my business and I would be constantly looking after you and not living my own life. "Mama, I appreciate the offer but we've talked about this numerous times. I'm living and working in Columbia now, I'm needed there. This is the next step up for me. I can't waste the opportunity I have at Takira's. It's too important." Wren sighed. "Why is it you never asked Val to move back in after her divorce finalized? You'd have had Val *and* Ana."

Her mother made a face. "Because your sister is not you, my dear. She's too much like your papa's mother. Cold, no sense of humor, and sometimes best seen in small doses." Her mother savored a piece of cake before continuing. "I know she's my daughter and I love her, but she can be very…unlikeable. Besides, she'd never let me spoil Ana like I'd want to."

"I wish you'd warned me she was coming today," Wren said.

"Then you wouldn't have come."

"Maybe. But can you blame me? She's on my back about my life every time she sees me. I know what I'm doing with my career. I don't need her advice on everything I do when she has no clue how to run a restaurant."

Don't let your family wear you down. Wren could hear Drew's words ringing in her head as her frustration began to mount. She silently thanked her yoga teacher for his patience with her and took a few, deep, calming breaths just like he'd taught her to do when anxiety rose within her.

"I know, sweetheart. Maybe today will be better?" Her mother tried to sound hopeful but even she knew it was a lost cause.

"Yeah, Mama, it's been a 'maybe today' day ever since I was in diapers." Wren returned to the kitchen, determined to enjoy the last remnants of peace in the house she'd get before Val and Ana descended.

Wren wondered how much louder the music in her niece's ears had to be before she seriously damaged her hearing. Ana was listening to Taylor Swift while seated at the table beside her. Wren could almost hear every word sung. She made a mental note to get Ana a pair of noise-canceling headphones so she could reach the age of eleven and still have some hearing left intact. She had to smile though. Ana was proudly wearing her new T-shirt over the flowered blouse Val had undoubtedly chosen for her. Val tried so hard to make Ana a pretty princess, but so far, Ana was still a rambunctious tomboy with a deep passion for superhero movies. Ana had been so excited to receive her gift and had scrambled into it. Wren had deliberately ignored Val's narrowed eyes at her as they watched Ana tug the tee on. She didn't want to use Ana as a needle to poke at Val. But it had been satisfying to see Val's resigned look at her daughter's obvious excitement for something Wren had given her.

"So, did you make the cake, Wren?" Val wasn't eating any of it. She'd already rattled off whatever fad diet she was embarking on this week. Val was leaning against a cupboard, her phone in her hands as always.

"Takira made it."

"And she's the one you've taken over from. Why is she still in the kitchen?"

Wren fought not to roll her eyes. "Because my taking on her role has freed her up to go back to cooking for the restaurant like she used to. And she now gets to spend more time with her family."

"The son that is really her nephew who she got when her twin sister died." Val looked up from her phone screen. "It sounds like something from a soap opera."

Her mother chided her. "Valentina…"

Val looked at her mother but remained silent. "I'm just saying. It's very admirable what she's done. And now, with Wren there, she gets to experience the joys of motherhood." Val looked pointedly at Ana who was blissfully unaware of the scrutiny. She sat bopping her head along to the music in her ears while eating her second piece of cake.

"Have you been able to implement any changes of your own, Wren? This restaurant would be a great testing ground for you to see what works and what doesn't."

"It works perfectly fine how Takira has it running. There's nothing that needs fixing. Takira has worked hard for years to get it to the well-oiled machine it is. Anything I tried to do to bring about change would be an unnecessary wrench in the works."

"Hmm. Are you noticing what the manager does? I've heard good things about her. She's the one that's with Takira, isn't she?" Val pursed her lips. "A little unorthodox working with a partner, but if it gets the job done…"

"It works well enough for you and Marco," Wren pointed out. Marco still worked with Val at the practice. Val gave Wren a small nod, conceding the point won.

"True. Still, in a restaurant, with such a massive turnaround in staff…"

Wren heard Drew's voice in her head again and decided, this time, she would bite back. She wasn't here to talk business today. It was the weekend. She was visiting with *family*, not consulting with her lawyer.

"Anyway, enough about my job. I haven't been there long and I'm still learning everything. But I love it. It's the best restaurant I've worked in. The family atmosphere alone is worth the hard work."

"You'll have to emulate that in your own place," Val said, tapping away at her phone again.

Wren wondered if she had a spreadsheet open, one she was filling in entitled *Things Wren Needs to Do in Life*. She gave Val a look when Val's head finally lifted from the screen.

"It's something that has to be cultivated. It's not just another box you can tick off. Takira has worked hard to grow this loyal customer base over time. It's not something that you can snap your fingers at and suddenly customers come streaming through the door and keep coming back." Wren was getting angry and her tone uncharacteristically biting. She'd really wanted this to be a peaceful visit.

Wren spotted Ana surreptitiously turn the volume up even louder on her phone. Wren deliberately reached over and paused the music. "So, Ana. Tell me *all* about school."

Ana slipped her headphones off and snuck a quick surreptitious look at her mom first. Val was looking back at her phone, a frown furrowing her forehead at being thwarted. "Well, my art teacher says—"

Val's phone rang out shrilly. "I have to take this call," she said, already leaving.

Wren blew out a puff of relief once she was out the room. Ana laughed at her.

"Go, Auntie Wren!" She cheered quietly. "You obviously had your Wheaties today! You managed to shut Mom up."

Wren shook her head, embarrassed by her outburst. "I'm so sorry, Ana. She just winds me up every time."

"Ignore her. She thinks she runs the world." Ana shrugged and rolled her eyes dramatically. "I was looking forward to seeing you today. I want to talk with you about my art project." She ran her hand down the print on her T-shirt. "And this. I *love* this. Thank you again. I'm never taking it off."

"Your mom won't take it away from you, will she? It's not exactly what she usually picks out for you to wear." Wren's confidence was beginning to crash after finally making herself heard. She blamed Drew. Wren would have just suffered in silence as usual if she hadn't had Drew's message rattling around her head like a rallying call.

No more cake for her.

"She'll have to fight me for it. Besides, she's finally getting the idea that I'm not a pastel shades kind of girl. I can always leave it at Dad's if she gets too controlling. He watches all the movies with me so he will love it." Ana mused. "He'll probably want one too, now. He's more a Black Widow fan though."

"Are we still speaking over Skype next week?" Wren was worried Val might stop that in retaliation. Wren rarely got the last word with her.

"Of course. Auntie Wren, no matter how terrible my mom is at being your big sister, I still love you because you're awesome. So, take a word of advice from the pop goddess, Taylor Swift."

Wren waited for Ana's obvious punch line.

"Just shake Mom off!" Ana leapt up from the table to perform a little dance to accompany her singing before she launched herself into Wren's arms to try to get her to join in on her impromptu performance.

Val came back in. "I have to go back to the office for an hour. Some idiot filed the wrong claim. I need to go put it right before it goes through Monday."

"Leave Ana here with us. You can come back for her when you're finished." Her mother smiled at Ana. "I got in your favorite ice cream especially."

"Mama, do not spoil her," Val grumbled as she kissed Ana. "I'll be an hour, tops."

Everyone waited for the sound of the front door to close. The second it did Wren shot out of her seat and raced Ana to the freezer that housed the ice cream.

"I want gummy bears on mine!" Ana shouted.

"I want chocolate sauce," Wren shouted back as she grabbed the tub and carried it back to the table in triumph. Ana gathered all the toppings.

"I want to dance in my kitchen with my favorite girls!" Her mother stood up and opened up her arms. "Miss Ana, if you please."

Ana switched her phone to speaker and, with a mischievous look at Wren, began playing a certain song. Her mother gathered Wren into her arms and began dancing.

Wren tried to keep in step with her mother's old-time waltz set to a very unsuitable song. "Are you singing 'Shake It Off' to me in Spanish?"

Her mother grinned. "Who do you think got young Ana hooked on her?" She continued to waltz Wren around the kitchen. Ana laughed at them, dancing on the spot, waiting for her turn in her grandma's arms.

The moment took Wren back to her childhood. Her mother singing and dancing with her while they waited for whatever was in the oven to bake. A time when Val was out of the house at one of her endless school clubs, and it was just Wren and her mother. That was when Wren's passion for the culinary arts was born. The simple connection between a young girl and her mother, creating something that brought pleasure and fulfillment.

Wren hugged her mother closer.

"You know what I wish?" Her mother asked.

That Val and I could get along? That Papa was still here? That I'd move back home so you wouldn't be so alone?

"What?" Wren braced herself for the answer.

"I wish I hadn't eaten all the cake. Cake and ice cream sounds *so* heavenly right now."

CHAPTER SIX

Drew never felt truly comfortable dressed in her costume until she was in line with the other costume players waiting to go inside the convention halls. Today was MoCon, a Missouri convention that would have TV personalities, comic books and memorabilia, and a costume party that rivaled the rest. Drew had been counting down the days to it, feeling both excitement and trepidation. The crowds were always a problem for her at first. Drew had to regulate her breathing and repeat a few mantras before she got into the right mindset to be among so many people jostling their way around the crowded halls. Drew all too easily remembered bad experiences as a child with crowds of people all hovering around her.

She shook the memories from her mind; they had no place in her world now. What got her through the day was the fact she was in costume. She wasn't there as Drew Dawes; she was whatever hero she dressed as. She straightened her shoulders in *their* clothes and walked in *their* footsteps. Her mother had never let her dress up for Halloween as a child. She never got to play dress-up because work came first. But now Drew was at every convention she could get to, hidden in plain sight. There in person, but never as herself.

Drew checked herself over in the bathroom mirror. She liked that she was almost unrecognizable wearing a blond wig where the hair fell to her jawline in a side-parted bob. It was weird seeing herself with long hair after so long having it cut brutally short. Drew wasn't keen on wigs, but this character called for it. She'd attached a chained earring set to her left ear. She'd had it especially made because she had no piercings so had to have one with cuffs instead. The blue T-shirt she wore had a rainbow stripe running across the chest. She'd tucked it into a pair of blue high-waisted, cropped-legged culottes. She had on a pair of warm, woolly blue-striped socks that she'd probably regret all the walking in and an oversized pair of brown boots that she had spent months breaking in so they looked well-worn but were still comfortable to wear.

Drew struggled to get a pair of yellow suspenders to fit right over her shoulders. She didn't need them to keep her pants up, but they were part of the costume. Drew was not leaving them out, no matter how awkward they were. She was eternally grateful she had very little in the breast department, otherwise the suspenders would have been a nightmare to keep straight. She checked her phone for the time. She had ten minutes before Dakota and Aaron were picking her up. Reverently, Drew picked up the last item she had to wear. A wonderfully long lilac-blue trench coat, with a hood, finished her costume. Monica Simons had made it for her and it had been worth every dollar it had cost. It was Drew's pride and joy, and wearing it made her feel empowered. Satisfied she looked the part, Drew gathered up her phone, wallet, and a curiously shaped object that she pointed at the mirror. The end lit up and it made a noise. The "real" sonic screwdriver was a masterpiece of craftmanship that housed components that made it a font of all knowledge and had the ability to scan objects and open locked doors. Drew's was an exact replica, just minus all the space-age tech and magic. She was just happy for the bright light and the buzzing noise.

Drew quietly crept around the apartment. Her grandma wouldn't be up for another hour. Drew had written her a note and had left strict instructions for Noah, who was looking after both the store *and* her grandma, until Drew returned in the evening. He did it every time there was a convention; he knew the drill. Drew hated leaving her. Grandma was her responsibility and one Drew took very seriously. Her grandma, however, had promised she'd be fine like she always was and wanted Drew to go and have fun.

Drew took one last look around the kitchen where she'd left out her grandma's breakfast fixings and her daily medication, then left before she found something else to fixate on. She ran down the stairs to go wait outside the store for Dakota and Aaron. It was barely seven o'clock but they all liked to get to the convention venue early so they could park, get in line, and start the day as soon as possible. Drew lifted her face to the sun that was already warmer than blue woolly socks required. She surreptitiously looked around, didn't see anyone anywhere, and began to sing. Her voice was quiet so as not to disturb the day and those still sleeping. It was quiet so she wouldn't draw any attention to herself. It was quiet because Drew didn't sing out loud any more. But some days the pent-up song in her heart screamed to be loose and Drew found a quiet space where she could be alone and release it for her ears alone. She knew her grandma mourned not hearing Drew's voice, but something stopped Drew from letting herself be heard, even by her. Being heard brought attention, and she'd learned the hard way that attention was something she just couldn't deal with. And nothing good ever came from her singing in public so Drew just...didn't.

Something on the store's shutters drew her attention and gave her something to mess with while she sang under her breath and waited for her ride to come. She was so out of it that she never heard someone walk across Takira's parking lot.

"Hey! The store's closed, numb nuts! Go hang around somewhere else!"

Drew startled so hard she feared she'd swallowed her tongue. She turned around to see Wren standing, hands on hips, ready for battle. For a moment, over the sound of her heart pounding in her ears, the fire in Wren's eyes seized Drew's attention and held her captive. She watched as Wren's face turned from indignation, to puzzlement, then to a startled recognition.

"Oh my God!" Wren sauntered closer, her gaze slowly and deliberately taking in Drew from head to toe. "Drew! I didn't recognize you at all! Wow, it's incredible how long hair totally changes you."

Drew reached for her hair self-consciously. "I haven't had long hair since I was a kid. I never liked it. Grandma let me have it cut when I went to live with her."

"Well, this look is certainly a great look, but I think I prefer your shaved hair. It's more you." Wren shook her head, obviously still surprised at Drew's unusual attire. "Let me guess, by day you're a mild-mannered comic book store owner but..." she squinted up at the bright blue sky, "by early morning you're some sort of superhero in pants that don't reach your ankles?"

Drew laughed. "I wish. I'm going to MoCon." She was surprised when Wren nodded in understanding.

"I know what that is. Believe me, I heard all about it last weekend from my niece." Wren blinked as a realization struck her. "Have I really not seen you since last Saturday? I needed to come over to tell you the T-shirt was a huge hit. I'm so sorry, my week has rushed past. We were incredibly busy."

Drew didn't say how much she'd missed seeing Wren wandering in and taking up space in her store. Or how many times she'd considered going to Takira's just in case she could catch a glimpse of the feisty head chef and say hi.

"My niece is going to it. Damn, I know she'd love to meet you. I'll have to bring her to the store...that's if her mom will let me after I stood up for myself for once. Not sure who was the more surprised, her or me."

Drew was impressed. "Good for you."

"Yeah, well, I'm blaming you for telling me not to let them get to me. So, I didn't. You're a bad influence on me, Drew Dawes."

Drew heard the familiar sound of Dakota's car heading her way. "You'll have to come into the store soon and tell me all about it." She hesitated but asked anyway. "What were you going to do if it hadn't been me fiddling with the shutter? I'm a whole lot taller than you."

"I'd have glared you down until you crumbled beneath my wrath," Wren said, glaring at her.

Drew had to admit it was an intimidating look.

Wren's smile appeared as the car pulled up and Dakota and Aaron leaned out the window to say hi. She waved to them and gave Drew one last look. "Okay, I give up. Who are you?"

"Yes."

Wren frowned at her. "Who?"

"Yes."

"No, who *are* you?" Wren was getting a little annoyed. Drew decided to stop teasing her.

"I am Thirteen. The thirteenth incarnation of Doctor Who." Drew held her arms out in a typical Jodie Whittaker pose.

"She dresses like that?" Wren considered this a moment. "Is she as cute as you?"

The hoots and hollers coming from the car made Drew glare at them. "She's way cuter," Drew said, meaning it.

"Guess I'll have to come see you to learn more about this Doctor, then." Wren started to walk backward, leaving them to it. "I'm on the early shift today. Have a great weekend. And, Drew?"

Drew stopped mid-step on her way to the car.

"No one could be cuter." With a wicked smile Wren waved her good-bye and headed toward the restaurant.

Stunned, Drew could only watch her go. Aaron waited until she finally got in the car before he spoke.

"Did she sleep over last night?"

"No, she did not!" Drew blustered. "She's just come into work. We're not like that!"

"Drew *wishes* she'd slept over last night," Dakota said, grinning knowledgably.

"Just drive, Vision. Wanda? Shut the fuck up." Drew sat back in her seat at their laughter. She didn't have time to be awestruck at how detailed their Vision and Scarlet Witch costumes were. She'd marvel at them later. They were too busy singing "It Was Agatha All Along*"* from the TV show *WandaVision*, substituting Wren's name in it instead until even Drew had to see the humor in it and accept their good-natured ribbing gracefully.

❖

Lost in a world of her own, Wren pored over the day's menu. She scribbled a note down to order more cilantro as their stock had dwindled faster than she'd anticipated. Her eyes darted constantly to the large kitchen clock, mindful that the breakfast customers would be coming in soon. Their breakfast bagels and doughnuts were a huge hit with the walk-in crowd and Wren was overseeing the breakfast crew who were baking everything fresh ready to fill the display cases. She grabbed a doughnut for herself for her own breakfast and stood back, out of the way, so her staff could work without her breathing down their necks.

"Ooh, that looks good," Takira said, leaning over Wren's shoulder and eyeing the doughnut. She wandered off to greet the staff and took two doughnuts off their tray, laughing when one of the bakers tried to slap her hands away playfully.

Wren loved the atmosphere in the restaurant. She'd never worked in one that was as hard working but still jovial. It said a lot about Takira's way of managing her staff and how she treated each and every one of them as important as the next. Wren was head chef, with all the prestige that came with the title, but the kitchen couldn't run without the waitresses, the cleaners, or the guys who brought the produce. Takira treated everyone who came to her restaurant, be it through the front door or the back, as family. Wren hadn't been there long but she felt a sense of belonging. This had become more than a job. It was a joy to create, and bake, and serve the food. When Wren had been with her mama in the kitchen, *this* was the kind of dream she had. A fun place to make food that tasted phenomenal and made people happy.

Takira guided Wren to join her to sit at the bar. "What are you thinking about that's given you a 'lightbulb' moment emblazoned on your face?"

Wren smiled. "Just realizing all my dreams have come true working here."

Takira's face lit up. "Oh, sweetie, that's so good to hear." She took a bite from her doughnut and sighed. "We make the best doughnuts. I'm biased but that doesn't mean I'm not right." She licked the powdered sugar from her lips then stilled. The look in her eyes grew intense.

Wren would have had to be blind not to see what was happening. She didn't even need to look to know who had captured Takira's attention. "Leave Dante alone. She's sorting out a snafu with the coffee company. We're a crate short."

Takira continued to eat her doughnut, her eyes not shifting from Dante. "But she's too good not to stare at. She's got her sleeves rolled up, and that new pinstripe vest, and those Chinos hugging all the right places..."

Wren handed her a napkin. "Here, you might need this. You're practically drooling."

Takira laughed and dragged her attention from her lover. "I don't think I'll ever tire of looking at her."

Wren envied Takira's utter confidence that Dante was her match. "You're lucky."

Takira finished off her doughnut. "No woman on the horizon yet for you, Wren?"

"I'm too work orientated. I put my heart and soul into my job. No woman wants to be second best to that."

Takira nodded. "That's exactly how I got where I am today. Give or take a scheduled booty call when the itch needed to be scratched."

Wren was so thankful she'd just swallowed her mouthful of doughnut or she'd have choked. "Takira!" she said. "TMI!"

Takira just grinned at her. "I don't need to worry about that now. I have the most gorgeous butch babe who caters to *all* my needs." Takira leaned in close to whisper, "If you get my drift."

"Sure, *now* you whisper when the words *booty call* still ring around the restaurant." Wren shook her head at her. "Seriously though, how did you ever make time? Before me, that is."

"I didn't and I suffered for it. No matter how big your dream, Wren, you need to have a life to go with it. It gets lonely real fast, otherwise."

"I flirted with someone today," Wren blurted out, wanting desperately to have someone to talk to about it. "Deliberately flirted, not as a tease. I never do that. I have zero flirt game. My mind is set firmly on my career goals. But I flirted and I don't know why. She didn't even look like herself. But the words just slipped right out of my mouth and now they're out there. I really, *really*, like her, but I don't think I have time to commit to someone when my job always has to come first."

"Okay, let's break that ramble down into bite-sized pieces," Takira said, leaning back on her stool like she meant business. "First thing, you flirted. You go, girl! Glad to know you have it in you."

Wren hated that she was getting embarrassed, but Takira's support was heartwarming.

"Now the whole *she didn't look like herself...*it's way too early in the morning to lay that on me so explain, please."

"She was dressed as Doctor Who."

Takira nodded sagely. "Which one?"

Wren sighed, exasperated with herself. "Am I the only person who doesn't know about *Doctor Who?*"

"You are very single-minded at times," Takira said. "It's endearing, if a little limiting. Anyway, who was she? Did she wear a long scarf, a leather jacket, a fez?"

Wren hoped the look she was giving Takira wasn't as goofy as it felt. What on earth was she going on about? A *fez?* "She said she was Thirteen."

"Ooooh." Takira's smile widened. "Jodie Whittaker. God, she owns that role. Tall, blond, gangly, kind of chaotic, deliciously gorgeous, sexy as hell, and the size of her hands..."

"You've just described Drew to a tee." Wren knew she was in trouble the minute her words escaped her. Takira pounced.

"Drew the comic book store gal was the recipient of your flirting this morning?"

Wren nodded. "She was going to a convention, all dressed up. She looked amazing, and I think she was singing."

"I didn't know Drew could sing." Takira looked surprised.

"I didn't either but it was really quiet. I could have misheard. And then I yelled at her and frightened her to death."

"You yelled, then flirted? Wouldn't have seen that as your dynamic but each to their own."

Wren huffed at Takira's teasing. "I yelled because I thought she was trying to break into the store. Then I saw it was Drew and the flirting was kind of a parting shot. I called her cute." Wren sighed. "I was way more confident doing it than I am now thinking about it."

"How did Drew react?"

"I kind of skipped out of there without waiting for a reaction?"

"Are you telling me or asking me?"

"*Telling* you?" Wren felt pathetic.

Takira reached over to pat Wren's arm comfortingly. "Next time, when you're getting your flirty game on, you really need to stop and see if it's working. It's kind of like you setting a pan to heat then walking away and not noticing it boiling over."

Wren nodded, chewing on her lip a little. "How do I see this *Doctor Who* thing?"

Takira never batted an eye at the non sequitur. "Do you have BBC America?"

Wren shrugged. "I have no idea. I barely turn the TV on."

"Bring your tablet in and I'll get Dante to set it up for you."

"And I'll be able to watch it on that?"

"Yes. Just start with Jodie's episodes though. The guys were good but she's way better. And I bet your girl is more interested in her anyway. We *all* are."

Wren nodded her thanks. "I'll do that." *Maybe then I'll have a clue about something big in Drew's life. It's what* friends *do, right?* Takira's words sunk in. "And she's not my girl."

"Not yet," Takira said with a sly grin. She took a big bite from her doughnut and just stared at Wren, daring her to argue.

Dante wandered over to them. "Ladies, Takira's is about to open for business."

Takira pretended to shiver. "I love it when you get all professional."

Dante leaned across the bar to kiss her quickly on the lips. "Go serve your customers. If you can spare any time today, Master Finn and I will be starting a marathon viewing of all the different incarnations of Spider-Man movies."

"Will there be popcorn?" Takira asked.

"I may have brought your favorite caramel popcorn just in case you could join us, yes."

"Will there be cuddling?" Takira's voice dropped a register.

Wren watched Dante's reaction to the sensual purr with interest.

"There'll always be cuddling." Dante's voice dropped too.

Wren shivered for real. She could almost feel the sexual tension between them sparking in the air. She threw her hands up in defeat. "Okay, that's my cue to leave. You two and your sexy shenanigans are way too much for me to handle this early in a morning when I'm still freaked about flirting. I'm seeking refuge in the kitchen where I'll be cooking up a storm."

"It won't always be your safe haven," Takira called after her.

"It is today!" Wren called back and threw herself into helping someone make a batch of porridge. Anything to keep her mind off Drew and likewise Takira's stark warning about Wren needing a life outside the kitchen to be truly happy. She looked around her. This had always been her safe place. The thought of needing more scared her.

Especially if *more* was starting to look decidedly tall and blond with a strange choice in role models who wore rainbow striped shirts.

Chapter Seven

Still high from a successful weekend at the MoCon, Drew wandered around her store, reminiscing. They'd had a great time mixing with the other conventioneers and Drew had been quite the hit in her costume. She'd had a few women show some interest in her, much to the amusement of Dakota, who had been urging her to use it to her advantage. Drew had politely declined every offer to have her "use" her sonic screwdriver on them. She knew all about people only wanting her for the image she portrayed and not for the real person behind it. It was all as fake as the wig she'd been wearing. Drew really didn't want to have sex with someone just because they wanted the fantasy of fucking the Doctor. That wasn't why she cosplayed and she wasn't *that* desperate for a bedmate.

The door dinging announced a new customer and Drew watched as Trent Williams wandered in, ushering her tiny daughter before her, followed by Dante with Finn. Harley and Finn ran around the shop to greet Drew excitedly before they hurried back to their parents. Drew bit back a grin at how well-mannered the children were, considering they weren't even four years old yet. She didn't feel on edge when those two were in her store. They didn't rearrange the Funko Pops, or wreck the covers of the comic books. They were welcome every time.

"Drew, how did the con go? I can't believe I couldn't get time off this weekend. I'm the manager, for God's sake!" Trent said, clearly unhappy. Trent, dark-haired, and handsome as hell, stood by Dante, who was older, grayer, and a calming influence to all.

"It was a good one. I didn't bother with many of the TV personalities though, they were a bit obscure and not from anything I was interested in. I did however find what you were after." Drew grinned at the excited reaction from Trent. For a moment she could see how little Harley Quinn favored her mama. Drew went back to her counter and pulled out a huge box from its carrier.

Trent let out a happy little sigh. "Will you open it for me so I can get a look inside?"

Carefully, as if handling something infinitely fragile and precious, Drew eased off the black slip cover proclaiming *Star Wars: The Child* on it. It revealed a box underneath with artwork on it.

"Look at that! Oh my God, the artwork on the box alone is fantastic. Sideshow always does a magnificent job." Trent rocked on her heels, anticipating the reveal.

Drew loved her response. She got the same way with her own statues that decorated the apartment. They were, to her, exquisite works of art.

Harley clung to Trent's leg. "What, Mama? What you got?"

Trent picked her up so she could see when Drew pulled out the packaging holding the statue inside. Harley squealed and clapped her hands in delight. "Baby Yoda!"

Dante snorted behind them. "Some things never change. Trent, you're still a big ol' Star Wars nerd."

Trent proudly owned it. "I'll be a rebel til the day I die." She leaned in to study the statue of Grogu from the TV series *Star Wars: The Mandalorian.* "I have a space ready and waiting for this little guy. Juliet is gonna love him." She put Harley down and reached for her wallet. "He's going to make my wallet groan, but he's worth every dollar. He looks so real."

Drew set to packing the statue back up as carefully as she'd unwrapped him. "They only had two so you were lucky. I grabbed him the second I saw him and ran back to the car to hide him away."

"You are fantastic," Trent said, counting out her money. "Thank you for getting it for me."

"It was no problem. Anything you ever want from a con I'm going to, just let me know." Drew put everything back in the bag and gathered up Trent's money. "Now you just need to make sure you have plenty of frogs to keep him fed!"

Harley's face lit up. "We're getting froggies?"

Trent shook her head. "Not real ones. Mommy wouldn't like it. Maybe a pretend one though, one that can go on the shelf with him so he has a friend."

Harley looked a little disappointed they weren't getting real ones to hop around the house. She wandered off to join Finn and Dante who were checking out the posters.

Drew pulled out two action figures from under the counter. She lowered her voice. "I found these for Harley and Finn. Can they have them?"

Trent looked them over and nodded, smiling at the Wonder Woman obviously for Harley as she was Harley's favorite superhero. She picked up the other box. "How did you know Finn is currently Miles Morales mad?"

Drew gave her a look. "I run a comic book store. I know all my customers' geeky needs." She relented under Trent raising an eyebrow at her. "He told me when he and Dante were in here last week that they were playing the game on her PS4 and how cool it is Miles looks like he does."

"I've played that game; it's brilliant. Miles is definitely a hero of mine too." Trent reached for her wallet again. "How much do I owe you for these?"

Drew shook her head. "No, these are from me. Those two are my best customers. They have a Gashapon capsule from the vending machines every time they come in here. They have their comic books pre-ordered with me. Finn's about to redecorate his room in Miles Morales posters. These are my treat for them. I found them at the con yesterday and couldn't resist getting them."

"Thank you." Trent called the children over. "Harley, Finn, come see what Drew has gotten for you."

Harley and Finn oohed and ahhed over their new figures. Before they started to struggle with the packaging, Trent told them they couldn't open them until they were at home so they wouldn't lose any of the pieces. They both gave Drew big hugs that she wasn't expecting and was a little startled by, but she was happy they liked what she'd found. Dante paid for the poster Finn had picked out and then they all stood by and watched while Harley and Finn seriously debated over which toy in a capsule would be suitable for today.

"I don't know why Harley ponders over it so long. We all know she'll pick the *Frozen* one and I'll end up with another Elsa to sell on eBay because she already has five of them 'letting it go' all around the house. She's after Olaf but he's a wily little fucker." Trent hastily smothered her last word as the children came running back with their choices in their hands. Dante and Trent helped open them for them. Finn proudly held up a Pokemon critter that Dante had no clue about. Fortunately, Trent did and named it. Harley opened her bag and let out a cheer when she finally found an Olaf.

"Oh, thank God," Trent muttered and cheered along with her.

Dante was about to steer Finn toward the door to leave but stopped. "Before I forget. Drew, this Friday we're meeting up at Monica and Elton's. Before you say you can't come, I know full well your grandma will be with Mrs. Daniels because they've already ordered their food from us to cater for their evening."

Drew rolled her eyes. "Those two might as well move into your place. Since when did canasta have to be a catered event?"

"Sooo," Dante drawled out, "when you close your shutters get yourself over to Monica's. I'll be there with Finn."

"Juliet and I too. Finn and Harley are having a sleepover with baby Natasha."

"My Tasha," Harley said, dancing Olaf around in the air.

"Takira's working so I'll be stagging it," Dante said. "This way, you, Trent, and Elton can actually see each other face-to-face instead of chatting through your headsets."

Drew was a member of the Baydale Reapers gaming clan that Trent and Elton ran. She played *Call of Duty* with them most nights. It would be nice to get out of the apartment and socialize with them, especially as her grandma would be equally occupied. Drew nodded. "I'll be there."

Dante looked surprised at her. "I was honestly expecting to have to cajole more and then resort to threats."

"Hey, I'm not *that* anti-social," Drew complained, knowing full well that yes, she actually *was* that anti-social, but she was making an effort not to be so obvious about it.

"Friday, seven o'clock. Takira's promised us a feast to make the night go with a swing."

"Then doubly yes, I'll be there," Drew said.

"It's never our company," Trent said, feigning hurt, "it's always the food."

"It *is* Takira's food," Dante said as if that explained it all.

"True." Trent smiled then pointed at Drew. "I'll see you Friday. Now Harley and I are going home to play with our new toys, thanks to you."

"Have fun." Drew waved them off and noticed how quiet and empty the store felt without them.

She'd made some marvelous friends since moving into the store. Trent had been one of the first customers through the door. She'd met Monica and Elton, and now their new baby, Natasha, through knowing Trent. She saw more of Dante now that she had Finn in tow. Her circle of people kept growing. It was something Drew had never had before. Her mother hadn't encouraged making friends. All of Drew's young life had seen her forced into pursuing her mother's ambition for her. What few friends she had soon fell to the wayside. Friends were of no use unless they did something for you, her mother drilled into her. Once her parents were gone and she'd had a second chance at childhood, it had taken a long time for Drew to make new friends.

She had been the shy, geeky tomboy. The one who was almost excruciatingly shy around people, and who would never sing in school. The one who was lean and lanky, lacking in any feminine curves. Her mother had hated that in her as a child. Drew dreaded to think what her opinion would be if she'd lived to see Drew reach adulthood. Especially her being an out and proud lesbian. Her mother would have likely disowned Drew in a heartbeat. She'd have held up pictures of other women and pointed out where Drew was lacking. She'd have constantly bemoaned the fact she didn't get a *normal* daughter like she'd hoped for.

Drew hated that something as brutal as a car accident had killed her parents but had left her free to live life how she chose. Drew could never come to terms with it. Her freedom had come at a terrible cost.

Grandma says everything happens for a reason.

Drew often wondered what *her* reason was as she stood in the comic book store she owned, living a life that was a million miles away from the future her mother had demanded of her.

But it's my *life and I'm living it. Free of spotlights and performances. Just me and Grandma and my growing circle of friends who like me for who I am. Drew, the comic book store owner. Where the only name in lights is Dawes & Destiny Comics.*

And Drew loved it that way.

The restaurant's kitchen was devoid of orders shouted out or the clang of pans. It was the strange lull in the middle of the afternoon when there were just a few customers already catered to and the kitchen could just *pause*. It wouldn't last long, there were always more customers in and out of the popular restaurant and meals to be prepared for the evening crowd. But the quiet moment gave Wren time to take a moment, lean back against a countertop, and just observe. She was watching Takira over on the other side of the room, decorating a cake for an anniversary. Takira, lost in a world of her own, was oblivious to how many of the staff were watching her. She swirled the icing bag with ease and styled fondant roses on a pretty pink slab of rich red velvet cake.

Dante sidled in beside Wren. Wren tried not to stand at attention and quickly find something to do.

"She makes that look so easy, doesn't she?" Dante said, watching Takira along with everyone else.

"She's a master at her craft. I can never get the icing to be so uniform in its swirls as she can. I can ice and it's edible, but it's a poor man's cake compared to what Takira can do."

Dante nodded, clearly proud of what her love could create. She never took her eyes away from the cake decorating. "Do you think she's happy?"

Wren turned to Dante. Her question had held a curious tone to it that intrigued Wren. "Professionally? I'd say definitely. She's still running the restaurant, but she's able to go back to how she started here. She's brought so many new dishes to the menu since she stepped back, and the customers can't get enough of them. She's gathering momentum in the occasion cakes side because people already love her desserts. Personally, though, I think she's eventually going to need to get someone in to work with her on that because she's getting a very long list of cakes wanted and there's only one of her to fulfil them."

"She tells me you're all helping her out with them."

"Yeah, some of us like to play with icing as much as the next chef. It's a nice break from what I usually do."

"Finn loves it when she's doing these cakes."

"That's because she lets him lick the spatula when she's finished before it ends up in the sink."

Dante laughed at Wren's blunt reply. "That's my boy!" She looked at Wren. "Am I going to need to get an extension to the building so she can do the cakes out of the way of the dinner preparation?"

Wren considered this a moment, weighing the options as she cast an eye around the kitchen. "Eventually...probably...yes. Let's see how regular the orders are first before an addition is necessary. It's a novelty at the moment, brought on by that grand wedding we hosted a month ago. For now, there's plenty of room where she is and plenty of hands to help." Wren shook her head, watching Takira in her zone. "She's amazing to watch. She was born for this."

Dante agreed. "A born provider." She nudged Wren's shoulder. "And you're exactly the same."

Wren nodded. "Ever since I was big enough to hold a wooden spoon, I wanted to be a chef. Mama said I flew past the Easy Bake Oven stage. I wanted the real thing." She smiled at the memories. "My childhood was cooking with either my grandma or mama.

Some of the best memories I have are of time spent with them, watching something rise in the oven."

"No wonder Takira hired you. You're her twin." Dante grinned down at her.

Wren felt her chest ache with a burst of pride. "Dante, you have no idea what a compliment that is to me."

"You fit into this kitchen like you were born to be here. You two make a great team. Don't think it hasn't gone unnoticed."

Wren's cheeks bloomed with heat. "Working here is my dream job. It was like winning a thousand lotteries learning I had the job."

"More than getting your own place?" Dante asked, her gaze sharp as she watched Wren, waiting for her reply.

"That's a 'one day' dream," Wren said. "But working here, with this staff? It's such a family affair that, to be completely honest? It may not be my name over the door but I feel like this place *is* mine. My place is *here*. My heart knows this is *home*."

Dante's smile almost made Wren melt. No wonder Takira had no defenses around her.

"That's exactly how I feel," Dante said. "This place has a magic to it I've never felt before. I've worked in other countries and just couldn't put down roots. It took me coming back to Missouri, stepping into this restaurant, and meeting the loves of my life to know that I was truly home."

Wren sniffed and surreptitiously wiped at her eyes. "Don't make me get emotional. The staff will think you're firing me!"

Dante's laughter caused Takira to look up and spot her. She smiled over at the two of them. "Should I be worried you two are watching me?" Takira narrowed her eyes at them playfully.

"Just admiring your...*talents*," Dante said, causing Takira's laughter to sound out in the kitchen.

"You'd better have your eyes on the cake, Dante Groves," Takira said, brandishing her piping bag at her.

"My eyes are always on the sweetest thing this kitchen has to offer."

Wren choked back a giggle at Dante's blatant flirting. The rest of the staff started to take notice and enjoyed their banter too. It was a usual occurrence once Dante left her office and Takira was in her sights.

Takira stared at Dante just a little longer than necessary then smiled. "You say the sweetest things." She looked a little flustered and shook her head at them.

Wren thought it was so cute. She stared up at Dante and watched her smile grow tender.

"I'm going to marry that girl one day," Dante said for Wren's ears alone.

Wren didn't doubt her. She whispered back. "She'll want to make her own wedding cake." She knew Takira's need to take control all too well.

"She can do whatever she wants so long as she says yes."

"Don't wait too long. She's a very independent woman. She's likely to propose to you before you even get a chance to get down on one knee."

She watched Dante's eyes widen as she recognized the truth in that. "Damn, you're right. I'd better hustle my butt!" Dante pushed away from the counter she'd been leaning against with Wren. She stopped whispering. "Before I forget, Takira has taken your shift Friday night, as you have been invited to a night of fun, frivolity, and food at Monica and Elton's with us all."

"The Friday Finn can't shut up about?"

"The very same. He gets a sleepover with his little buddies, and we get to eat, drink, and be sober for the children but merry at heart."

Wren snorted. "Yeah, no. The kids are your responsibilities. I hear a bottle of wine with my name on it Friday night."

Dante patted her on the shoulder. "I'll come pick you up, then you can be as obnoxiously merry as hell as you wish."

"There's no need. I have the early Saturday shift so I'll be as sober as a judge." Wren made a face. "Unless you think my manager would alter that for me if I had to be carried home?"

Dante shook her head. "Nope. But she'd tuck you in on the sofa upstairs so that Saturday morning you'd be woken up by Finn's cartoons and him sitting on you because you're in his spot."

"That's a mean way of making sure I drink responsibly."

Dante laughed at her. "Wren? You're the most responsible person in this room. The bottle may be calling but you'll still make one glass last all night."

"You make me sound so dull. Pretend I'm wild and crazy for a moment."

Dante paused, considered that for a moment, then shook her head. "Nope, that was too scary a thought."

Wren picked up a spoon and brandished it at her. "Scoot out of my kitchen before I unleash my crazy on you."

Dante raised her hands and disappeared into the hallway, laughing all the way, to go back to her office.

I'm going out Friday night, Wren thought with an excited inner squeal. She always had fun with Monica and her friends. She'd become a part of their group without even realizing how but she was grateful for their friendship. This time, in this job, she wasn't lonely for company if she wanted it.

She got back to work having something to look forward to. There was just that small voice in the back of her head. She tried to hush it, but it kept niggling at her.

I wonder what Drew will be doing Friday night?

CHAPTER EIGHT

The Simons' home was one of Drew's favorite places to be. It was a welcoming place, even with its spooky *Nightmare Before Christmas* theme. Inside was a mixture of Monica's unique Gothic style, Elton's fascination with *The Crow*, and baby Natasha's bright colored toys scattered amidst it all. The three children present that night were already in bed inside. The adults sat outside around a large table covered in empty plates. They sat resting their appetites and enjoying more grown-up conversations.

Trent and Juliet sat close together, laughing at Elton's spirited rendition of a customer he and Trent had dealt with earlier that day. Monica sat beside him, crocheting a blanket. Drew watched her nimble fingers fashioning the cream wool into intricate patterns. Drew was fascinated how quickly she could do row after row. Drew was lucky if she could thread a needle without sticking herself.

Idly, Drew swirled her straw in her drink, laughing at Elton's theatrics. Across the table she could see Dante seated with Wren. Drew had been surprised when Wren had turned up too but was secretly pleased and had enjoyed surreptitiously watching her all evening. Wren was laughing too, her dimples creasing her cheeks in her mirth. Drew wanted to run her fingers over them, trace the little indentations and then cup her cheek and…

"Drew, I wanted to thank you for getting Baby Grogu for us," Juliet said, smiling across the table at her, startling Drew from her musings. "Trent is having so much fun recording Harley talking to him. She's already told him, months ahead of time, what she wants for Christmas. I just hope Santa ignores her wish for a real lightsaber."

"I have a friend who has the same Grogu model. Her cat keeps head-butting Grogu's hand that's shaped like he's using the Force. It's just the right height for Leonardo to get head scritches from Baby Yoda." Drew stopped swirling her straw and addressed Wren. "I bet you don't know Grogu either, do you?"

"I'm not totally pop culture impaired," Wren argued. "I've seen the memes and I have Ana who's educating me in all things Star Wars, Marvel, and CD."

"DC." Everyone around the table corrected her as one.

Juliet laughed and reached out to pat Wren's hand. "It's so nice not to be the only odd one out here." She rested her head back on Trent's shoulder. "Believe me, you'll learn everything quickly in order to stay in on any given conversation with this lot."

"She's a whiz at baking Spider-Man cookies though," Dante said. "She and Takira did a batch for the kids at play group this week and they were fantastic. I managed to grab two before they were gone."

Juliet nodded. "Harley ate her weight in them."

Wren shook her head. "I'm not taking the credit for those. It was Takira who iced them to perfection. I just prepared the dough."

Drew hummed under her breath. "I like cookies as much as anyone, but those sound fantastic. Peter Parker or Miles Morales cookies though?" She looked to Dante for her answer.

"Who do you think?" Dante laughed. "He's obsessed with Miles. It's so fun to see. Every kid needs someone they can see on the screen and identify with. I've promised him on our next trip to the barber's I'll have them etch a spiderweb into where he's shaved."

Drew loved the sound of that. She ran her hand over her own shaved hair. "That sounds so cool. I wonder if I could get a Wonder Woman W cut into mine?" She rested her drink on the table and quietly addressed Monica. "May I use your bathroom, please?"

"Drew, you don't have to ask. You know where it is." Monica waved her off.

Drew got up to enter the house. She knew her way around well enough, having been a visitor many times before. Her favorite part of the house was the staircase. The walls, covered in a multitude of different frames, charted the Simons' family history. Drew stopped as she always did and looked at a photo obviously taken very early on in Elton and Monica's relationship. They shared a look of new love blossoming. There were a lot featuring them with Trent and Juliet. Drew knew that Elton and Trent had a friendship that started way back in school. There were pictures of them at parties, weddings, Elton holding baby Harley as she tugged on his beard and, as the photo snapped, made his smile look more of a grimace of pain. Newer photos of Natasha appeared, some highly professional which Drew knew came courtesy of their friend Scarlet. She was an artist who used every medium to showcase her creativity. Drew loved the one of Harley, Finn, and Natasha all posed for the camera. Drew had a feeling those three were going to be a barrel of fun growing up together.

The pitiful wail of a baby's cry pierced the air and made Drew jump. Natasha was *loud*. She grimaced in sympathy as she finished walking up the stairs. The noise was even worse the closer she got. Drew figured Monica or Elton would come see to her. Didn't parents have a sixth sense when it came to a crying child?

Drew didn't expect Harley and Finn, dressed in identical Spider-Man pajamas, to be waiting at the top of the stairs for her.

"Drew! She's crying. Make her stop," Harley demanded, reaching for Drew's hand, and pulling her into the nursery.

Drew hesitated by the door. She looked over at the crib. "I think maybe she needs her mommy."

"No, you can do it! Get her out." Harley's voice brooked no argument.

Drew entered the room cautiously. She peered into the crib and found Natasha, red-faced, wet-faced, and clearly unhappy. Drew hesitated, but the baby was obviously in distress so Drew slowly reached into the crib to pull out a crying Natasha. She held her awkwardly at arm's length, unsure what to do next. She had zero experience with holding babies. She usually only saw them at a distance in someone else's arms. She'd been happy with that.

Harley huffed. "Hold her like a mama!"

Drew looked down at Harley. "I'm not sure how. I'm not a mama."

Finn leaned around Drew to address Harley. "She needs a mommy to be a mama. She don't got one."

Drew found herself decidedly nonplussed as to how this child knew she was single.

"On your shoulder," Harley instructed her, dishing out her orders like a pro. Drew tentatively rested the now screaming child against her shoulder. Natasha laid her head into Drew's neck and sobbed as if her heart was breaking.

"Does she need changing?" Drew asked, hoping to God she didn't. She'd break her neck running down the stairs for help if that was the problem.

Finn shook his head. "She's not stinky."

"She probably had a nightmare. She needs a cuddle," Harley said. "And pats. Pat her butt."

Drew clumsily shifted the child in her arms so she could cup a hand to cradle the baby's butt. She began patting slowly. Natasha's volume diminished a touch, but she was still loud. Drew couldn't hold back a grimace at how ear-piercing Natasha's crying was right next to her head. She feared she'd lose her hearing if the baby didn't calm down.

"No! You have to do it a little harder. Pats like when my Tasha was in Auntie Monica's tummy. Her heartbeat patted baby Tasha."

"And rock her," Finn said, rocking himself to show Drew how.

Drew quickly found a tempo that seemed to calm Natasha down a little more. She looked down at Harley. "Now what?"

"Sing to her."

Drew froze mid rock. Her body started shaking and she gripped a little more to Natasha. "I…I don't sing," Drew said, shaking her head furiously.

"Sing anyway. Auntie Monica always sings her to sleep," Harley said.

Drew closed her eyes against the blackness that threatened to steal her sight as panic set in. She felt the familiar tremor that rooted her to the spot and flirted with making her pass out. Drew knew she couldn't let herself fall because she held Natasha in her arms. Willing herself not to let the fear overtake her, Drew sucked in a few shaky breaths. She felt Harley's and Finn's little hands clutch at her jeans as they crowded in while Natasha continued to cry. Drew opened her eyes to find Harley and Finn looking up at her, expecting her to fix this, trusting she could do this.

Just sing.

Drew stood a little straighter and started to pat out a rhythm against a diaper-covered butt as the music took shape in her brain. She was hesitant at first but then, with more confidence, she began to sing. Her voice was low and husky as she sang about a young child's innocence and her wanting to run away with her little friend who didn't have a happy home life. As the song progressed, Drew lost herself in it, just as she used to, back when singing was a pleasure and not the nightmare it became. Drew hummed the instrumental part of the song's ending before eventually falling silent. Natasha's crying had stopped and Drew honestly couldn't say when that had happened.

Carefully, Drew knelt down to Harley's and Finn's height. "Is she asleep?" she whispered.

Finn nodded. "She's dribbled on your shoulder. I fix it!" He grabbed a cloth from the changing table and dabbed at Drew's shirt. "All clean. Might be sticky though. Her drool is worse than Spider-Man's web." He pretended to shoot web from his wrists in demonstration.

Drew carefully got back up and slowly eased Natasha away from her to lay her back down in her crib as carefully as if she were handling something explosive. Drew watched her for a moment. Natasha's face now looked peaceful as she slept, sucking on her little fist for comfort.

Harley tugged at Drew's pant leg. "She woke us up. Come read us a story now." Harley and Finn pulled Drew away from the nursery before she had any chance to refuse.

Drew welcomed the distraction. The haunting melody of the song she sang lingered in her head. This time she didn't chase it away. She welcomed it like an old friend and found a semblance of peace in it.

❖

Wren was glad she wasn't the only one left dumbfounded by what they had just witnessed. Everyone had congregated around the tablet Elton used as a baby monitor, watching the performance that had just taken place in the nursery on it.

"Oh my God," Monica whispered in awe. "She sang Taylor Swift to my child."

Wren quickly looked to Juliet, wondering if this was some kind of huge dishonor in the goth rock Simons household. Juliet just smiled and explained.

"Taylor Swift is Monica's guilty passion."

"She sang 'seven' from *folklore*," Monica said. "That's my favorite track. God, she was *amazing*." Monica turned to Wren. "Did you know Drew could sing like *that*?"

Wren shook her head. Singing had never come up in any of their conversations. Drew was the comic book geek. Wren had no idea that inside the geeky store owner *that* voice hid. Wren wondered what other surprises she had in store.

Everyone looked up at Drew when she finally made her way back to the table.

"I'm sorry. Two very persuasive children apparently needed to hear *The Gruffalo* tonight and then proceeded to fall asleep just as I was getting to a good bit." Drew sat down and reached for her drink. "For a moment, I thought they meant *Mark Ruffalo* and I was all set to do my best Hulk impressions." She finished off the last of her soda from her glass and only then realized that everyone was silent and staring at her. "What?"

"You sing like an absolute superstar and ask us *what*?" Elton shook his head at her. "Dude, I had no idea that kind of voice could come from you."

"That's because you usually only ever hear her say 'fuck you' when someone shoots her when we're playing," Trent said.

Color drained from Drew's face. "You...heard me sing?" She tried to sound nonchalant but the words sounded strangled to Wren's ears.

Monica turned the tablet around so that Drew could see the nursery and the room she'd left Harley and Finn snoring in. Wren saw Drew's hands dig into her thighs as she struggled to take in air. Her breath wheezed out from her, becoming erratic and panicked. Wren shot out of her seat to get to her before the panic attack brewing hit full force. She knelt at Drew's side and placed her hands over Drew's own, stilling them.

"*Drew.*"

Blindly, Drew gaze sought out Wren's. Her hands grabbed onto Wren's and held on a fraction too tight. Drew's eyes looked wild and dark with pain.

"It's okay. You're among friends here. I need you to take a deep breath. You're hyperventilating and I'm too short to carry your lanky ass out to the car if you pass out."

Drew smiled through her panic. She fought to get the panic attack under control. Wren prayed that the touch of her hands would anchor Drew to her. Drew's breathing finally evened out, but she couldn't look up to meet anyone else's gaze as embarrassment engulfed her.

"I'm sorry," she whispered. "You didn't need to see me like this."

"Don't ever apologize, Drew," Dante said, coming to her other side. "We're sorry we put you on the spot about something that obviously is a touchy subject for you. I'm sorry the kids asked you to sing. I'll have a word with them—"

"No," Drew cut in. "Don't. They couldn't have known." She looked around at everyone's worried faces. "No one was supposed to know. I've managed to keep it secret for years. I never expected to out myself being asked to sing a baby to sleep." She looked sheepishly at Monica. "I couldn't say no. They had such faith that I could do it, even though I was totally useless holding the baby to pass Harley's apparently high standard of baby management."

"You were fucking great at it though," Elton said. "The singing, I mean. If it wasn't such a trigger for you, we'd move you into the spare room and pay you to do it nightly for when Natasha is crying fit to wake the dead."

Drew smiled. "I couldn't leave my grandma. I have enough with getting up in the middle of the night to help her. And who'd open my store bright and early to get your comic books in?"

Monica shook her head. "Drew, forget the comic books. You could have been famous doing anything you wanted with that voice."

Wren felt Drew's whole body stiffen at Monica's comment.

"Yeah, that was what my parents had high hopes for. But I started to get crippling stage fright and just couldn't perform anymore," Drew admitted. "*My* dreams were realized when I signed the papers for my own comic book store. That's where my hopes and dreams lay."

"How old are you, Drew?" Monica asked.

"Thirty-one."

"Oh my God, you're the same age as Taylor Swift! You could have been running in the same circles as her now if you'd have continued singing and gotten the fame that voice of yours deserves."

Drew grimaced. "My mother would have just loved that. Pitting me against someone pretty, intensely charismatic, and able to write her own songs. I'd have never heard the last of my long list of shortfalls." Drew shook her head. "No, I'm happy just to be a huge fan of hers instead. She brings more to the music industry than I could ever have achieved. And I'm more than happy to be this side of the music fence looking in."

"Yet you still can't sing," Wren said, "Not without it taking the light from your eyes."

It was obvious to Wren that she'd shaken Drew with her perception. Drew tried to shrug it off as nothing. "We've all got that one thing from childhood that haunts us and becomes excess baggage as we grow older."

Trent raised her beer bottle in the air. "Oh, I'll drink a toast to that."

Dante reached for her bottle and held it aloft. "I second it."

Wren stood up, squeezed Drew's hands before reluctantly slipping from their hold, then reached across the table to snag her own glass to raise.

Monica leaned into Elton whose bottle was still on the table beside her own. She looked over at Juliet. "Are we the only ones here who escaped relatively unscathed from our childhoods?"

Juliet snuggled into Trent's side, lending her support. "I guess so, but…" she raised her own glass, "I'll raise my glass for the strong women at this table who struggle, but survive. Love, and are loved."

Monica and Elton reached for their drinks. "Cheers to that," Monica said. The sound of their glasses clinking rang out into the night.

Wren didn't leave Drew's side. She leaned into the chair Drew sat on and rested her hand lightly on Drew's shoulder. Monica leaned over to speak to Drew while conversations started up again around the table.

"Anyway, thank you for getting Natasha back to sleep. You saved me having to come see to her and ending up dropping a stitch. She's usually a good baby, but when she wakes up crying it sometimes takes both of us to get her calm again."

Drew smiled. "Glad I could help. I'm sorry I freaked everyone out though."

Monica waved her hand dismissively. "You should have been here the night Elton, drunk off his head, screamed that the flowers were talking to him. *You* have a legit reason to feel how you feel. *He* was just fucking stupid."

"Hey!" Elton said, overhearing the disparagement. "You always say that the flowers you work with are living things. I just happened to hear them holding conversations after a particularly strong fermentation of beer that dumbass Eddie Gray brewed."

"Yeah, three barrels of that lethal stuff he brewed in his mother's basement," Trent said, laughing. "He stunk of hops for weeks!"

Wren listened to the story and laughed along. Drew was laughing too at their silliness, and Wren couldn't help but notice how attractive she was when she smiled. Drew caught her looking and grinned at her before ducking her head away in a rare instance of shyness between them. Wren really wanted to tell her she was beautiful. Instead, she just smiled and tried not to dream about them going back home together, falling into bed, and greeting the next day rumpled and giddy from lack of sleep.

Wren enjoyed the daydream for a moment. It left her yearning for something she knew she could never have. Their lives were too different, *they* were too different. But that didn't stop Wren from wishing she could feel Drew's large hands caressing her skin and bringing her to the heights of pleasure. She'd felt the slight roughness of calluses on Drew's fingertips and wondered how they'd feel brushing across her nipples and setting her flesh ablaze. Wren tried to shake herself free of those thoughts and pay attention to her friends. She held her glass out to receive a top up and ignored Dante's raised eyebrows.

It was definitely a second glass kind of night.

CHAPTER NINE

A multitude of stars shone in the night sky. Drew sat on a reclining deck chair on the balcony of her apartment, trying to count each and every one of them to delay conversation. Wren sat beside her, quiet and still. She'd insisted on accompanying Drew home in her car once the evening at the Simons' had drawn to a close. Drew knew Wren's car was still in the restaurant's parking lot. From her view off the balcony, she could see it left in its usual space. Drew had started checking it was there every morning. And every morning she told herself today was the day she'd go next door and greet Wren there and maybe, *maybe*, ask her out like she wanted to. She hadn't worked up the courage to do so yet. She looked to the stars above for guidance, a sign. They were as silent as she'd become.

"I don't think I could have made a bigger ass of myself if I'd tried tonight." Drew finally spoke, keeping her voice low in the darkness. She shifted her gaze to look over the mass of trees that gave the balcony a fantastic visa to view.

"No one thought that of you at all," Wren said, shifting on the deck chair to look at her. "We were all torn between worrying about you and being shocked that voice came out of you."

Drew couldn't help but smile. "Yeah, it's a singing voice that's wasted on me." She could still feel the bruising grip from her mother's hands. The sharp sting of her mother's nails deliberately digging into Drew's flesh as she dragged Drew off every stage she'd frozen on again. Stood in the spotlight, an audience awaiting, Drew with her guitar in her hands and her throat closing up. The lights blinded her, the sound of the crowd terrified her, and her mother's wrath afterward left Drew hiding the bruises under long sleeves and thick sweaters.

"Did you ever enjoy performing?"

Drew nodded. "At first it was great fun. I was a child who thought nothing of the fact I could handle a guitar twice my size and play it. I could hear a song on one play through and then play it and sing it."

"That's an amazing talent."

"It was." Drew remembered that time. Her mother and father had been so excited, and pushed Drew to perform in front of everyone who came to visit. They'd been so proud of her. *Look at what our child can do.* It was only later, as Drew grew, the sound of the money they were making off her started to deaden the sound of praise and Drew only heard threats. She spared Wren a glance. She didn't want to see the pity in her eyes. "My parents would have made Britney Spears's folks look altruistic."

Wren grimaced at the analogy. "Fuck, Drew. I know my parents were ambitious for Val and me but never at the use of abuse."

"Mother thought I was 'being awkward.' I was a kid, one who didn't have any friends because I was constantly practicing on the guitar or piano. Mother deliberately sabotaged any friendships I had because they got in the way of my performance." Drew shook her head at the memories. "I just wanted to be like all the others, getting dirty at the park, playing fetch with a dog, riding a skateboard and taking the skin off my knees."

Wren chuckled. "Wow, I never wanted to do any of that when I was a child."

"Yeah, but you're a *girl*." Drew made it sound like a bad thing and laughed when Wren swatted at her arm in retaliation. "My mother was so sure when I hit puberty all her hopes and dreams would come to fruition. At the advent of my first period, she fully expected me to change overnight. She expected me to grow boobs and sprout curves and become Pamela Anderson." Drew swept a hand over herself. "As you can see, that still hasn't happened. Instead, I grew taller, barely made an A cup, and started to resemble Grandma." Drew closed her eyes and tried not to flinch at memories of her mother telling her how ugly she was. It had taken years for her to regain the confidence to look in the mirror and not shy away from herself.

"You don't need the frills and layers of makeup to be you. The androgynous look works *very* well on you," Wren said.

"My mother thought I was a freak. It made puberty very difficult, trying to understand all the changes my body was going through, none of which I liked."

"No one likes periods. As someone who ends up in bed with a heating pad for the first day of agony, believe me when I say they are obviously a cruel joke played on women."

Drew sympathized with her. For a moment she imagined looking after Wren when she was hurting, the two of them cuddling up under a blanket and watching a marathon of Marvel movies together. Or plying Wren with so much comfort food and chocolate she ended up with a different kind of belly ache.

"Let's just say I wasn't the child my mother thought she was getting. But I was the one Grandma wanted and she repaired a lot of the problems I had as she steered me through becoming a teenager and beyond."

"What happened to your parents, Drew?"

Drew looked up at the stars. "There was an accident. We were in a car and came off the road. My parents died instantly. Grandma escaped with numerous broken bones and problems that have worsened throughout the years. It's why she has so much trouble walking now."

"And you? What happened to you?"

Drew remembered everything that happened that night with stark clarity. "Grandma shielded me from it all. I barely got a scratch. She held me the whole time we waited for someone to come find us. She never let go of me."

Wren's eyes filled with tears. "And that's why you're so close to her."

Drew nodded. "I owe her everything. My freedom, my sanity, my life."

Wren reached over to clasp Drew's hand. "Everything happens for a reason."

"Funny, that's what Grandma believes too."

Wren squeezed Drew's hand gently. "She's missing seeing us out here, bathing in the moon glow, surrounded by a million stars." Wren sat up a little to look out over the balcony. "This is really a great view. I know Takira and Dante have a balcony from their apartment above the restaurant. I'd never really given the view from it any thought." She lay back and wriggled into the soft cushions on the chair. "This is nice. I could get way too comfortable here."

"Grandma sits out here way more than I do."

"You're too busy running your store."

Drew nodded. She was enjoying the feel of Wren's small hand holding her much larger one. Wren really was small and delicate, in looks at least. Drew knew she could handle her own in a kitchen with no problem. She wouldn't be working at Takira's otherwise.

Wren let out a disgruntled sigh. "I have the early shift tomorrow. As much as I would enjoy staying and having you name all the stars above for me, I need to get some sleep so I don't put salt in the wrong dishes."

"What makes you think I can name all the stars?" Drew was curious about her assumption.

Wren gave her a look. "Because you're a huge geek, which means you're probably a giant nerd too and have a telescope somewhere so you could try and find aliens on one of those planets out there."

"Hey!" Drew huffed at her. "I resemble that remark!" She gestured back inside the apartment. "The telescope is inside so no one climbs up here to steal it. Grandma bought it for my thirteenth birthday. The stars do seem so much prettier from here, but I've yet to see an alien waving back at me."

Wren got up and stretched. Drew unashamedly took in every inch of her while Wren's attention was on fixing her hair.

"They're prettier because this is your home and everything is better seen from where your heart rests."

Drew nodded, but it wasn't the beauty of the stars that held her attention now. She stood up and grew more aware of just how much bigger she was than Wren. "Are all your family tiny like you?"

Wren bristled. "I am not tiny!" She balled her hands on her hips in indignation.

Drew just laughed. Wren looked adorable. "Next to me you're tiny."

Wren conceded that. She took a deliberate step closer to Drew. Drew swallowed hard at the look in Wren's eyes.

"I may be smaller, but that doesn't mean you're out of my reach." She reached up to gently pull Drew's head down to her, giving Drew the chance to stop what she was doing. Drew didn't offer any resistance so Wren kissed her.

Drew was certain her head exploded. The touch of Wren's lips on hers was warm and soft, and made her see stars ten times brighter than the ones above them. She felt Wren deepen the kiss and heard her moan. Or was that Drew moaning? She couldn't tell. All she knew was she wanted more and was about to pull Wren into her arms when Wren stepped back. Drew shivered from the loss of Wren's lips on hers.

Wren smiled at her, obviously enjoying the dazed look Drew had no doubt she wore.

"I think our second date went well, don't you?" Wren fished out her car keys from her jeans.

"Second date?"

Wren carefully traced the pattern of the Punisher on Drew's T-shirt. Drew barely felt Wren's fingertips brush over her, but her body reacted all the same to the touch.

"You're wearing your serious date T-shirt. So, I'm counting tonight as our second date."

Drew's head spun. "And our third will be…?"

Wren stood on her tiptoes and planted a little kiss on Drew's cheek. "When you summon the courage to come into the restaurant next door and ask me out properly. If you want to. Or we could just remain friends who do the occasional lunch and keep circling around this obvious attraction we have. Think about it." Wren flashed her a devastating smile and went back through the apartment to leave.

I've thought about nothing else, Drew thought as she dutifully followed her. Mesmerized by the way Wren's jeans fit and showed off her curves perfectly, Drew purposely walked a few steps behind her. Drew wasn't about to let Wren walk back to her car alone so she accompanied her, holding her hand the whole way.

The night had been a roller coaster of emotions for Drew, but the simple act of holding Wren's hand in her own soothed her like nothing else did. She watched like a lovesick teenager as Wren drove off. Only then did she head back to her apartment.

Drew meticulously locked everything up, activated the alarms, and then set about getting ready for bed. Once she was under the covers, Drew couldn't settle. She was restless, worked up, and needy. Wren's kisses had awakened a hunger inside Drew that she'd never felt before. With a groan, Drew dug out her vibrator from her bedside drawer. Grandma wasn't home; Drew could be as loud as she wanted to be. Before, her fantasies as she touched herself were always of faceless women. This time, it was Wren. Wren's hands that ran over Drew's nipples, down to tease her clit, and added the fuel to her wildest dreams. Drew gave herself over to everything she dreamed of having Wren do to her. She knew in Wren's small hands her breasts would be more than big enough. She imagined Wren's tongue tracing over the budding six-pack Drew exercised so hard to get. Drew worked herself up, teasing herself with the vibrator until it made her tingle and ache for a firmer touch. *Wren's* touch. Drew chased the need to come, with her fantasy Wren urging her on. She ran the vibrator through her wetness and then centered it on her aching clit. She altered the setting to a higher pulse that all too soon sent Drew tumbling over the edge. Wren's name escaped from her lips, leaving her panting and wrecked on the sheets. Finally, Drew settled down to sleep with the memory of Wren's sweet lips on her own.

She had been content to have Wren as nothing more than a friend, but to know she considered Drew worthy of more filled

Drew's lonely heart with hope. In her drowsy state Drew was sure she heard a love song playing. She let her inner voice sing along with it before tumbling into sleep.

Nine-year-old Drew loved school. She had a voracious thirst for knowledge and was never happier than when a book was in her hands. School was learning, and friends, and freedom. For the time she was at school Drew could just be a kid and lose herself in the crowd. But the minute the end of school bell rang, Drew's shoulders tensed and her smile disappeared and she knew who would be waiting for her at the gate.

Drew sat at her desk with a piece of paper clutched in her hand. It was a lifeline, a hope. A promise of a day spent doing something other than guitar practice, scales on the piano, or singing. It was an invitation to a birthday party. Mandy, the little red-haired girl she sat next to in biology, had handed her the invite with a smile that left Drew desperately tongue-tied as usual. She was noticing that more now, pretty girls made her shy and as stupid as the boys were around them. Drew wanted to go to the party so bad. She remembered her own parties years ago, when she'd been really little. They'd stopped once Drew reached five because her mother said she wasn't ruining her diet with cake and ice cream. Eventually, Drew's friends stopped asking her because she always had to say no.

Maybe this time it will be different, Drew hoped, knowing deep in her heart it wouldn't be. But if she held onto the paper hard enough the promise was still there, right in the palm of her hand.

Drew watched as everyone raced out of the class, glad to be going home. Drew dragged her feet. She took her time getting her backpack on and then checked her clothes over for any stains. All hell would rain down on her head if she got ink on a cuff or food on her dress.

One must always be presentable was just one of her mother's many mantras. Drew tried so hard to adhere to the list of dos and don'ts she had drilled into her, each and every day.

The corridor was awash with children pushing their way out the doors. Drew stood back and watched them. The boys with their gelled hair, the girls with short skirts that made them look years older than they were. Drew detested the clothes her mother picked out for her. She didn't feel comfortable in dresses. She watched one of the boys walk past and coveted his jeans and oversized letterman jacket. He'd obviously stolen it from his big brother. In Drew's eyes, he was the coolest thing ever. But girls shouldn't dress like boys. Drew had heard her mother's opinion on that subject loud and clear.

Once outside, Drew couldn't miss her mother waiting for her. Front and center of the other parents as usual, dressed as if she'd just come from a meeting, all power suit and high heels. She stood out amid the more casually dressed parents waiting. Mary-Louise Dawes, talent scout to the stars.

Or so she claims, Drew thought with a hint of vitriol. She walked over to her but, as always, her mother didn't acknowledge her. Instead, she parted the parents like Moses parted the Red Sea, leaving Drew to follow in her wake. Drew got in their car, careful not to slam the door too hard and be the recipient of *that* look. Her mother pulled out into traffic without a care for whoever was already in the lane. Drew slid down in her seat as a car horn blasted and an angry driver swerved around them, nearly clipping the back of the car.

"Stupid fucking woman!" he screamed out his window at them.

Her mother paid him no mind. "Drew, sit up. You'll wreck your posture slouching like an old man."

"That man nearly hit us." Drew was still shaking from the near miss.

"But he didn't and I had the right of way."

Drew looked out the window, back up the street. "I don't think so…" She *felt* the look before she even heard a word from her mother's lips.

"Really? *You* don't think so?" Her mother's face hardened. "Are *you* driving this car? What have I told you about thinking?"

Drew sighed. "That I can't possibly know what's best because I'm just a kid."

"Exactly." Her mother took her eyes off the road for a second. "What are you holding in your hand?"

"An invitation to a party. May I—"

"You know you're busy, Drew. You have guitar practice and piano lessons. I have that audition for you too."

"You don't even know what day the party is on," Drew argued. Just once she wanted to be like the others. To have cake, and ice cream, and sing something silly like 'Happy Birthday' instead of the songs her mother forced her to memorize and perform.

"Whatever day it is, you can't go. You seem to forget what we're working for here. Do I need to remind you *why* you can't waste your time on trivial things?"

"No, Mother." Drew knew her argument was dead in the water before she even started. She balled the paper up in her hand and crushed it. The sharp edges cut into her palm, but Drew welcomed the pain. It was hers. It was *her* choice to feel it.

"You have a God-given talent, Drew. Your voice will take you places those silly little children will never go. What have I told you about friends?"

"That I don't need them."

"And why is that?"

Drew took a deep breath. "Because they are a distraction and I can't afford to be distracted if I want to fulfil my dreams." *But they're not my dreams, Mother, they're yours.*

"And what do we want?"

Drew stared out the window, watching the streets fly by as her mother drove way too fast as always. "We want me on stage at the Grand Ole Opry, singing with Dolly Parton, and signing a record deal with the biggest and best producer so I make enough money so you can retire from your job and manage me." Every word cut like razor-sharp knives across her tongue. She'd had this drilled into her from a very early age. Drew wished she'd never expressed an interest in playing the guitar. Her pleasure at mastering it and finding her singing voice didn't last long. The tidal wave that was her parents seeing dollar bills at her obvious talent soon swept it away. Drew knew she could sing, she wasn't stupid. But doing it for fun was a whole lot different than her forced to sing on a stage in front of people critiquing her style when she was just a child. Their criticism hurt her feelings. They were disparaging of her looks. They expected everyone to look and act like Britney Spears while Drew's mother pushed her doggedly toward a career in country music. Drew was lean and lanky, and one old man had gone as far as saying she looked "like a boy in drag." That last comment had her mother so incensed she'd grabbed Drew hard to pull her from the stage. Drew bore the bruises in the unmistakable shape of a hand on her arm for weeks. Now her mother fought to tease Drew's long hair into something fashionable, no matter how much pain each brush stroke cost or how much Drew choked on the hairspray. She used makeup to hide Drew's natural beauty and instead painted her a new face. And she beat Drew where no one could see the marks. Beatings given because the gift Drew undeniably had did not come packaged in a more feminine daughter.

"Distractions stop you from fulfilling your obligations. What are *your* obligations?"

Drew rattled them off by rote. "To God, to family, to fame and fortune."

Her mother looked at her after they'd screeched to a halt at a red light she'd almost run through. "Give it to me." She held out her hand.

Drew dutifully handed over the crumpled invitation.

"You have a voice that will sell millions of CDs worldwide. I'd stake my career on that, and I am. What's the point of being a talent scout when my daughter has the biggest talent of them all? I just hope when you reach your teens your looks change because that voice is wasted on you otherwise." She looked Drew up and down critically. "The rest of you needs to fill out too so you can attract the guys. Sex sells. You're never too young to learn that." She pushed her foot on the gas pedal and peeled away the second the traffic light turned green. She wound down her window and tossed the invitation out.

"No more making friends you're just going to leave behind anyway. No more distractions."

Drew felt the weight of the world press down on her, trapping her, driving her breath from her lungs.

"Just God, guitar, and good press." Her mother laughed at her own wit. "Your singing is your destiny, Drew. And I'm going to make sure you fulfil it." She patted Drew roughly on her knee. "Even if I have to drag you, kicking and screaming, every step of the way."

❖

Drew woke with a start as the nightmare faded on her mother's threat. It hadn't been an idle threat either. She had literally pushed Drew on stages after Drew had barely been able to stand after throwing up from nerves. She played the oh-so-proud mother, always at Drew's side, at photo ops and interviews. Then beat her black-and-blue in the dressing rooms while Drew begged to go home, growing more and more terrified of stepping on the stage and singing for an audience.

Drew's father had been no help. He left everything to her mother and just spent Drew's earnings on new cars and alcohol-soaked parties for their friends.

Drew rubbed at her eyes and tried to wake up more so she could chase those memories from her head. She hadn't had a dream like that in ages. Her mother always haunted her dreams when Drew tried to let go of her fears and dared to sing again.

Drew sat up and ran a hand through her short hair. No more brushes caught in tangles and her head smacked with the brush in retaliation. "I never wanted my hair long, Mother. I bet you're turning in your grave at how I have it now."

She padded into the bathroom to splash water on her face, then quickly dressed. She reached into her closet for a clean T-shirt and didn't miss the unmistakable shape of the guitar case hidden way in the back. Drew hesitated for a moment, then pulled it out. She stood at the end of her bed, her hands lightly resting on the battered brown case she'd laid on her sheets. Slowly, Drew flipped open the catches and revealed the guitar inside. The acoustic guitar had a light brown body with dark brown accents. Drew's name was curlicued across the body in slick black ink. She took it out carefully, giving it a once-over for any damage left in her neglect of it. The guitar felt familiar in her hands, it molded to her body like a lover, and Drew felt like she was embracing an old friend. She instinctively began to tune it, easily plucking at the strings as if it hadn't been years since she'd last picked it up to try to play. That time the memories had rushed back and overwhelmed her so she'd hidden it out of sight again. Nervously, Drew looked over her shoulder, almost expecting her mother to come storming in at her for playing a chord wrong. Thankful she was home alone, Drew began to strum the guitar strings, practicing her scales from an ingrained memory, and then just played. She hadn't lost her touch with her favorite instrument. She rarely faltered as she ran her fingers over the strings and familiarized herself with its tone again. She linked melody after melody, old songs she'd played as a child and new ones she loved now, until she'd played for over half an hour without stopping.

But she hadn't sung a word.

Her stomach started to rumble, reminding her she needed to get ready for the store's opening. She quickly put the guitar away, shoving it back into the wardrobe, out of sight. She winced as she realized she'd cut open her fingertips. They were no longer callused enough to sustain the plucking of a guitar string for an extended use. She quickly put Band-Aids on the worst ones to stem the blood weeping out. She tried not to remember her mother screaming that Drew obviously hadn't practiced enough if her fingers weren't bleeding.

Her grandma was still at her sleepover so Drew puttered around not having to worry about getting breakfast ready for anyone but herself. She reached into the fridge and paused, leaving her juice untouched. The dream lingered in Drew's head and she needed to ground herself again in the reality that was hers *now*. She dashed down the stairs, let herself out the back door, and walked around to the front of the building. She raised the shutters early for once then stood for a long moment just looking at the sign hanging over the store.

"Here's my true destiny, Mother. My name, not in stage lights, but above the door of a career I built for myself. *Dawes & Destiny Comics.* Not the destiny *you* wanted from me, but the one I made for myself instead. With the help of *your* mother-in-law, who was a much better parent than you and Father ever were."

Someone called out to her and Drew turned around to wave at the man across the road. He was taking his dog for a walk and mercifully couldn't hear Drew talking to herself.

"Hey, Drew. Have you got any *Deadpool* comic books in? My kid saw it last night and now he's obsessed."

Drew nodded. "I've got a whole section devoted to him."

"I'll be by once I've dropped the dog back home. I'll probably bring the kid in with me. Might be the only way to get him out of bed on a Saturday morning!" He waved good-bye and Drew just smiled.

Her life wasn't the bright lights, packed stadiums, or million-dollar deals her parents had demanded of her. It was the giving of an escape from the real word, a *distraction* from it, if only for a while. To worlds of heroes who fought for those who couldn't fight for themselves.

She wouldn't trade that for anything. For Drew, no stage, however prestigious, compared to a comic book store filled with a multitude of fantastic stories.

She glanced over at Takira's, imagining Wren hard at work inside. Drew ran a fingertip along her lips, remembering the kisses they had shared. Friends might be a distraction, but when they looked and kissed like Wren did?

They were a welcomed one.

Chapter Ten

Drew was having a fantastic morning. She'd sold a plethora of Deadpool comic books to a teenager she knew would be coming back for the rest in a very short time. His father had opened his wallet willingly.

"I'd rather be buying him comic books than having him hanging on the streets smoking and drinking. Besides," he handed over his credit card, "if he gets a taste for this then there's the Punisher, Daredevil..."

"Jessica Jones," Drew added. "If you're going the more mature Marvel route then you can't leave her out."

The man nodded. "I don't think I have those on DVD." He looked up at Drew who grinned and pointed to the DVD section. He sighed. "I'll just leave you my wallet, might be easier." He paid for the comic books, handed them to his very appreciative son, and then directed his attention to the DVDs. "Let's go find something we can watch next weekend."

Drew bounced on her toes. She felt strangely energized and just a touch giddy. Dakota, dressed in a steampunk-inspired dress and wearing a tiny top hat covered in watch faces and cogs, stared at her with a curious gaze.

"If I didn't know better, Drew Dawes, I'd swear you were high on something. You're only missing the munchie phase. What has gotten into you?"

Drew shrugged at her. "I'm just enjoying the day. The sun is out, I have a full store of customers buying my wares. What's not to be happy about?"

Aaron wandered past with a stock replenishment. "You went out last night, didn't you?"

Drew nodded. "I do that sometimes. It's allowed."

Dakota snorted inelegantly at her. "Yeah, but it's not that often and you're usually grumpy about it."

"Well, this time I wasn't. I had fun." Drew ignored the part in her brain that reminded her of her panic attack. She was too busy dwelling on the feel of Wren's hand in her own and the kisses they'd shared. Her thoughts, obviously emblazoned all over her face, made Dakota squeak.

"Oh. My. God. You got some!"

Drew's head whipped around and she hushed her quickly. "Will you not...!"

Aaron quickly put everything down and hurried to Dakota's side. They both stared at her expectantly, waiting for her to spill details.

"Stop looking at me like that. You're like the freakin' Grady Twins from *The Shining* standing there."

Aaron gasped. "Ooh! That would make a great Halloween cosplay for us. I'd probably have to shave my legs...but stop distracting me. *You* went out last night."

"Yes, I was at a house with some married friends."

Dakota looked scandalized for a moment. "You didn't..."

Drew shook her head at her. "I swear to God, Dakota, your imagination is way too active. I was with Dante, Trent, Elton, and their wives. It was not some illicit wife swapping party."

"Annnnnnd, so?" Dakota pressed for more. Drew gave in way too easily.

"And Wren was there."

Aaron looked thoughtful for a moment. "The little chef from next door?" He and Dakota shared a joyous look between them. "Free food!"

Drew closed her eyes briefly. "Once again, I am regretting hiring you two at the same time. I should have known better the second you both laid eyes on each other."

"You love us. We're as weird as you are." Dakota stuck a model pose. "Well, maybe just a tad weirder."

Aaron shushed her and leaned into Drew's personal space. "Grandma was out of the apartment last night, wasn't she?"

Dakota squealed like a child who'd scored a ton of candy at Halloween. She inadvertently pulled the attention of every customer in the store to the three of them standing behind the counter.

Drew quickly waved them off. "Nothing to see here, folks, just Dakota being overdramatic as usual." She turned to her and hissed. "Will you quit it? Anyone would think I never go out or get a night alone."

"But you don't," Aaron pointed out. "It's about as rare as a Sasquatch sighting."

Drew grumbled at him. "I'm not *that* bad."

Dakota nodded. "Yes, you actually are. So, yay you for going out last night and then bringing a gorgeous woman back and—"

Drew stopped her there. "No! Nothing happened. It was a perfectly innocent night. She came and looked at the stars, then I walked her to her car and she left. Nothing else." Drew wondered why she had to explain herself and her pitiful life to these two kids. Both of whom were looking at her with disappointment coloring their faces.

"Oh." Dakota looked crestfallen. "You didn't get the telescope out and go all science nerd on her, did you? That's not going to win a woman's heart."

"Wait, that was part of *my* strategy when we were dating," Aaron blustered.

"Yeah, but I was too busy checking out your butt every time you bent over the telescope. The stars were the last things I was interested in that night."

Drew had to laugh at Aaron's conflicted face, being both complimented and dissed at the same time.

"But I thought," Aaron sputtered, but Dakota stopped his lips with her fingertips.

"You charted the skies for me and then mapped out the constellations again using the freckles all over my body." Dakota let out a breathy sigh at the memory. "It was magical."

Aaron's face reddened and his eyes softened. His face got the goofy lovesick look he always sported around Dakota. Drew decided that was way too much knowledge for her to be privy to and decided to take a break. She left them looking starry-eyed at each other.

"Just remember to serve the customers," she said. "I only needed to catch you in the storeroom once to know that was one time too many."

Dakota waved her away. "Go eat," she said dismissively. "It's your break time. We have everything under control."

Drew snorted but walked away. For once she didn't go upstairs to grab a bite to eat. Drew straightened her *Doctor Who* T-shirt and headed toward Takira's before she talked herself out of what she was going to do.

I can do this. I'm a grown woman with romance on my mind. Wren is beautiful and smart and I have to do this right. I just need to prepare for the right time and the right place and get some intel from ones who know her.

With a newfound determination, Drew walked into the restaurant as a woman on a mission. I'm so doing this, she thought, until the loudness of the restaurant and the choreographed chaos of the wait staff buzzing from table to table halted her in stride. For a moment, Drew was terrified. So many people. She clutched at the edge of her T-shirt as if drawing power from the blond-haired Doctor on it. In her own store, if the customers got too much for her, Drew sought sanctuary behind the counter and listened to the music to center her. Here, she was a small fish in the mighty ocean, frightened to swim in case the fierce tides pulled her under.

Zenya appeared by her side. "Hey, Drew. Long time no see. Can I help you?"

Grateful for her distraction, Drew nodded. "I need someone's advice on something for a special occasion. Do you think Dante is free?"

Zenya guided her around the tables and made her sit at the bar. "I'll find out for you."

Drew didn't have to wait long. Dante came out from the back of the restaurant to see her.

"Drew, it's not like you to venture in here on a Saturday. Is your grandma okay?"

Drew nodded. "I love how when I come in, everyone immediately thinks there's something wrong with my grandma. I do come in here myself, occasionally."

Dante laughed at her. "So, what brings you in here today?"

"I need some advice about an employee of yours."

Dante smiled. "Oh, this sounds intriguing. Follow me. This kind of conversation is best had away from multiple ears." She guided Drew through to a hallway and into her office. Drew's attention caught on a canvas painting featuring the characters from *Mulan*. It was an explosion of color. Bright cherry blossoms hung from a tree. An array of multicolored flowers lined the bank to a stream. Mushu, Mulan, and Li Shang took their places amid the splendor.

"This is beautiful," Drew said, fascinated by all the detail.

"*Mulan* is one of my favorite Disney films. I have a *Fantasia* one upstairs. I had this one put in here so, when suppliers are giving me a headache, I can look at this and channel only positive energy."

Drew reluctantly moved away from the artwork to sit opposite Dante at her desk.

"You're here to ask about Wren, aren't you?" Dante said. She frowned as a thought struck her. "Why do I suddenly feel like asking what your intentions are toward her?"

"God help Finn when he starts dating," Drew muttered, trying to ignore Dante's humor at her expense.

"No!" Dante raised her hands to ward that thought off. "Do not go there! I'm having to gear myself up for him going to school, I'm not ready to lose him to some girl...or boy. Not yet. He's still my little buddy."

It was obvious how much Dante loved Finn. There was no blood between them, yet their bond was undeniable. Drew was in awe of it. Her mother had given birth to her yet had never shown even a fraction of the adoration Dante had for little Finn.

"I just wanted a bit of advice. I want to ask Wren out for a meal, something informal, nothing too fancy, but how can you do that with someone who works all day in a restaurant? Any place I take her, will she critique it? If I get a bottle of wine from the store, will she judge it beneath her?"

Dante laughed. "Are we talking about the same Wren? I've seen her dunking her doughnut in her coffee."

Drew made a face. "Eww. Who does that?"

"Apparently, the girl you have your eye on does. She's not a food snob, Drew, just because she works in a restaurant. I'm sure whatever you decide to do for her she'll love, because *you* have taken the time to do it for her."

Drew wasn't so sure. "I'm a Cheerios and Doritos kind of gal. I haven't been on a date in forever. I'm kind of out of practice for selecting a place to eat that doesn't involve tater tots at some point."

"Forget Wren, I'm setting you up on a date with Finn. He hasn't met a meal yet that doesn't need tater tots as a side dish."

"I'm just worried if I offer to take her to a restaurant, it's never going to match up to this one."

"You could always dine out here."

"But then is she going to think I'm being lazy because, for one thing, she works here? And also, I literally live next door so I wouldn't even have to bother using my car." Drew slouched down in her chair like a grumpy teenager. "And I can't cook anything as fancy as Wren could prepare herself, and Grandma used to cook but that's fallen aside since she's taken root in *your* dining room."

"She's *our* grandma now!" Dante grinned at her then tried to be serious. "Okay, so you want to impress the lady but not really move out of your own comfort zone. Well, I know her favorite wine. It comes in a box and will last forever because she only ever has one drink from it at a time."

"So, not a heavy drinker. That's a good sign." Drew knew she'd inadvertently sparked Dante's curiosity judging by the raised eyebrow look Dante gave her. "I'm uncomfortable around people who drink just to get drunk. My father used to drink heavily. I don't think I remember him without a glass in his hand. He could be an aggressive drunk on the rare occasion. He and Mother used to fight like crazy over money, and if he had been drinking all day, he'd smash the room up. He never hit her, but the things he threw came close enough. I learned very early on that hearing their raised voices meant run and hide. Mostly, though, he ignored me except for when he could brag to his friends about how rich I was going to make him." Drew tried to hold back the memories that were rushing to break free. It was like her daring to sing had opened up old wounds and the memories were pouring out. "Grandma has no clue how he turned out so bad. She and Grandpa were the kindest, sweetest folk you could ever meet. She blamed Mother. She deliberately got pregnant so he'd marry her and they were never truly happy. I can't help but think he drank to escape my mother's obsessive attention. And that, unfortunately, landed all on *me*."

"I have to be honest, Drew, from what I heard last night? You have a beautiful singing voice. I'm sorry your parents bullied you to the point where it became impossible for you to use it anymore."

"I have other priorities now. My store, which is my pride and joy, and Grandma. She needs me. I couldn't be managing a singing career and looking after her at the same time." Drew couldn't see that as her life's path at all. She felt perfectly settled doing what she was doing now. Even if she was about to take a tentative step back into the world of dating. It was a daunting task. She'd been single for a long time and Drew had been perfectly content with that. But Wren called to her, no matter how hard she tried to ignore the pull.

"How did you ask Takira out that first time?" Drew needed all the help she could get.

"I brought her a bouquet, some of her favorite candy, and told her I'd cleared a space on her calendar for us. Then I took her to the hidden theater tucked away under the bar I used to work at and we watched a movie together."

Drew knew the place well. Takira had thrown a surprise birthday party for Dante there and Drew had gone along to celebrate. Whatever the theater lacked in size, it made up for in atmosphere.

"I can ask Roller, who owns the bar, if you want to book it."

Drew mulled that over for a while. "Maybe, if I manage to get past this date without screwing up. I know she's not a big movie fan though. At least, not of the superhero variety."

"If she's the right girl for you I'm sure she'll garner some appreciation of what you like. It's a huge part of who you are, after all."

"She likes the Dan Brown movies. I wonder if she's seen the new TV series, *The Lost Symbol?* Grandma and I love it." Drew nodded to herself. That might be a nice relaxing way to be together without the formality of dating in a crowded area.

"Could you plan a romantic meal at home? If it was something simple? Maybe even catered by your friends next door to your needs and hers?" Dante asked.

"That would solve another dip in the dating road that has to come up sooner or later. Grandma has to figure into the Drew Dawes dating experience. She always has to figure into the equation." Drew made a rueful face. "Which is just one of the many reasons why I'm single and have been for waaaay too long."

"Dating Takira meant I had to adjust to suddenly having a kid too. Takira had never wanted children. I hadn't had much to do with them, but Finn was left in her care and now neither of us can imagine life without him."

"I've been my grandma's primary caregiver for years now. I'm not pushing her aside for any woman who can't understand my duty to that. Inviting a woman home to meet my live-in grandma usually puts them off. Especially when I can't always stay out overnight. Grandma isn't always mobile and I can't leave her in pain just so I can sleep with someone. She's the only family I have left. She and Grandpa were the best things in my life. Grandma let me be me, finally. I owe her everything."

"So, a meal at home would test Wren's true intentions…I think she might surprise you."

"I hope so because I could get extremely serious over her. She's beautiful, and sweet, and feisty. And she's an amazing kisser."

Dante looked surprised. "She's kissed you already?"

"Last night, under the stars, out on my balcony." Drew knew her voice sounded dreamy but she was past caring.

"Could she reach you?" Dante asked with a chuckle.

"I think she might have stood on tippy toe," Drew said, sniggering a little. "She's very tiny but don't tell her that. She gets all riled up and that's just too cute for words."

"She *is* a little firecracker," Dante agreed. "How about this? You and I sort out a menu for your evening together, for *all* of you, then all you need to do is go ask the girl out."

Drew grimaced. "Sure, like that's going to be the easy part."

"Drew, it's as simple as, 'Wren, would you like to share a meal with me at my apartment on insert date here?'"

"*Insert date here?* Fuck, I've got to work out a day we're both free now. Do you have her schedule handy?"

"I'm her manager, of course I do. See, that wasn't so hard, was it?"

"I've still got to ask her." Suddenly Drew felt daunted by the task. She hadn't asked anyone out in *years*.

"I'm certain she'll say yes. I saw her last night, Drew. She never left your side after you were upset. She could have stayed on her side of the table and left you to it."

"But she didn't," Drew realized.

"And she had you drive her back here, not me. She was concerned for you."

Drew knew all this, but it was still good to have someone else notice. Drew pulled out a pad from her pocket and a pen and began scribbling on the top sheet. Dante peered over to see what she was doing. Her voice was incredulous.

"Tell me you're not asking Wren out using a children's party invitation?"

"They don't do them for dates, I checked at Hallmark."

Dante let out a long-suffering sigh and rubbed at her face. "Okay, we have way more work to do here than I expected. You can't ask her out like that!"

Drew looked at the invitation in front of her. "Why? Should I have brought the Disney Princesses one? I liked this Marvel one though. Look, it has Captain America on it. She knows who he is."

Dante looked completely at a loss for words before Drew burst out laughing at her. "You should see your face! Of course, I'm going to ask her properly. I just got this as a bit of fun."

It had more meaning to Drew than Dante would ever know. Drew wasn't ready to open that particular Pandora's box yet.

"I'm going to have the chef spike your tater tots with hot sauce." Dante blew out a breath. "Brat!"

Drew chuckled, pleased with herself. "Just find me a date she won't be working, please. Then you can tell me which fork I need to use to eat my tater tots correctly." She ripped off the top sheet that was filled in.

Dante held out her hand for the pad. "Give me the rest of those. I can use them when we plan the double party for Harley and Finn when their birthdays are due. Something tells me they'll be far easier to deal with than a nervous non-dater."

Wren often felt like the conductor of a vast symphony, knowing that one wrong baton sweep could bring the whole symphony screeching to a halt and cause the melody to die. Fortunately, everyone at Takira's knew their jobs. That made one part of her job easy, but the sheer volume of meals they were creating meant Wren barely had a second to think. The dining room was full. There were spaces on the display cases that needed filling. The home delivery team was ready and waiting to take food to those using the new app that Dante had implemented. Takira's staff had little time to pause and breathe while customers needed feeding. Lunchtime on a Saturday always gave Wren a rare moment when she'd take a breath, watch the madness swirling around her, and wonder if there wasn't something a little less manic she could have turned her talents to. She'd always dismiss the idea as soon as it hit. This was what she'd trained for. A highly successful business with a loyal customer base and no letup in the demand for more food.

Wren was preparing three meals herself. She barely acknowledged it when Zenya sidled up beside her, tray in hand, to take away the plates Wren had just added the finishing touches to. Wren merely picked up another order and prepared to fulfil that.

Zenya came back within a few minutes and leaned against the counter Wren was working at.

"Mae's granddaughter has just come in to talk to Dante. What do you think that's all about?"

It took a second before Wren's brain processed that query. "Drew's here?" She quickly looked over her shoulder and scanned what she could see of the dining area.

"She's in Dante's office. Told me she was here about a 'special occasion.' Guess it's Mae's birthday or something." Zenya chuckled. "I still can't believe Mae asked me out for her."

That brought Wren to a sudden stop. "Excuse me?"

"Yeah, her grandma asked me out for her not long after they first moved in. Kae was furious about it. She stormed off to the comic book store and was about to get all up in Drew's face when she realized Drew had zero clue what her grandma had done. Mae apologized to me and Kae the next day." Zenya laughed. "Her grandma is quite the character. I swear she and Mrs. Daniels are plotting something every time they get together. Old ladies are scary in groups."

"Mae tried to set Drew up with me," Wren admitted.

Zenya shook her head. "Guess Mae didn't learn her lesson after all. What did you do?"

"Went around to the comic book store and told Drew what was happening. Made a friend, had my lunch break there with her. Took her cake and chatted." Wren didn't look up from her task. "Might have kissed her last night under the stars."

Zenya nearly dropped her tray. "You *kissed* her?"

Wren winced at the volume of Zenya's voice. "Yeah, and I'd appreciate it if the whole of the restaurant didn't have to find out."

"Sorry!" Zenya whispered and bounced beside her, her excitement making her giddy. "What was it like? I mean, the girl is mighty fine. Tall, blond, she's got that masculine thing going on that is sooo sexy. And her hands. Have you seen her hands?"

Wren wished she'd kept her mouth shut. But now she was curious. She recalled Takira had made a comment about Drew's hands too. "What about her hands?"

"They're so big! And her fingers are long." Zenya winked at her salaciously.

Wren *really* wished she'd kept her mouth shut now, but her memory was replaying the feel of Drew's hands in her own. Wren's hands had been engulfed by them. She'd felt protected when Drew took her hand to walk her back to her car. A simple gesture that had meant so much. There'd been a strength to them, she'd felt calluses amid the softness of Drew's skin. Wren hissed as she nearly caused her sauce to burn due to her inattention. Mind in the moment, Wren, she scolded herself and hastily got back to work.

"I wonder why she's here," Zenya said, looking down the corridor to where Dante's office lay. "Maybe she'll tell you, you know, in between more kisses."

"Maybe," Wren said, trying to get her mind back in the kitchen and not thinking about Drew. "Here." She handed Zenya the plates filled with food. "Quit gossiping! And don't make me regret telling you."

"Yeah, I know. But now you're intrigued, right?"

I'm always intrigued by Drew Dawes, Wren admitted to herself. If she had to hazard a guess as to why Drew was there then it was probably to do with her grandma. Drew seemed to do a lot for her. Wren wondered if she'd be able to convince her that Drew was as important too? She was quickly becoming someone very important to Wren, after all.

Dante's voice sounded out across the noisy kitchen. "Hey, Wren! You got a second?"

Another chef moved into her space to take over the pot she was stirring and motioned for her to go. Wren wiped her hands on her cloth and made her way over to where Dante stood.

"How can I help?" she asked. Dante gestured with her thumb back down the corridor toward her office.

"I have someone in my office who'd like a brief moment of your time."

Wren nodded, not quite sure what was going on, but headed that way. She found Drew there, her nose nearly pressed up against a painting.

"Drew?"

Drew pulled back and grinned sheepishly. She pointed at the painting. "Mushu has a gong in his claws."

Wren had no clue what she was on about. "The only mu shu I know comes with pork."

"I didn't come here to disturb you at work, but Dante was adamant I did this now before I chickened—" Drew hastily shut her mouth and instead handed over a folded-up piece of paper to Wren.

Wren opened it and laughed. "It's not going to be hearts and flowers with you, is it, Drew?"

"I can do them, if you'd prefer that?"

"I'm never home long enough to look after flowers. They're pretty but they fade so fast." Wren read the invitation. "This sounds great. I'm guessing Dante told you I was off next weekend?"

Drew nodded. "Helps to have friends with access to your shifts. Is that okay? I know it's soon but…"

Wren was thrilled. "That's more than okay. I'm looking forward to it already." Wren reread the paper again. "Seeing as the invite is the Dawes *family*, I'm guessing Grandma is included too?"

"Two for the price of one," Drew said, watching Wren intently for her reaction.

"A threesome for a third date. Inventive. I like that." Wren loved how red-faced Drew got at her teasing.

"I promise I'll try to have her on her best behavior."

"No, please don't. I'd like to see *Grandma*, not just Mae the customer. Just ask her to get all the photo albums out for me. I want to see everything from baby Drew to now."

Drew took a step closer. "You don't need a photo to see me as I am now."

"You stay right where you are," Wren said, taking a step back toward the door. "Just stay over there with Mushu whatever, because if you come any closer Dante is going to kill me for what I'm considering doing in her office." Drew's laughter lightened Wren's heart. "I'll see you next weekend for our date, but I intend to see you before that. Lunch in the comic book store with its handsome owner is becoming my favorite time of day."

Drew looked so happy that the temptation to just give in and kiss her senseless left Wren not caring what Dante would do if she found out.

"Do I need to bring anything? For next weekend I mean?"

"Nope, I have that all under control." Drew looked mighty pleased with herself.

Wren had a feeling she knew what was going to happen, but she didn't want to deflate Drew's smug little bubble. "Guess I'll go back to the kitchen, but I'll see you for lunches next week. Wren turned to leave but had to ask. "You've used up your Punisher T-shirt. What's a third date tee?"

"Guess you'll just have to turn up to find out, won't you?" With a handsome grin that did curious things to Wren's insides, Dante sauntered past her, planted one long, soft, deliberately sensual kiss on Wren's lips, and left.

Dante came back in to find Wren just standing there, eyes glazed, and her heart racing.

"Were you two kissing in my office?" she asked gruffly, pretending to be annoyed.

Wren shook her head. "She kissed me; it doesn't count."

Dante sat back behind her desk. "I'll be sure to ask the chefs next Sunday preparing the takeout not to include too much garlic."

Wren appreciated that, but she still made a face at Dante's sly dig. She hastened out of the office but stopped for a moment to properly look at the invitation decorated with superheroes. It was *so* Drew.

"Drew Dawes, you are definitely one of a kind."

CHAPTER ELEVEN

Wren could barely keep up with the excited chatter of Ana as she skipped beside her. Her father walked with them, totally at ease with her exuberance.

"She's been excited all week about today," he told Wren. "I'm glad this fell on a weekend I could join you."

Wren agreed. "There's no way in hell I could have asked Val to this."

"Yeah, imagination and fun aren't really her thing, are they?"

Marco's eyes darkened with memories, and Wren felt desperately sorry for him. He'd loved Val, but it hadn't been enough to keep them together, not even for Ana's sake. But Marco's love for his child was unmistakable. Wren had always liked him. She'd feared from the start that her sister would lose him with her mind always fixated on work. Wren was glad she'd gotten to keep in contact with him after the divorce and even happier that he'd agreed to spend the day with her today. When she'd explained where she wanted to take them, he'd been as excited as Ana was.

Wren cast a critical eye over what he was wearing. "So, who are you again?"

Marco, dressed all in black leather, held up his left arm artfully wrapped in silver foil. Even his glove had silver on the fingers. "I'm Bucky Barnes."

"He's the Winter Soldier, Auntie Wren. He's the best friend of Captain America."

"And the silver bits?"

Ana eagerly explained, rattling off the details in quick succession. "He fell off a train and lost his arm. Then the big baddies called HYDRA kidnapped him and they made him a new one of vibranium that makes him really strong. Then he became a bad guy because they brainwashed him, but Steve Rogers helped him get his memories back and saved him."

Wren waited for Ana to catch her breath. "And Steve Rogers is?"

"Captain America!" Ana cheered. She stopped her dancing and struck a pose in her own Captain America suit, complete with the shield she had insisted on bringing. Ana gave Wren her best pouty face. "You didn't come in a costume, Auntie Wren."

"That's because I don't know as much about all this as you do, Captain Ana-merica."

Wren and Drew had been talking over lunch earlier in the week when Drew had casually mentioned a big event she was hosting at the store that coming Saturday. Comic Cosplay Saturday. From what Wren could gather, it was an event held four times a year. Drew invited customers to come dressed as their favorite heroes, anti-heroes, monsters, or Manga characters, and she gave them twenty-five percent off all purchases in the store. She also posted their pictures on the store's website for viewers to see, vote on, and the winner got a thirty-dollar voucher to spend in store. It was a bit of fun that started off small but had gained a following and now Drew hosted quite the go-to event. Wren had casually mentioned it to Takira who had gotten very excited because, when the costumers left Dawes & Destiny Comics, they usually made their way into the restaurant. Takira had told Wren to look out for Finn at the store. He'd be wearing his Miles Morales Spider-Man costume. Trent had promised to take him and Harley in before it got too hectic so they could experience the fun for themselves. Seeing others' excitement for the pleasure Drew brought to them made Wren feel so proud of her. She was starting to understand the attraction these fantasy worlds had on people. Her niece especially, who was already having her best day and hadn't even stepped foot in the store yet.

Wren couldn't wait to see Drew. She wouldn't tell Wren who she'd be dressing up as, but she could tell Drew was looking forward to the event just like everyone else. Dakota and Aaron had been busy working out their costumes, in between teasing Wren and Drew for sitting behind the counter eating the burritos Wren had brought for them from the restaurant, and complaining they never got to eat in the store.

Ana rushed up to the comic book store's main window and oohed and ahhed over the display. She turned around and grinned at Wren. "This is going to be so cool!"

Wren laughed and ushered them through the open door. She had to look past Stormtroopers, Hobbits, Wonder Women, and a few little kids all dressed as Iron Man before she finally spotted Drew. She had that damned wig on again and it always threw Wren off.

Drew looked up as if sensing Wren was in the shop. Wren hoped her mouth hadn't fallen open at the sight of her. Drew had her Thirteenth Doctor wig on but no rainbows today. Instead, she wore a long black tuxedo jacket, with a crisp white shirt, and a muted color bowtie at the neck. Black pants cut off at her calves, and dark socks were in the familiar heavy boots. She looked so dashing. Wren hoped she wasn't drooling.

"She's the Doctor!" Ana exclaimed. "From the episode 'Spyfall'!"

Wren sighed, turning her eyes heavenward. "Am I literally the only one who didn't know this character?"

Marco laughed beside her. "I'm just getting into it too. Ana wasn't interested in *Doctor Who* when it was men in the title role, but having a woman in the lead caught her attention very quickly." He eyed Drew as she came closer. "My God, she almost looks like her too. She's got the same shape of nose and everything. That's kind of spooky."

All Wren saw was Drew. Drew looked over Ana's head to smile at Wren, but her attention quickly returned back to Ana.

"Welcome, Captain, to Dawes & Destiny Comics. I see you have Bucky with you." Drew leaned down a little to talk to Ana confidentially. "Is he still with HYDRA or has he left the Falcon for a while to accompany his best buddy to my store?"

"He's a total good guy now. That's my dad."

"Then welcome all. Ms. Banderas, you seem to be missing a costume." Drew sounded quite put out.

"I'm not quite as adventurous as you all are," Wren said, feeling out of place in her regular clothes. "I should have asked for your help with one."

"If you really want to fit in, I think we can help you. *Zantanna*, can you please come and work your magic on this customer?" Drew beckoned Dakota over.

Wren was sure she heard Marco audibly swallow as Dakota stepped out from behind the counter. Dressed as a magician, Dakota wore the black top hat and black tuxedo jacket with style. Attached to her lapel was a blood red rose. Her white shirt, coupled with an ornately patterned vest, somehow pushed her breasts up to make them *very* noticeable. The cut of the sheer shorts Dakota wore showed off way more leg than Wren realized Dakota even had. Black fishnet stockings and over-the-knee, high-heeled boots, finished the ensemble. It was strange seeing Dakota with jet-black hair, and Wren again recognized how wearing the costumes changed the person, letting them take on another persona, just for a while. She'd be sure to ask Drew just who it was Dakota dressed up as at lunch next week.

Dakota sketched a bow at Ana. "Captain America, how wonderful to see you here." She eyed Marco who was still staring. "Bucky, still rockin' the bad boy look, I see." Her gaze rested on Wren. Dakota started to singsong, "One of these things is definitely not like the others. *You* need a makeover, Chef Wren." She sighed dramatically. "Damn, I wish I'd brought an extra costume." She looked over at Drew, then back at Wren, with an exacting gaze. "Oh, *Doctor*? Team Tardis is on the way!" She ran a hand over Wren's long hair. "With your gorgeous skin, you're already perfect for who I have in mind. This won't take long at all."

Wren found herself unceremoniously herded into the staff bathroom. A makeup kit and brush rested on the cupboard in there.

Dakota stood Wren in front of the mirror and began working on her hair.

"Drew was so excited you were coming today," Dakota confided. "And that she gets to meet Ana too. Did your sister name her after the *Frozen* character?"

Wren watched how swiftly Dakota was shaping her hair. It was fascinating to watch. "No. My sister wouldn't be that whimsical. I don't think *Frozen* was out when Ana was born."

"I'm guessing that gorgeous hunk of a man is the ex?"

"Yes, that's Marco. He's a good man."

Dakota reached for some pins out of her case. "Your hair is perfect for this. It's so nice to work with someone with long hair. We have to get Drew's wigs made for her to cosplay. I couldn't wear my hair as short as hers, but it suits her so much."

"I have trouble recognizing her when she's in her Doctor costume."

"I know, right? Totally changes how she looks. But she loves this Doctor so she braves the wig. But the minute she can take it off she runs her hands through her own hair and just sighs like she's released from bondage."

"What's this hairstyle you're doing for me?"

"Space buns, my dear! As worn by the wonderful Yasmin Khan." Dakota stepped back to eye her work.

Wren looked in the mirror. "There's no way in hell I could ever do this style on my own." She turned her head this way and that, checking out the two high buns fashioned on the top of her head. "*Space buns?*"

"An homage to Princess Leia, though she had hers on the sides. This was the style Yaz wore when she traveled with the Doctor in their first adventures. She dresses casually so we don't have to change anything there, but her hair is rather distinct. She's darker skinned like you so you're perfect as the Doctor's companion."

"Companion?"

"Travel buddy, fellow explorer, human along for the ride in the Tardis." Dakota giggled to herself. "Thasmin lives!"

"What's Thasmin?" Wren didn't understand half of what Dakota was talking about.

"A shipping name for the Doctor and Yaz." Dakota stared at her. "Fans wor*ship* them together as a couple. Thasmin is for the *Who* fans who like their lovable lesbians out having adventures in time and space."

"So, you've done me up to look like the Doctor's girlfriend?" Wren gave her a suspicious look.

"Seemed appropriate. She lets you bring food into the store, and you sit for an hour and talk more than I have ever heard Drew talk. And she watches you leave and it isn't just her staring at your very nicely shaped butt."

"Thank you...I think."

Dakota's face turned serious. "Just promise me something. If you can't accept that a great deal of Drew's time has her wrapped up in fantasy, then step away now before you break her heart. You're the first woman I've seen her with, Wren. She's letting you into her world. She's trying to make a space for you."

Wren took the words to heart. "I want to be in that space. This isn't my kind of thing, but I am willing to learn. I don't want to miss out on what's important to her."

Dakota looked relieved. "Then, Yaz, your *Doctor* is waiting in what looks like a great suit to be worn at a wedding." Dakota gave her a sly look. "Don't you think?"

Wren laughed. "My God. I'm sticking you and my mama in a room together. You can share notes on how best to marry me off."

"I'd love that! Sign me up!" Dakota patted Wren on her cheek. "You are ready. Go out there and help your niece find something cool to get her twenty-five percent off."

Wren came back into the store to find Drew and Marco chatting with Trent and Elton. Dakota quickly explained everyone's costumes to Wren so she wasn't clueless. Trent was The Mandalorian in a full silver armored set that shone under the store's lights. Wren had to admit she looked dashing in it. Elton was the Crow, looking suitably creepy dressed in a T-shirt full of holes. His face, covered in white makeup, emphasized his dark shadowed eyes. Wren was surprised he didn't frighten the children. She looked around and found Harley dressed adorably as Grogu to match her mama's costume. Finn was beside her as always, dressed in his customary Spider-Man costume, pretending to shoot web around the store. Wren knew exactly who he was; he never seemed to wear anything else.

"And who is Aaron today?" Wren could see he looked like some kind of robot. He was all in white, from his form-fitting one-piece suit, to the cape on his back. "Fuck," Wren whispered so as not to offend anyone nearby. "His eyes look super weird."

Dakota nodded gleefully. "Yeah, don't they just. He's the Vision. I've told him to keep those contacts in for tonight!" She shot Wren a cheeky wink.

Wren laughed with her. "You pair are perfectly matched."

Dakota readily agreed. "Oh, here comes Drew. The Doctor will see you now."

Wren loved Drew's smile. It grew bigger the closer she got.

"Yasmin Khan, Yaz to her friends. Fancy a trip in the big blue box?"

"I don't know what you're talking about, but I'm going to say yes anyway." She reached out for Drew's hand and squeezed it tight.

The store had a steady stream of people coming in and out. Wren had never seen so many costumes in one place. She said as much to Drew.

"I'll have to take you to the next MoCon," Drew promised. "We can grab Marco and Ana and just geek out there. I'll promise you any meal you want afterward in case it's not your thing."

"Anywhere with you seems to be my thing." Wren leaned into Drew and just marveled at the ingenuity of the costume wearers and how proud they all were and excited to see each other.

"Doctor," Aaron called out. "Dakota says for you and Yaz to come have your photo taken for the site."

Drew picked a comic book from off a shelf and showed it to Wren. "This is who you are."

"Wow, she's very pretty." Wren studied the young woman with the beautiful big smile.

"Think you can copy her pose?"

"She looks like she's ready to take on all those monsters on her own."

"She's no damsel in distress. She's capable of standing up for herself, right by the Doctor's side." Drew held out her hand. "Care to take your place by mine?"

"You do realize this will be our first photograph together?" Wren said, standing on the mark on the floor to be in frame.

"I wish it were my own hair showing, but only one Doctor had a shaved head. I loved Christopher Eccleston, but I don't want to cosplay as him. Jodie's *my* Doctor."

"Team Tardis, strike your pose!" Dakota said.

Drew struck a pose and Wren, not used to this kind of thing, did her best Yaz impression and hoped she didn't look as self-conscious as she felt. She really needed to watch the show so she knew whose buns she was wearing.

Dakota snapped off a few shots then leaned over the camera. "How about one of the two of you together? Just for you, being yourselves."

Drew put her arm around Wren and pulled her close. Wren snuggled into Drew's lean body. She placed her hand on Drew's chest. Drew's hand covered it.

"Two hearts, both happy, beating for you," Drew said, enigmatically.

Wren heard the snap of the camera capturing them. Dakota grinned and let out a squeal at the shot, flipped them a thumbs-up sign, and skipped back to the counter. Wren stared up at Drew.

"*Two* hearts?"

Drew nodded. "There's more to the Doctor than meets the eye." She pulled Wren after her to rejoin their friends. "Didn't I tell you she was an alien, too?"

Wren let Drew guide her back into the busy store. She could see her friends talking with Marco as if they'd always known him. Ana was knelt on the ground chatting with Harley and Finn. She was tying Finn's shoelace for him, the little boy hanging off her every word. They'd slotted into this world with no effort at all.

Family, Wren thought. It could be blood or it could be a weird collection of friends. Wren was thankful this was beginning to be hers. Drew had to release her hand to go serve a customer, and Wren watched her behind the counter, smiling and happy. She was talking to a little girl dressed as Wonder Woman, holding a cardboard sword and hand-drawn shield. Drew complimented her as though her costume was worth a million dollars. The little girl beamed at the praise.

I could fall in love with her so easily, Wren realized.

In her heart, though, she already knew she was halfway there.

❖

It was strange being in the restaurant as a customer and not as one just wandering in to order food for her grandma. Drew had closed the store after a very busy, lucrative day. She was trying not to think of all the re-stocks she had to order in. The wall of Funkos alone had been severely depleted. She sat at a table, still in her *Doctor Who* costume. She'd taken the jacket off, rolled up her sleeves, and removed the wig before they left the store. Drew ran her hand through her hair again, free from the confining wig, and enjoyed the feel of the bristles against her palm.

"You do that as a soothing gesture, don't you?" Wren asked, her chin resting in her palm as she gazed at Drew with happy but tired eyes.

"I hated my hair as a kid. I always had to wear it long. Mother shaped, styled, and fixed it so much with hair spray it's a wonder it didn't fall out in clumps." Drew's memory darkened. "Or I had it used as a means to control me. In braids it became a leash to call me to heel."

"I could kill your mother," Wren said, the truth of her words in her eyes.

"She wasn't the best. I wish I could have been the daughter she wanted but I couldn't. I wasn't pretty, I wasn't curvy and feminine, and I didn't want to be anywhere near the boys at the circuits we performed at just to generate publicity. I didn't know what I was then, but I knew I didn't like boys that way and that was another mark against me in my mother's eyes." Drew ran her fingers through the longer hair on her crown. "Grandpa cut it for me that first time. He got that damn Rapunzel braid and the kitchen scissors and hacked the thing right off. I cried and cried in relief." Drew smiled. "He let me set fire to it in the garden, warning me not to tell Grandma he'd let me play with matches. Then he sat us on the ground around this hole he'd dug to set the hair alight in, brought out the fixings for s'mores, and we roasted marshmallows over the flames. He said it was no use letting a good flame go to waste." Drew laughed at the memory. "Grandma was still stuck in the hospital and they'd sent me home to be with Grandpa. I found out later, Grandma had begged him to cut my hair and to go buy me the clothes I wanted to wear. It was weird shopping for clothes with Grandpa. He was a very quiet man, but he made it fun and let me pick what I wanted from the boys' section without saying a word. I got my first pair of Converse high-tops that day and waved good-bye to the Mary Jane shoes my mother forced my less than dainty feet into."

"And so baby butch Drew was born." Wren speared a piece of her cherry pie on her fork. "So, this whole Doctor in a tux get-up, is it the clothes or the Doctor you like?"

"Both. It's easy to dress as a man in cosplay, but to be female and dress as a woman who dresses androgynously like I do is just fantastic. I don't want to be a man. I just don't want to look female. Does that make sense?"

Wren nodded. "You wear that tux *very* well."

"That's the fun in dressing up. I'm surprised Marco came in costume. I wouldn't have expected he'd have such a creative or fun side. And Ana...I love Ana to bits. She was so cute and so fierce with her shield." Drew sucked at her milkshake through the straw. "I can see you in her, especially around the eyes."

Wren looked thrilled to hear that. "I'm just glad she follows her dad and not Val. We do not need a Mini-Me of Val."

"Is she really that bad?"

"It was just difficult growing up so far behind her in age. We never had anything in common. She saw me as a nuisance from the second I was born." Wren looked around the restaurant. "I am so proud of working here, but she can't see past that it's not *my* restaurant. My papa had high expectations of me getting my own restaurant one day. Val seems to have taken that mantle up now. I sometimes feel I'm not working hard enough to reach either of their expectations in me. This morning she'd sent me an email, detailing investors interested in my restaurant. I don't have one yet, nor will I have one in the foreseeable future, but she's already lining them up for me. I'm not ready for that responsibility yet."

"She sounds charming," Drew said, anger building inside her at the callous way Wren's sister treated her.

"She and your mother would probably have got on like a house on fire." Wren chewed at her pie. "No, I take that back. Val isn't that bad. She's just not mindful of the fact I might want to live my life at my own pace before I tackle the huge responsibility of running and financing a restaurant." Wren waved her hand dismissively. "Enough of them. I have a question I've wanted to ask for ages now."

Drew sat back in her seat. "Ask away."

Wren reached over to trace the tattoo on Drew's arm. "What is this? I can see the stars and space surrounding it, but what is this?" She tapped at the blue box-like object.

"This is the Doctor's Tardis, her spaceship. It's designed from a British police box that they used years ago. Inside, it's huge. Outside, it's supposed to be innocuous. Something you wouldn't look at twice because it blends into the background."

"A large blue British police box? I'd think people would notice it."

Drew laughed. "I guess it was more subtle when the show started back in 1963."

"It's *that* old? And it's *still* going?" Wren looked surprised. "Wait, and they've only had *one* female in the lead since then?"

"Don't get me started on that," Drew said, knowing this wasn't the time or place to start on *that* particular rant. She ran a fingertip over her tattoo. "I got this done earlier this year. It's not the traditional blue box. I had it done like the Thirteenth Doctor's so it's more a blue/green than the usual dark blue."

"What did your grandma say? My mama would go ballistic if I had one done."

"She was sitting in the seat opposite me, getting her own done." Drew grinned as Wren nearly choked on her pie. "She said she'd always wanted one and if I was going to do it then it was high time she got one too."

"What's hers of?"

"A vine of ivy that covers the scars on her hip and leg left by the accident."

"Your grandma is an amazing lady."

"Yes, she is. She can't wait to see you tomorrow. It's all she's talked about this week. Getting to meet you."

"Meet me? But she knows me."

"Meeting you as my *girlfriend* for the first time." Drew loved the flush of color that darkened Wren's cheeks.

"So, is that what you're calling me now?"

"I'm counting every lunch break and kissing session at your car before you drive home from your shift as stepping-stones to us taking that title, yes." Drew had gotten into the habit of waiting at Wren's car to say good night to her after the restaurant closed. Her grandma thought it was chivalrous. Wren had told her it was sweet and her face lit up every time she saw her. Drew lived for the kisses she got and the feel of Wren in her arms.

"Who knew the woman of my dreams was a Tardis-tattooed geek?" Wren smiled at her from across the table. Her foot nudged at Drew's boot.

"And who knew mine was a head chef at a restaurant that gives us extra sides and desserts when we eat here? If I'd known that I'd have come in more often to try to snag a cook." She laughed as Wren delivered a gentle kick to her shin. "Hey! No kicking, I have bare legs on show here."

"And you look so cute in those weird short pants too." Wren stifled a yawn in her palm. "Geez, I am so tired. Ana ran me ragged today. First at your store, then on the picnic we had at the Rock Bridge Memorial State Park. Ana wanted to see the caves and the underground stream. I'm surprised I haven't fallen asleep in my pie yet." She reached over to take Drew's hand in her own. "Must have been the amazing company I'm keeping." She yawned again. "Goddammit!"

Drew sucked her milkshake dry and tried to catch the eye of a server so she could pay the bill. "I think you should let me drive you home so you can leave your car here."

Wren shook her head. "No, I'll perk up once I get out into the night air. You need to go check on Mae anyway."

"Did you see her at the store?" Drew tried to remember if it was after Wren had left that her grandma had rolled up in front of the store on her mobility scooter. The wheels bore giant Xs like Professor Xavier's wheelchair from the X-Men. She wore an old secondhand suit but had refused to wear a bald cap. The customers knew exactly who she was and had swarmed around her for selfies.

"Damn, I missed her."

"Don't worry, Dakota took her photo so she'll be on the website with us all."

With the check paid, Drew walked Wren to her car. They shared a kiss that made lightning race over Drew's skin and left her shaking. Reluctantly drawing back, Drew looked up at the night's sky.

"We always seem to be kissing under the stars," she said.

Wren caressed Drew's tattoo. "Seems appropriate given your love of star gazing and for a traveler through space and time. Will you be wearing these funky pants tomorrow?"

"No, I'll wear my big girl pants for you." Drew opened Wren's door for her and stood back as Wren prepared to leave. "Drive home safely. Send me a text when you get in and I'll see you tomorrow evening."

"I have my invitation stuck to my mirror. I won't forget. Sweet dreams, Drew."

Drew watched her go then wandered home.

❖

"That you, Drew?" Her grandma called from the kitchen as soon as Drew turned her key in the door.

"I'm back. Sorry I was a little longer than I promised."

"You were with Wren. I'm not going to time you when you're with your sweetie." Her grandma limped over to her. "You've been alone too long, my girl. You take all the time you need. You really like this one, don't you?"

"Yeah, I do." Drew's feelings were becoming way more complicated than just *like*.

"Then I look forward to her coming tomorrow and my getting to embarrass you by telling stories of you as a little girl. Like that one time you swung your little guitar like a baseball bat smack bang into that judge's balls when he got a little too handsy with his prepubescent girl singers."

"I hid the photo albums," Drew said without remorse.

"Good thing I found them then, isn't it? I'm sleeping with them tonight. Good luck trying to wrestle them off me." Her grandma sat on the sofa. "I think Wren likes you enough not to be put off by pictures of you with your hair gussied up like Tammy Wynette."

"God bless Grandpa and his kitchen scissors," Drew preached dramatically.

Her grandma played along, as she always did, and put her hand on her heart. "Amen to that."

Drew sat beside her. "I really like her, Grandma."

"Then all you can do is show her that." Her grandma gestured to a shirt hanging up in the room. "You're employing the big guns, I see."

Drew looked over her shoulder at the black shirt pinstriped with green. Only on closer inspection did the green reveal itself to be the Matrix code. It was Drew's only concession to anything like a *serious* shirt.

"It's a third date kind of shirt, don't you think?"

"I think it's perfect. And if she thinks you're the *One*..."

"She might just see it as a regular shirt though."

"Sweetheart, she's spent time with you. She knows there's nothing regular about you at all."

Drew smiled at her. "I'm taking that as a compliment."

"Good. It was meant as one. Now, are you going to help find a third date suitable flannel shirt for your ol' grandma to shine in?"

"Do you want to come across as a feisty old lady or lull her into a false sense of security?" Drew knew her all too well.

"The baby blue one it is, then," her grandma said with a wicked glint in her eye. "I can't wait for tomorrow."

Neither could Drew.

CHAPTER TWELVE

Wren had changed into three sets of clothes before she'd finally found something she judged casual but girlfriend-y. She didn't know why she was so nervous. It wasn't like she hadn't been exchanging kisses with Drew for a while now and she knew Mae from the restaurant. But this was different. This had a label attached. This was Wren, *the girlfriend*, meeting Drew's *family*. That thought brought Wren up short as she reached to ring the doorbell to Drew's apartment. *If I'm meeting her family that means I need her to meet mine. Oh God, I wonder if we can get away with just doing Mama because Val will be Val and that never ends well. She'll send Drew running for the hills.*

Wren pushed that thought out of her head as she pressed the bell. She heard footsteps, the door opened, and Drew's welcoming smile pushed all of Wren's fears aside.

"I'm so glad you're here." Drew pulled her close. "Grandma is driving me crazy. She's like a damned puppy with two tails waiting for you."

Wren pulled Drew down for a kiss. "I'm glad I'm here for *this*." She kissed her again and Drew melted in her arms. It was a while before they pulled apart.

"Do you want to just leave? I'll take us to McDonald's, get you a burger and fries," Drew said, sounding desperate.

Wren scolded her. "No mentioning another eatery within earshot of Takira's. And, no. I'd like to think I'm strong enough to take on your grandma."

"Famous last words," Drew teased her and let Wren enter.

Wren picked her way carefully up the stairs past the stairlift.

"Hurry up, you two, don't keep an old lady waiting!" Mae's voice rang out from the door half open at the top of the stairs.

Wren laughed. "Two tails and a yippy bark to match." She walked inside and found Mae at the kitchen table.

"There you are!" Mae's smile was welcoming. "Come give me a hug. I'll expect it now that we're family."

"Grandma! We've literally only just started to call it dating," Drew grumbled.

"Nonsense. You pair have been dillydallying eating lunch together for weeks now. You just didn't make it official." Mae hugged Wren close and whispered in her ear. "See? I told you that you two would be perfect for each other."

Wren kissed her cheek. "Thank you. I agree."

The doorbell sounded out in the apartment. Drew bounded out the door again. "That's our meal."

Mae took hold of Wren's hand. "You're making her very happy. I can't thank you enough for that."

"She makes me happy, Mae. She's becoming my everything."

Mae squeezed her hand gently. "You hold on to her. She's a good girl, she just doesn't realize that she is."

"I will, Mae. I'll hold on for as long as she lets me."

Drew pushed open the door with her butt and staggered in with bags of food. "I don't remember ordering this much."

Wren hurried to help her. "You know Takira will have added extra for us. She's such a sweetheart."

Mae rubbed her hands together gleefully. "That looks like a feast!"

Drew pulled a chair out for Wren. "Let's tuck in while it's still hot, then we can sit like beached whales on the sofa afterward."

Wren and Drew sorted out the cartons of food so everyone had their choice. Wren noticed that their names were on the lids but one had DREW written in big bold letters. She handed it to her. Drew peeled off the lid and burst out laughing. She showed the contents to Wren and Mae.

"Dante is such a smart-ass," Drew said, fishing out a tater tot. She tossed it into her mouth, and gasped as it burned her. She sucked in air quickly to cool her mouth down while Wren laughed at her.

Wren placed a scrumptious looking cake to one side, along with the fruit and pretzel bowls that were for snacking on later. She knew Drew hadn't ordered those; they were an off-the-menu item Takira occasionally made for the staff as snacks. It was one of Wren's favorites. Wren would be sure to thank Takira when she went back on shift tomorrow. Satisfied everyone had their meal to hand, Wren checked her own fried chicken, mashed potato, and assorted greens over.

"Quit critiquing the presentation. It got squished into a take-away foil," Drew said, chewing on a long green bean.

"I can't help it. I always want our food to look its best."

"And it does," Mae said, looking blissed out with a forkful of creamy mashed potato. "And it tastes delicious. Takira's food is never anything but that. You must love working there."

Wren nodded. "It's the best job I've had so far. The staff are fantastic and the food is outstanding. The menu switches around a lot too, which is fun for me as a chef, but also gives the customer a lot of different choices each visit. We're not a restaurant that has the same old menu trotted out every week."

"Was it hard, taking on Takira's role?" Mae picked up a large fried chicken wing and tore into it.

Wren loved seeing people enjoying their food and relaxed finally. "It was, but it's a challenge I was prepared to shoulder. If I open my own restaurant one day, I'll need to know I can stand the pressure it takes to do that." Wren tried to ignore the acid in her gut that always appeared when she thought about starting her own business. It used to be a dream, her end goal. But all her career so far had shown her that it wasn't as simple as her father had led her to believe. He'd never seen her anywhere but in her own restaurant. Wren's stress levels rose now at the mere thought of her having to shoulder everything.

"You'll need a Dante." Drew tipped her tater tots onto her plate to mix in with her meal. She pushed them around to soak up gravy with a contented sigh.

"I need a Dante *and* the whole catering staff and waiting staff. Takira has an excellent team in place. I literally walked in to an already well-run kitchen. If I had my own restaurant I'd be starting from scratch and would have to interview hundreds of applicants in the hopes of finding even a quarter of that level of competence." Wren frowned a little and felt her heart ache at the amount of work it would take to get anything even close to the setup Takira had in place. "I admit, sometimes, I think the dream of my own restaurant is harder to achieve than I originally thought."

"No dream is impossible. Sometimes you just have to wait for the right time and everything falls into place," Mae said, wiping her fingers on a napkin before reaching over to pat Wren's arm.

"It's finding a good place that's assessable. Then there's the appliances, dinnerware, gathering my kitchen staff, setting up reliable food deliveries. Then there's health and safety to consider. All that and more, before I even get to the fun part of deciding menus." Wren sighed. "Papa saw me owning my own restaurant by the time I was forty. I can't see myself in one before I'm even the other side of fifty."

"My bank manager was very reluctant to give me a mortgage for a comic book store." Drew gestured around her with her fork as she spoke. "I told him I'd be the only store of its kind in the area, and there was a large market for what I was aiming to sell. But it still helped I had an inheritance to pay the bulk of the costs."

Mae huffed. Her mouthful of chicken muffled her angry words. "That's the one good thing your parents ever did for you."

"I have some money my papa left me but it's my safety net in case the worst happens. Like, what if I wake up tomorrow and decide that being a chef is no longer what I want to do? I'm due a midlife crisis at some point." Wren grimaced, dreading the thought.

Drew raised her eyebrows at her. "I think you've still got a few years before you hit that mark. But, if it happens, I could stretch to a part-time job for you here. I'd have to warn you though that Dakota would try everything to get you wearing her costumes."

Wren balked at that. "Some of what she wears is very suggestive."

"And you'd carry them off even better than she does." Drew's eyes shone at her with a gleam that wasn't exactly family friendly. "But then you wouldn't get a whole load of work done." Her wink emphasized her meaning.

Wren knew she was blushing. "Drew! Not in front of your grandma!"

Mae waved her hand dismissively. "No, go right ahead. I've waited years for this to happen."

Wren laughed at them both and continued with her meal. "Enough about me." She looked around the room properly for the first time. The decorating was undoubtedly Drew's influence. The walls were a plain pale blue. The vibrant colors in the room came from the many framed photos and shelves full of ornaments and collectibles. On one wall, obviously Mae's wall, Wren could see photos of Mae, someone she guessed was her husband, and a little Drew. No other family were on display. The rest of the room appeared dedicated to Drew's passions.

"Are all the figures in that glass case yours, Drew?"

Drew nodded. "That's just the case out here. I have another in my bedroom."

"No doubt she'll show you that later," Mae said wickedly.

Drew cut her a look but continued as if she hadn't said a word. "The statues are damned expensive so I'm picky over what I get. If I had all the ones I wanted, we'd be sleeping on the balcony."

Wren noticed a painting that looked a little out of place amid the framed signatures of various characters. "What film is the farm scene from?"

"No film. That's where we used to live. Arthur, my husband, painted that years ago," Mae said. Her eyes grew distant as she reminisced. "It was the farm he grew up on. I lived on it with him until we just couldn't make it work anymore. We got a little house with the proceeds and kept a nest egg safe for our son, Bradley. He nearly blew through the whole lot until he met Mary-Louise and married her. She earned enough for him to be a stay-at-home husband." Mae shrugged, her expression resigned and unhappy. "It was her money he drank through then." She looked over at Drew who remained silent. "And then they both tried to blow through what Drew made for them." She looked guilty for letting that slip out.

"Wren knows I used to sing," Drew said, reassuring Mae it was okay. "But that's the past. Now, I'm your friendly neighborhood source for all things geeky."

"She had a beautiful voice." Mae mourned for a brief second then brightened, switching tracks. "But her talents lay elsewhere. This store is never empty of customers. And thank God that we moved here, right slap bang next door to a restaurant where I can meet my friends, eat, and catch up on the gossip. And then *you* appeared!" Mae gave Wren the biggest smile. "And just look at us all now. Destiny *and* Dawes, mystical fate at work!"

Drew's indulgent face at Mae's excitement made Wren chuckle.

"Told you." Drew eyed Wren ruefully. "Two for the price of one."

"And here I thought you were going to be more than a handful on your own," Wren said to Drew before giving Mae a considering look. "I know *you're* trouble already. You and Mrs. Daniels, sitting together like two crones stirring a cauldron."

Mae pretended to be astonished by the description. "Honey, I wish we were up to no good. It's mostly gossiping and planning our next canasta night."

Wren wasn't sure if she believed the innocent tone. "You know, when I first saw you two together? I thought you were lovers."

Drew nearly spit her drink clear across the table. She barely managed to swallow in time and began to choke. Mae dropped her fork with a clatter. Wren was satisfied to have gotten both reactions. Drew started laughing so much she had to remove herself from the table and ended up hanging onto the sink. Mae blushed a deep red and, uncharacteristically, didn't utter a word. Wren was incredibly intrigued. At least Mae hadn't taken offense.

Drew wiped at her eyes. "Oh, she's got your number, Grandma!"

Mae huffed at her. "You know damn well that's not going anywhere. Mrs. Daniels is just a friend."

Wren looked to Drew for more information.

"Grandma's unrequited love has been simmering for a few years now. We're waiting for Mrs. Daniels to grab a clue because Grandma here won't woman up and tell her."

"Does Mrs. Daniels even have a first name?" Wren asked, totally curious to the mysterious moniker no one in the restaurant knew.

Mae nodded. "Of course, she does."

Wren pushed. "And?"

"A gentlewoman never reveals another woman's secrets." Mae picked up her fork and deliberately stuffed her mouth with a large bite of mashed potato to effectively seal her lips.

"The mystery continues," Wren sighed. "Drew, are you okay over there?"

Drew was still snickering. She retook her seat and reached for Wren's hand. "Congratulations. You're the first woman to ever render my grandma at a loss for words. You're definitely a keeper."

Wren liked the sound of that. Her eye caught something on Drew's shirt. "Come here a minute."

Drew leaned forward. The look on her face said she thought she was getting a kiss. Wren put her hand over Drew's puckered lips, making Drew let out a disgruntled huff. "I'm not trading kisses with you over the dinner table. I've traumatized Mae enough for one night." She pulled Drew closer so she could look at her shirt. "I thought I was seeing things at first. Your shirt has the green writing from the *Matrix* as stripes. See, even *I* know that movie." She shook her head at Drew, indulgently. "Only you."

Wren wondered at the significant look exchanged between Drew and Mae before she tugged Drew in for a kiss anyway.

"Definitely a keeper," Mae said.

Drew couldn't remember a more entertaining evening. Her grandma had been having the time of her life showing Wren through the family photo albums. Drew hadn't missed the looks Wren had given her as her grandma guided her through all the photos of little Drew on stage at various places, standing alongside the well-known adults who'd been performing. Her mother had loved using her power to wrangle a spot for Drew in any and every country music event that would have at least one big name headlining. Drew appreciated Wren not laughing at some of the ridiculous costumes Drew wore. Gingham dresses, making Drew look like some old-fashioned farm wife or Dorothy from *The Wizard of Oz*, had been her mother's staple. Drew knew her mother had been waiting for Drew to start filling out so she could pimp her out another way. She just wished her mother had realized that Drew would be more k.d. lang in looks than Dolly Parton. She also wished her mother had let her grow up first, let her grow and mature at her own pace, and just have the chance to be a child first. Maybe she'd still be singing now, headlining at festivals, shifting from country to pop, treading similar pathways as Taylor Swift had traversed. Drew almost shuddered at the thought. The woman Drew had grown up to be couldn't have handled the limelight and the pressure that came from having to perform and constantly reinvent oneself in order to still be relevant in the pop industry of today.

Drew watched her grandma and Wren chatting together. Not once had Wren left her out of the conversation and Drew loved her for that. They were currently poring over the photos that showed the construction of the store. It seemed so long ago now. Drew really couldn't see herself doing anything else. This was all her hopes and dreams rolled into one. Her *home*.

Wren nudged Drew's knee, bringing her out of her thoughts. She was pointing at a photo from the opening day of the store.

"Trent and Elton were here when you first opened?"

Drew nodded. "All the folks in that photo still come to the store. I have the best customers, loyal and true."

"Ana says she wants to visit more now that she's been. I don't think she's going to be the next generation of lawyer in our family. Val won't be very happy. Marco will be the one to let Ana decide her own path without an argument."

"Was your father okay with you not taking a job in his firm?" Drew asked, trying not to think of what would have happened if Wren had been a lawyer instead. They'd have never met. The realization of that hit Drew like a Hulk fist to the chest.

"Papa always had Val snapping at his heels so I think he was content enough that she would undoubtedly follow in his footsteps. When my love for the culinary arts became more than just something I did with Mama, he indulged it. But, when I got old enough to understand that I couldn't just cook with Mama forever, he sat me down and showed me his blueprint of my future." Wren shook her head, smiling. "He had it all plotted for me, the best schools to go to, the courses I would need to take. All culminating in my running my own restaurant by the time I reached a certain age."

"Did *you* want to own your own restaurant?" Drew asked, curious to know the answer. To Drew's surprise, Wren hesitated.

"I've grown up knowing that is my ultimate goal."

Drew pushed a little at Wren's answer. "Yeah, but *do* you want to run your own restaurant? Do you actually *need* to? To be happy in your work?"

Wren was silent for a long moment. She raised her gaze to Drew and seemed to be searching her eyes for an answer.

"I thought I did. In every kitchen I've worked I've had the belief that it was just a stepping stone to get me toward my own." Wren made a disgruntled face. "Val has always been so sure of what she had to do to succeed. She was destined to fill Papa's role at the firm. I've never felt that certain. I'm not like her." Wren looked back down at the photo album. "I've given myself an ulcer worrying about only having ten years left in which to gather the experience and money to get my own restaurant. I'm thirty now, I should be further along the path Papa envisioned for me."

Drew sat back in her seat. "Is the dream of your own restaurant yours, or is it to fulfil your papa's expectations of you?"

Wren's head shot up. At first, Drew thought she was going to argue with her. Wren's face was stormy, but then, just as quickly, Wren's defensive posture dropped. She lowered her shoulders and just stared at Drew.

"I don't honestly know," Wren said, her voice quiet as if admitting it out loud would be a desecration.

Drew reached out to tuck a long swath of hair back behind Wren's ear so she could see her face. "Take it from someone whose childhood was taken over by someone else's expectations and wants, you have to do what is in *your* heart."

Wren let out a long, gusty sigh. "And what if I don't know what's in my heart?"

"Then you take one day at a time until your heart decides your path," Grandma said, patting Wren on her knee.

Drew remembered those words well. The loss of her parents had also ripped Drew from the world they'd forced her to perform in. It was all she'd ever known. She was suddenly her own Drew, not the one her parents had been molding her into. It had been a jarring transition for her. Going from an abusive household to the unconditional love and support of her grandparents had been one hell of a mindfuck. Drew had a lot of baggage to unpack. Her grandparents had helped her every step of the way, but Drew still bore the scars to this day.

Drew had a horrible feeling that Wren had been set on a career path that wasn't entirely of her own making either. To Drew it was a very familiar song, just sung with a different tune. Encouragement, love, and praise colored the footsteps leading Wren to her destiny. It was still someone else's roadmap for her to live her life to, though.

Her grandma shared a look with Drew. She had obviously reached the same conclusion.

"I realized, just the other day, that everything I've wanted in my career I have at Takira's." Wren leaned back against the sofa and closed her eyes for a minute. "I've felt at home there from the moment I took my place in the kitchen."

"But…" Drew asked, sensing the word unsaid.

"But what if I'm just settling?" Wren opened her eyes and looked at them both. "Val would call me lazy."

"Honey, I've seen you in that restaurant. You are anything but lazy. You have taken Takira's role and it's all on your shoulders now. That's a major commitment, a ton of work, and you still come and smile at the customers." Grandma smiled softly at her. "The way I see it, if you're lucky to find your happiness, you need to grab it in both hands before it slips away. It doesn't always stick around."

Wren smiled at her and squeezed her hand. She turned to look at Drew, her eyes soft and shining.

"I might just have to do that," she said, giving Drew a significant look. She turned her attention back to the album on her lap, a small smirk curving her lips. Drew just knew it was because Wren had caught the heat suddenly coloring Drew's cheeks.

Drew stayed quiet, willing her blush to dissipate, and letting Wren pause that topic of conversation for now. She watched her turn the pages until Wren stopped on the latest additions.

"I'm in your album."

"Of course, you are. Those are our first official pictures together." Drew leaned into Wren's side and relished the warmth that came from her. "You make a fantastic companion."

Wren pressed more into Drew. "Just for the Doctor?"

"Maybe for me too," Drew admitted, bumping her shoulder playfully, then pressing a soft kiss to Wren's temple.

"I'll need a copy of these," Wren said, tracing the edge of one of the photos.

"I have them already printed out for you. Dakota did them in her lunch break yesterday for me."

Wren's sweet smile did curious things to Drew's insides. She was frightened to speak in case the thousands of butterflies beating their wings inside her burst out and filled the room.

"Who wants cake?" Grandma asked, breaking the spell.

Wren laughed at the way Drew's head whipped up.

"Mae, how many times did you get Drew to be good by offering cake as an incentive?"

Her grandma laughed at Drew's embarrassment. "More times than you'd believe. Really, she should be the size of a house."

Drew waved for her grandma to stay seated and got up herself to see to the cake. Grandma and Wren began talking among themselves and for a moment Drew just watched them. Maybe she could have it all. The girl to love, her grandma reasonably mobile and healthy, the kind of happy ever after that Drew never let herself dream of.

Her mother had tried to condemn her to a life of solitude for her own gains. Drew hoped, with the help of these two women, she could accept love freely given and be able to give it back without fear.

CHAPTER THIRTEEN

With her eyes half closed, Drew languished in the sensory delight that was Wren lying in her arms. She idly ran her fingers through Wren's long hair. They lay sprawled out on the sofa with the TV on quietly in the background, but neither watched what was playing. Instead, they had shifted and turned until Drew lay back and Wren had melted into her. Her grandma had gone to bed an hour ago, bidding them good night and hugging Wren close. Now they were alone, content in the stillness.

"The beat of your heart is going to send me to sleep," Wren said, stirring a little. "For a lanky thing you're surprising comfortable."

"Must be all the cake I eat, padding me out in all the right places for you," Drew said. "You're welcome to stay here. You can take my bed. I'll sleep out here on the sofa."

Wren shifted to catch Drew's gaze. "You wouldn't sleep with me?"

"I'd be a gentlewoman and save that for when we'd want to do more than sleep." Drew tried not to laugh at Wren's pouty bottom lip. "Besides, I know we're not in the most ideal of situations…"

"You mean with your grandma sleeping just down the hallway?"

"It can be something of a mood killer." Understatement of the century, Drew thought to herself.

"How many girls have you brought home, Drew?"

Drew thought she heard a hint of jealousy in Wren's tone. She had to think back to her last date. It had been a long while ago. "One here, not counting you. And she never slept over. She never got past the meet and greet."

"Did Mae welcome her?"

"She did, but didn't welcome her back. The woman knew of my circumstances and talked around Grandma as if she were deaf or stupid. It would have been funny if it hadn't been so mortifying how she shouted at Grandma like she was senile."

"Senile is the last thing Mae is." Wren snuggled back down onto Drew. "I have to ask. Are you usually so...*reticent* in touching someone?"

Drew sighed quietly. She knew Wren would notice. It was kind of hard to miss for someone as tactile as Wren could be. "I like to get to know someone first, spend time learning about them. I find intimacy a little...intimidating. I never really learned when it was appropriate to instigate it."

"You usually wait for the other woman to touch you first?"

"Kind of. I mean, it's difficult to know when a hug can mean something more. I always err on the side of caution." Drew laughed at herself. "Not that I have been flushed with much success with partners."

"You're not a virgin though?"

Drew shook her head. "No, but I could count on one hand and still have fingers to spare how many women I've been with." Drew nervously ran a hand over her hair. "It's not like my situation is ideal. We could sleep together here. Grandma's hearing is not so good that she could hear every moan and scream coming from behind closed doors. But, she's my main priority. *My* hearing is perfect. If I hear her having a nightmare or if she needs help getting out of bed, I will go to her. I offered to get one of those baby monitor things so I could hear if she needed me without her calling out. Grandma said she didn't want anything that could inadvertently switch on and have me listening in on her, and I quote, 'getting in touch with her *feminine* side.'" Drew grimaced as she remembered wanting to bleach her brain after *that* particular conversation.

Wren shook with laughter in her arms. "Your grandma is something else."

"Isn't she just?" Drew agreed ruefully, shaking her head to rid herself of the word masturbation and her grandma in the same thought.

"Does she have nightmares a lot?"

"Sometimes, when she's stressed or hurting."

"Nightmares about the car crash?" Wren's question was quiet as she traced a finger down a line of code on Drew's collar.

Drew wasn't surprised at how intuitive Wren was. She rested her cheek against Wren's head and nodded. "Yeah."

"I wouldn't expect you to stay in bed with me if Mae needed you."

Drew didn't know why she was surprised. She hugged Wren closer in gratitude for her understanding.

"My grandma lived with us when I was younger. Her husband had died years before I was born and she just couldn't manage on her own any more. She and Mama shared all their cooking secrets with me. I know she wasn't my responsibility like Mae is with you, but I made sure she always knew she wasn't in the way. I learned so much from her and I treasure that time I had with her." Wren smiled against Drew's chest. "She was the one who shortened my name to Wren. She said I was her little bird, always fluttering around her."

Drew was surprised. "I thought that was your name."

Wren shook her head. "No, I'm actually Florencia."

Drew loved how Wren said her full name. It held just the hint of an accent, the rise and fall of her voice sounding, to Drew's ears, like a beautiful melody.

"*Florencia*," Drew said, liking the sound of it on her tongue. "That's such a pretty name."

"I don't use it much. Everyone started to call me Wren from childhood."

"Flor*en*cia." Drew used the same inflections Wren had used. She imagined Wren's full name played out in a musical composition. "Florencia" sung as a repetitive stanza, a love song weaving its story, accompanied by a twelve-stringed guitar. Drew wondered if she could write it, if her meager talent for composing even existed any more after she'd neglected it for so long.

Wren eased her head off Drew's chest and shifted to press a gentle kiss on her lips. "Is Drew shortened from anything?"

"Nope. I'm just surprised I got such an androgenous sounding name from a woman who was so determined to make me the epitome of femininity." Wren smiled at her and Drew had to chuckle with self-deprecation. "I know, right? I'm more Drew Carey than Drew Barrymore." She reached up and tenderly brushed Wren's hair back from her face. "You are the most beautiful woman I have ever seen."

"I'm sure you've seen lots of beautiful women before," Wren said. "All those women at the cons you go to, dressed like Dakota."

Drew shook her head. "They're not like you. None of them ever see *me*."

Wren sat up to straddle Drew's hips. Once settled, she cupped Drew's face in her hands. The look in her eyes kept Drew motionless beneath her.

I could lose myself in her gaze, Drew rhapsodized, memorizing every tiny fleck of gold that sparkled in Wren's brown eyes.

"I see you, Drew Dawes, and if you need to go slow then I can do that." Wren leaned down to kiss her again. Slow and gentle at first, but swiftly changing to hot and demanding. "Though, it might be very tempting to see how long it takes before you break."

Drew grabbed Wren's hips and clung on for dear life. Fireworks exploded behind her eyes and her whole body came alive under Wren's touch. She slipped her hands under Wren's blouse and got to feel her heated skin for the first time. Wren was soft and silky. Drew was desperate to flip Wren under her so she could run her tongue across every inch. She smoothed her fingers up Wren's spine, watching as Wren arched and moaned when Drew ran her blunt fingernails back down again. Wren's mouth was hot and desperate against Drew's cheek as she drew in a quick breath and then began gently pressing kisses around Drew's face. She ran her hands along Drew's shoulders, then down, spreading her fingers to follow the lines of neon green code that decorated Drew's shirt. Wren's fingers brushed over Drew's nipples and Drew reacted like a live current had struck her. She moaned and Wren quickly kissed her again, muffling the sounds of Drew's pleasure. Wren deliberately brushed her fingers back and forth, driving Drew to distraction and making her writhe.

Wren began to tease open the buttons, one by one, on Drew's shirt. She pressed kisses down Drew's straining neck and nuzzled the shirt open. Wren pressed agonizingly soft, slow, wet kisses down Drew's chest and pushed the shirt aside just enough to expose the outer curve of Drew's breasts.

Before she went any further, Wren stopped. She gave Drew an innocent look. "Am I going slow enough for you?"

Drew growled as Wren's sweet smile turned deliciously smug. Drew roughly pulled Wren back up in her arms so she could wipe that all too knowing look off her face. Drew kissed her firmly, loving the feel of Wren's mouth under her own, drinking in her gasps and groans. She pressed her tongue between Wren's lips to deepen their connection. The faint fruity taste of fine wine clung to Wren's tongue as Drew swept hers over it. This time it was Wren who drew back, panting and writhing atop Drew.

"Fuck, you're way too good at that," Wren muttered, sweeping her hair back over her shoulder out of her way, before taking control once more.

The slight sting of Wren's teeth biting down on Drew's lower lip awoke a myriad of pleasure points Drew had never known existed. Wren's touch was opening her body up to new sensations and Drew couldn't get enough of her.

Wren shifted again, whispering in Drew's ear as she nibbled along its edge. "This heat between us means you can touch me *when* you want, *how* you want, and for as long as you want."

"I'll remember that," Drew said, relishing the sight of Wren poised above her, her face flushed and eyes glazed with arousal.

The soft chime of a clock signifying it was eleven o'clock made Wren moan pitifully. She glared at the clock accusingly before giving Drew a look of utter regret.

"Damn the fact I have an early shift tomorrow. Even though it will kill me, we'd better stop before we go past the point of no return." After stealing one more kiss, Wren stood up. She wobbled a little as she stood and began pulling her blouse down from where it had ridden up her back thanks to Drew's wandering hands. Then she tried to tame her wild-looking hair with little success.

Drew groaned as she struggled to sit upright and looked down at her gaping shirt that almost exposed her breasts. She heard Wren chuckle.

"To be continued," Wren said. "But I'm enjoying the view from here."

Drew barely managed to fasten one button before her trembling hands made the rest impossible to tackle. She sat looking up at Wren, dazed at them stopping so abruptly.

Wren must have read the confusion on Drew's face. "I'm sorry for calling for a time-out. I'd really like our first time together to be hours spent exploring each other with no distractions. Not a quick fumble on the sofa with the fear we might disturb Mae." She trailed her fingers through Drew's hair. "I want a big bed, soft sheets, my being able to scream your name and not worry who can hear us. After that we can stay here and you can 'show me the statue case' in your bedroom." Wren winked at her. "I just want that first time to just be all about us. You not worrying about Mae or the store, me not worrying I'm going to be late for work. So, we need a plan of strategy that has Mae safely in someone else's care while you come to my apartment where we can eat pizza, sitting butt naked in the kitchen, then you can fuck me on the table."

Drew loved the sound of all of that. She understood the need for privacy but was grateful Wren had no issue with them spending the rest of the time here at the apartment over the store. Painfully aroused and in need of relief, Drew knew a quick fumble now would take the edge off but it wouldn't satisfy her craving for Wren. A stray thought struck her and she found herself torn between frowning and laughing.

"What's wrong?" Wren asked, smoothing the furrows in Drew's forehead.

"I'm wishing you had a bigger car because there is no way I can squeeze myself into the back seat of what you drive for a quick fumble."

Wren laughed at her. "The restaurant certainly doesn't have a license for the entertainment we'd be providing out in the parking lot if we tried it."

"Your apartment it is," Drew agreed. She stood up and shook herself as if she was preparing for an athletic event. "Fuck, Wren," she grumbled, "You've got me all gassed up with nowhere to go."

"I'm sorry, Drew. I didn't think we'd go that far. You're very addictive. I couldn't stop myself." She burrowed herself into Drew for a hug. "My car's parked in your lot. Walk me to it?"

Drew didn't want to watch her leave. She could still feel every place where Wren's lips had marked her. Drew escorted Wren out of the apartment and out the back door.

"I had a fabulous night," Wren said, unlocking her car and looking reluctant to leave now.

"As third dates go, I'd count it a great success," Drew said.

"Only our third? I feel like we've been together longer."

"If we counted all our impromptu lunch break dates then we have been."

Wren smiled. "I don't think forever would be long enough."

Drew swallowed hard at the longing and sincerity in Wren's voice. Drew desperately wanted to drag her back to the apartment. Instead, she deliberately peered into Wren's car and pretended to work out if she could fit with a little maneuvering.

Wren laughed at her and gave her such a sweet kiss good night that Drew was certain she heard a choir of angels blasting out a hallelujah. She forced herself to step back and let Wren go. She waved her off, quietly singing Katy Perry's "I Kissed a Girl" under her breath.

CHAPTER FOURTEEN

M onday lunchtime found Drew sitting at her counter, her eyes firmly fixed on the door as she waited for Wren to come in and make her day a little brighter. Drew kept checking her watch as the minutes ticked by but Wren didn't appear. For a moment, Drew started to worry she'd inadvertently done something wrong the previous night. She was second-guessing herself and running through the previous evening, searching for any misstep she had made that would warrant Wren not coming to see her. She was getting more and more worried until the door chime rang. Drew was grateful for the noise cutting through her inner voices.

It wasn't Wren though. Instead, Zenya wandered in, carrying a cake box. Drew was surprised, pleased that cake was involved, but disappointed it wasn't Wren bringing it.

"Chef Wren has asked that I deliver this to you along with her apologies for not making your lunch date today." Zenya handed over the box. "We're a bit short staffed this week so she's helping out so we can manage." Zenya couldn't miss Drew's disappointed face. "If it's any consolation, she's not happy either, but she didn't want you to think she'd forgotten you. So, she's just shoved me out the back door with this and threatened me not to linger. But I'm going to linger anyway. The peaceful vibe in here is healing my soul and it's so much cooler than the kitchen."

"Thank you. I was wondering where she was. Tell her thank you for me, please, and that I'll see her tonight when she leaves."

Zenya laughed. "Yeah, she's the talk of the restaurant, having a handsome woman waiting for her every night. Wren romancing next door's comic book geek has changed our head chef."

"Changed how?" Drew was intrigued.

"She's happier, doofus. *You* make her happy. And a happy head chef means a little more breathing room for the staff." Zenya pushed herself away from the counter. "But not if I don't hustle my butt back. Enjoy the cake!"

Zenya hurried out the store, but Drew was too busy opening her goodie box. She eyed the two slices of cake with delight and grabbed her phone to dash a quick text to Wren to say thank you. She received back a *sorry I can't share it with you* and lots of crying emojis. There was a red heart and kisses at the end too that made Drew's own heart lift. Drew looked across the store to where Aaron was dealing with a customer. She caught his eye and motioned she was going on her lunch break. Aaron gave her a thumbs-up and Drew went upstairs to the apartment.

Her grandma sat at the kitchen table, tapping away on her laptop. Drew had taught her how to use one and now Grandma had the whole internet at her fingertips, and Mrs. Daniels on FaceTime.

"Hi, honey. No Wren today?" Grandma peered at her over her glasses.

"Zenya came by to bring me this," Drew held up the box. "Wren's having to cover for low staff." She grabbed a salad box from the fridge and a fork from the drawer. "Might as well eat properly before I have dessert." She noticed her grandma's less than subtle interest in the box. "She's sent two slices. I think one is yours."

Her grandma pushed aside the laptop and took her glasses off. "Grab me a glass of milk, Drew, and a fork. I'd just finished my lunch so her timing is perfect." Her grandma eyed Drew knowingly. "Unless you want to keep both pieces to yourself. I mean, you're a growing gal…"

"I can share." Drew sat down and set everything out. "I'm not *that* bad with cake."

Her grandma snorted. "It's your favorite food. Young Wren cottoned on to that real quick." Her eyes widened at the large slab of cake she was handed. "Geez, I wish I'd pestered her about dating you sooner. We could have been having cake like this months ago!"

Drew waved her fork at her. "I am not dating her for her culinary skills, or the great food the restaurant has."

Grandma looked up from admiring her cake. "How did last night go?"

"You were with us for all but an hour of it. I think it went great, embarrassing baby pictures aside. I particularly liked her calling you out on your crush."

"Shush. We're not talking about that." Grandma waved her fork threateningly at Drew. "Did anything romantic happen after I left you two love birds alone?"

Drew tried so hard not to reveal anything. She wished she had the ability to pull back a blush before it bloomed on her skin. Her grandma's chuckle made Drew curse her lack of superpowers.

"Well, judging by how rosy your cheeks are getting I'd say you got some smoochies and maybe a tad more." Her grandma, looking mighty pleased with that outcome, tucked into her cake with gusto.

"We may have kissed," Drew admitted.

"Well, she wasn't here this morning fighting me for the bathroom so I'm guessing she didn't stay to continue your *conversation* in your room."

Drew shook her head. "No, she had an early shift at work and besides…" Drew wondered how to broach the subject without it sounding wrong. "She kind of wants us to erm…I mean, I understand why she does…" Drew was floundering under her grandma's steady gaze. "Will you stop with the supportive looks?" Drew sighed.

"Does she need me out of the apartment while she has her wicked way with you?"

Drew felt she could heat the entire block with how much her face was flaming. "She kind of wants me at her place for the first time."

Her grandma nodded. "I'll text Mrs. Daniels and ask if I can sleep over there so you and Wren can get better *acquainted*."

Drew squirmed in embarrassment. "Please don't! Don't tell Mrs. Daniels you need to sleep over there so Wren and I can have sex!"

"I'm sure I can find another excuse if you're going to be all prudish." Her grandma just grinned at her, unashamedly enjoying teasing Drew way too much.

Drew rolled her eyes at her. "Grandma, it's just…she's so special. She really is. And I'm so damn nervous. She's already noticed I'm not the kind of gal who rushes in and touches without permission."

"Some folks would find that an admirable trait."

"And others think I'm either an ice queen, a stone butch, or uninterested." Drew stared down into her salad bowl. "It's hard to explain to someone without me sounding like an abuse victim."

"But you are one, Drew. For all my sins of not getting you away from your parents quick enough, you are."

"It wasn't your fault, Grandma. You couldn't have known, and I wasn't telling anyone about what was happening. I just don't want it to be all I identify as. I'm the geeky comic book fanatic. I don't want to add 'used as a punching bag by my mother because I didn't grow big enough boobs' or 'virtually ignored by my father unless there was money to be cashed' to the list."

"I should have had you taken off them at birth. They didn't deserve to raise you as they did."

"You know their story like I do. Mother lied about being on the pill to force Father to marry her when she got pregnant with me. He told me that every chance he got until I started to sing and mother began feeding him stories of me being a superstar. Then, suddenly, I was his precious daughter who brought rich folk to come see us and beg to sign me up. He latched onto them like a leech, sucking everything he could from them, but giving nothing in return."

"And drained you in the process too."

"I still had some money left when they died. But I'm prouder of the money I make now. It's ours and this place is mine. Their money-grabbing hands never got to twist this place to their advantage."

"I wish you'd told me sooner about how she was hitting you and his vile mental abuse. I would have done something…anything." Grandma's eyes watered in guilt. "I can't believe a child of mine would turn out so rotten. Bradley was such a good boy as a child, but as a teenager he became selfish and hateful. And as a man he became detestable. He broke your grandpa's heart not looking after you right."

"They had me so twisted up in how I thought a family worked that I didn't realize not all kids experienced what I did on a daily basis. It drives me crazy I still can't instigate a hug because mother used that as a means to get me close. She'd lure me in with her kind voice and then she'd beat the living daylights out of me for some imagined thing I'd supposedly done wrong. She isolated me from the kids who could have told me that wasn't how family worked. That instead, affection is something freely and innocently given, not used as a bargaining chip until I gave in to their demands. I wish it had been different, but it wasn't. Mother was a tyrant who was determined to sell me to the highest bidder. She happily sat back and watched me act like a performing monkey, raking in the money for them both to squander." Drew revealed a fear she'd long believed her parents would have done, given the opportunity. "I just dread to think what altar they'd have sacrificed me on if I'd been the pretty girly-girl they had expected. That guy I hit with my guitar? Mother had stood by to let him feel me up before he signed me up. Said he wanted to 'test the merchandise.' But I smacked him in the junk so hard before he got a chance to even lay a finger on me. He squealed like the pig he was, clutching at his balls. Mother beat me so hard that night for ruining the chance of a trip to New York. It was worth it. We both know, as horrible as it sounds, the car crash saved me."

Drew knew the bruises she'd endured had faded in time, but the mental scars, left by the acts that caused them, didn't. "It just ruined your life in doing so."

"I'm okay, kid. I'm just a little creaky and can now forecast the weather better than any of those guys on TV with their fancy equipment can."

"You shattered a hip and leg, Grandma. You're the *Terminator* from the waist down because you shielded me in the crash."

"Honey, I'd have died for you in that damn accident."

"I know you would have, but I'm so glad you didn't." Drew reached over to clasp her grandma's hand. "You and Grandpa got to show me what a real family was."

"And now, maybe, Wren can show you another side with her." Grandma squeezed Drew's hand between both her own. "I'd really like that for you. I can't bear to think of you alone." She looked around at their home. "Arthur would have loved this place. He'd have sat, quiet as a mouse, in the store with you and just read through every comic book displayed. When we first got you? I remember wanting so much to be out of that damned hospital and to go shopping with you instead of you having to take Grandpa. I remember asking you what you wanted to buy first because you brought so little from your home when we had it cleared out and sold."

Drew remembered too. "There wasn't much in possessions for me to bring. They didn't allow me toys or games. They were a distraction from my singing. I remember you saying I could have anything I wanted and I had no clue where to start. I'd never had so many choices before. I was so frightened to ask if I could wear jeans and T-shirts. I fucking hated those damn dresses mother forced me into. And I wanted to wear boy's clothes so desperately. I wasn't sure why but I wanted to."

"And then you asked for a comic book. Just the one so you wouldn't use all our money. My heart ached for you, sweetheart. When you came back to the hospital that evening, you'd gotten your hair cut properly, had your first pair of blue jeans on, and that Lord of The Rings T-shirt your grandpa had to wrestle you out of every time he needed to wash it." Her grandma shook her head in remembrance. "So many things you were making up for lost time with. How you could dress, what you could read, finally going to a movie." Her grandma wiped away a tear. "And I remember how you sat by my bed side with a lap full of X-Men comic books because Arthur made you buy more than just one to read. You looked like you'd won the lottery."

"And I read them to you." Drew smiled at the same memory.

"You did and I saw how captivated you were by these people with magical powers. And I wished so hard that one day you'd realize how special *you* truly are, without a spider bite to trigger you, or you having to dress up as a bat to save the world. You're amazing at everything you turn your hand to, Drew." Her grandma hesitated a moment then said what was obviously on her mind. "I admit, I do miss your beautiful singing, but I kind of understand why you've kept that part of you silenced."

Drew reached for her cake and deliberately didn't answer. She chose instead to just enjoy the rich icing and decadent three-tiered peach-filled cake. She heard her grandma sigh softly as they ate their cake in silence for a while.

Drew finally pushed her plate aside and stood up. "I'm going back to work. Just press your button if you need me."

"And you'll come flying up here, faster than a speeding bullet?"

"You know it."

"You'll always be my superhero, Drew. You lived through hell and still came out on top. Look at you. You were the apple of your grandpa's eye."

"And to you?"

"You're the pain in my ass. You've haven't brought any new ice cream in a week. How can I watch my soap operas and sneak a tub of it if you haven't restocked?"

Drew laughed at her. "I'll go pick up some of *my* ice cream later. I'd hate to deprive you."

"You're a good girl," Grandma said.

"And you're *my* pain in the ass. It's a good thing I love you." Drew pecked a kiss on her grandma's forehead as she left.

"Love you too-oo," Grandma singsonged after her.

Drew checked her watch as she walked back down to the store. Visions from her childhood rolled around her head like a massive boulder intent to crush all her dreams. She stepped into the store, greeted by the riot of wall-to-wall fantasy. With glee, Drew pictured the boulder deflating noisily like a tired old balloon. She checked her watch again and started counting down the hours until she could go see Wren.

Everything Drew had gone through had led her here, to this moment. To having her own store and to finding Wren. It had been a rough road to travel, but she wouldn't change it for the world.

Work conspired to keep both Wren and Drew busy all week. Wren hated the fact she'd only managed to get one lunch break in with Drew since their third date. Two people were still off sick, and a family emergency had forced another member of staff to take time off, leaving the restaurant staff working hard to cover for them. If it wasn't for Drew determinedly waiting at her car to say good night then Wren would have gone insane missing her. She'd lost count of how many times she'd left the restaurant only to find her colleagues chatting with Drew when all Wren wanted was to throw herself into Drew's arms. She'd taken to shooing them away and launching herself at Drew. Drew caught her every time and seemed to relish the attention.

"You look lost in thought."

Takira's voice pulled Wren out of her mental musings. Wren quickly checked that what she was doing hadn't boiled over while her mind was too busy wishing she was next door in the comic book store. She had never been this distracted before, and she hoped Takira wasn't about to take her to task for it.

"This week has been brutal. Just three workers down, yet the difference it has made has been noticeable. How did you know exactly how many staff it takes to run this restaurant to its peak proficiency?"

Takira sighed. "It took years. You have to find a fine balance of cooks to servers. I wish I could say it all came together easily, but I'd be lying. You're seeing the culmination of my building this place up from scratch, four years swapping and changing staff, and having my first manager nearly bankrupt me and my having to start all over again." Takira passed Wren the plates she needed and helped her dish up the meals. "Once Dante took over, things improved so much. Sometimes, just one person can make a huge difference."

Wren handed the plates over to a server and gathered up the next order. "All my life I have had one goal set for me—to have my own restaurant. It's seemed like an impossible dream but I've followed the plan my papa set out for me diligently."

"Here, in this position, being your last step?" Takira worked beside Wren and they quickly got another meal ready to serve.

"Supposedly. I love what I'm capable of doing. I'll admit, it's one hell of a power trip some days, watching this kitchen working at full capacity and knowing I'm steering it. But, the thought of doing all that *and* dealing with the restaurant as a whole…frankly, I'm afraid I'll get another ulcer stressing over it."

Takira nodded. "Oh, I've had years of that stress. You definitely need a manager who can work miracles, one who can take a lot of the load off your shoulders. Dante did that, both in business, and in our personal life. She took over the management of the restaurant and pretty much Finn until I decided to take a lateral move to free up my time. Now I have more time with both of them." Takira looked pensive for a moment. "You know, I had my heart set on being strictly a career girl, no entanglements, definitely no children, just running my restaurant, and relying on no one." She laughed. "Life had other plans for me, however."

"I never really saw myself as a mother. When Val had Ana I got a bigger glimpse into that world and I soon wiped it clear from my to-do list. But I'd like a partner, someone I can go home to and share my victories with."

"Someone tall, blond, and handsome maybe?" Takira said with a knowing smile.

"Let's face it, the odds of me getting my dream job, right next door to one who could be my dream woman? I'm seeing a fate or destiny at work here."

"And Dawes & Destiny Comics is literally right in the next parking lot. If you get your own restaurant, you'd have to move away." Takira bumped Wren with her hip. "Because, as much as I love you, Wren Banderas, not all is fair in love and competing restaurants."

Wren laughed out loud but recognized the seriousness behind Takira's teasing. They'd be competitors. Wren hated to think about that. She loved the synchronized comradery she and Takira shared.

"Drew said something the other night. She asked if my dream of owning a restaurant was my dream or my papa's plan that I've followed without thought."

Takira didn't stop in her chopping of an onion and tossing it into a waiting pan. "And do you know the answer?"

Wren shook her head. "She made me question my whole life's plan, damn her. But now there's a part of me that can't help but wonder if what Papa said was my ultimate goal in becoming a chef wasn't what *I* wanted after all. That I just did what he expected of me, like the dutiful daughter I am."

"Then it's a good thing you're in no great rush to decide. You're still young, Wren. You could decide tomorrow that you're done in this business and go study paleontology."

Wren stared at her. "Fossil hunter? *That's* the job you'd choose for me?"

"It was the first thing that came to mind," Takira said, laughing. "Finn is all Spider-Man and dinosaurs. We've had to stop him from digging the backyard up in search of fossils."

Wren thought this over. "So, you're saying I'd at least have a fossil buddy in Finn if I chose to take this new route in my life?"

"Absolutely. You wouldn't have to get your hands dirty. He'd happily dig through the dirt for hours if you let him."

"I don't think I'm ready to quit my current day job just yet."

"I'm glad to hear that. Don't think I wouldn't fight Finn tooth and nail in order to get you to stay here." Takira's face turned serious. "You're a valuable part of my restaurant, Wren. If you choose to leave at some point then I'll respect your decision, but I'd also use any bribe possible to keep you working here. We're a family here. I need all of you to make this work. That means this is *your* restaurant too. It can't run with just me in it, can it?"

Wren's heart squeezed in her chest. "You know I love working here. It's all my dreams come true. God, Takira, what am I going to do? I'm so damn confused."

Takira set her pan alight and tossed the ingredients with a skilled hand. "You're not going to think about it anymore today. You're just going to continue as normal, spinning the plates in this circus of a kitchen, and when the time comes for you to make a decision you and I will talk it through."

"How are you so awesome?" Wren said.

"I surround myself with fellow awesome beings." Takira added some extra oil to her pan and the flames rose.

"What if my papa's dreams weren't mine after all?" Wren had to ask. The realization had been gnawing at her for days now.

"Then you'll always have a home here to realize *your* dreams." Takira tossed the vegetables one last time and spread them out on a waiting plate with finesse.

Wren honestly couldn't think of anywhere else she'd rather be.

Chapter Fifteen

The heaviness of the oversized guitar in her small hands was nothing compared to the weight of responsibility that threatened to crush her through the stage floor. Drew, just twelve years old, stood waiting in the wings for the band that was playing to finish their set. Her mother stood behind her, her hands heavy on Drew's shoulders, holding her firmly in place. Drew knew her father was somewhere out in the audience, propping up the bar as usual.

"I don't want another occurrence of last week, Drew," her mother said, curling her hands into claws. "You will not let me down again."

Drew felt her mother's finger nails dig through her thin blouse. She'd learned the hard way not to flinch at any pain inflicted when they were out in public. Drew kept her eyes on the drummer on stage, watching him play with a smile on his face. She remembered a time when she could do that. All she felt now was tired. Her grades were failing, she had no friends to confide in, her parents had forbidden her grandparents from coming near her after Grandma had noticed how pale and thin Drew was getting on their last visit. Drew had wanted so desperately to leave with them. Her grandma knew it, too. She'd promised Drew she'd be back. It had been two weeks. Drew feared she'd never return and things were getting worse, at home and on stage.

The sound of the audience's applause was deafening. Drew started to shake. She was up next. The band all rushed past her, nearly knocking her and her mother over in their haste. She heard the crude words her mother flung at them and the derision she got back. Drew's legs started to collapse under her and her mother forcibly dragged her back up.

"You'll perform or else, young lady. I worked fucking hard to get this gig for you and you will not disappoint me any further than you already do. You will *not* pass out again or I will make your life a living hell." She shoved Drew forward, toward the curtains that draped the side of the stage. "Do your duty."

To God, to family, to fame and fortune, Drew finished silently. The unforgiving obligation stabbed her in the heart a hundred times over.

Drew heard her introduction, heard the audience cheer. She had her loyal fans. She had fame building steadily. She could be someone of note in the music industry if she continued on this path.

Drew just wanted to go home, curl up in a corner, and die.

She took her place on the stage, plastered a smile on her face, and spoke as if nothing was wrong. Professional Drew took over while the real Drew hid in a sealed off room in a corner of her mind. The guitar was Drew's solace and her voice a soothing balm. With no orchestra or backing singers, the spotlight firmly fixed on a lonely girl with just her guitar. Dutifully, Drew sang. She sang the well-known songs from Olivia, Shania, Garth, and Reba. The staples for her Country audience, the songs her mother drummed into her. She sang songs of broken hearts that held little meaning for a twelve-year-old who had very little life experience outside of what her mother had planned for her. The audience clapped and cheered anyhow. Drew couldn't see them anymore. The lights that shone on the stage blinded her. What little of the people she could see blurred into fractured patterns. Her eyes became unfocused as her nerves jangled and the stress of the performance took its toll. Drew knew she could end soon. She had two songs left. She didn't want to sing them. They had no meaning for her. The guitar felt heavy, weighing her down like a millstone around her neck. Her voice never wavered, but she tired of hearing it. She missed the carefree singing when she was just discovering her talent and every new song was an adventure. She missed learning how to hit the high notes. She missed the fun of high-fiving her grandma when she could keep up with Olivia Newton-John's exemplary voice singing "Xanadu." She missed the peace her grandparents gave her most of all.

Without a second thought, Drew changed her set list. She knew she would pay for it later, especially as the song was by someone her mother detested. But Drew could feel the stress taking its toll and she'd black out soon enough, just like she'd started to do. Blacking out to stop the pain, to appease the fear, to just make it all *stop*.

Drew started to strum out k.d. lang's "Constant Craving." She ignored her mother's angry hiss from the wings as Drew blatantly disobeyed her. With a soulful voice, Drew sang the song that called to her heart. She understood it to be about being brave through the darkest of times and that her need, her desire, her *desperation* to be free of that darkness would always be a constant craving. Whether that was the artist's intention, Drew would never know, but the song presented itself to Drew that way and with a voice full of emotion, she sang it.

The audience was on its feet cheering, but for Drew it was just a dreadful white noise. The stage lights were dimming as Drew started to lose consciousness. Fight or flight. Drew's response was to pass out. Her body, overloaded by the pressures of performing, starved of nourishment because of the restrictive diet her mother had her on, shut down abruptly as if someone flicked a switch inside her. She collapsed to the floor, dimly hearing a voice calling her name before she was out.

"Drew? Drew! Wake up! You can't sleep the day away in your bed when you have a chance to test the sheets out in someone else's!"

Drew startled awake to find her grandma leaning over her, shaking her roughly. "Grandma? What the hell?"

"Up and at 'em, girl! It's your day with Wren! You need to get yourself ready and exfoliated."

Drew rubbed at her face as she struggled to sit up. "Do you even know what exfoliated means?"

"No, but then I don't have a date lined up for today either." Her grandma poked at her again. "The hot water is on. Your shower is ready." She ruffled Drew's newly shorn hair. "Look at you all neat and tidy. Wren is going to be impressed you took the time to smarten up."

Drew slid out of bed and stretched. "If I find it's only seven a.m. I'm going to be so annoyed with you. She's not coming for me until ten."

"It's nine o'clock," Grandma said.

Drew instantly woke up. "Oh my God! Why didn't you get me up sooner? I haven't decided what T-shirt to wear or anything." Drew hurried toward the bathroom and spared a quick look at the clock. It was eight thirty. Drew directed a dirty look over her shoulder at her grandma. "That was not funny," she grumbled.

Her grandma was laughing anyway. "Yes, it was. You were nearly shucking out of your pj's to leave a trail on your run to the shower. Go wake up, Sleeping Beauty. You're not gonna get any sleep tonight!"

Drew regretted, for the millionth time, ever letting her grandma in on the reason why she was taking today off.

"Keep it up, Grandma, and I'll spill the beans to Mrs. Daniels about the photo you have by the side of your bed." Drew grinned in satisfaction as she heard her grandma squawk behind her.

"Don't you dare, Drew Dawes! I will come in there and flush the toilet while you shower if you even consider doing that!"

Drew pretended to reconsider and took a more leisurely walk into the bathroom to start getting ready. She showered, washed her hair, and dried off in record time. It was while she was brushing her teeth that the magnitude of the day really sunk in. She stared at herself in the mirror, her mouth frothing with toothpaste. How did you dress for a "going to make love with my new girlfriend for the first time" date? All her T-shirts and sweatshirts had superheroes on them. She couldn't remember the last time she'd worn a plain T-shirt. The jeans had been easy to pick out. New socks and her

Rainbow Pride Converse were a no-brainer. Boxers and a bra of course, but a T-shirt that said "I am quietly confident and ready to take that next step into intimacy" was proving impossible for Drew to narrow down.

She wandered into her bedroom and opened her wardrobe that was pretty much nothing but T-shirts. She began flipping through them.

"Which one will suit the mood for today? The Flash? No, that red is too bright. I need subtle. Wonder Woman? No, today my mind focuses on just one woman. Superman, Batman, Antman, Aquaman, Spider-Man, Ironman." Drew flicked through them all with speed. "Geez, I have way too many men in my closet." She ran through her Star Wars ones. "No, not feeling the Force today." She looked down at herself, half dressed with just her bra on. "I could go like this and save us some time." She drew out a black T-shirt, saw it had Venom's terrifying face on and hastily pushed it back. She was just getting ready to get out a coin and flip for it when she spied something she hadn't worn yet. She took out a black T-shirt emblazoned with The Scarlet Witch in all her red horned glory. Drew smiled as she put it on. Wanda Maximoff was becoming a mighty force in the Marvel Universe. Drew always had room for another heroine to adorn her clothes. She wondered if Wren knew anything at all about the females of the MCU.

"Can that be used as foreplay, I wonder?" Drew ran back to the mirror in the bathroom to check herself out. "Yes, I am the living embodiment of geeky seduction."

Drew wandered back into the kitchen. Her grandma looked her over with an approving eye. "You look fantastic, my girl. Wren is a very lucky woman."

"I think I'm the lucky one, Grandma."

"Are you wearing the new socks I bought you?"

Drew pulled up the leg of her jeans to flash an ankle encased in brightly colored Pac-Man socks.

"Perfect. You're going to knock her off her feet. You're so handsome and it's about time you got some lovin'."

Drew narrowed her eyes at her. "Sometimes I wish you were the kind of grandma who just sat and knitted."

Her grandma waved a hand dismissively. "That's for the old ladies. Me? I want to cheer my granddaughter on as she rides off with her girlfriend to spend the day—"

"Okay!" Drew butted in, knowing exactly where Grandma was going with that train of thought. "Changing the subject swiftly to you. Mrs. Daniels is coming for you in ten minutes. If you need me for anything, you have my number. Do *not* hesitate to call it."

"I am not phoning you while you're otherwise engaged." Her grandma was outraged. "Wren would think it rude of me to do so!"

"I don't care. If you need me, you call."

"Nothing's going to happen to me. You just enjoy yourself for once. Get out, let loose, stop worrying. *Live*, Drew."

"I'm trying." Drew's phone rang. Wren's name appeared on the screen. She wasn't due for another forty minutes. *Oh no, is she having to cancel?* Drew hesitated a second before answering, fearful of what she might hear. "Hello?"

"Hi, Drew. A bit of a change in plans, if you're agreeable. Mama has asked me to go over and get her laptop set up to her new internet provider. Val switched it for her but didn't think to do the laptop. I've tried to talk her through it this morning and it was like banging my head against a wall. So, do you mind?"

"I get to meet your mama?"

"Of course, you do. I'm not leaving you in the car with the window cracked open like a dog."

Drew loved Wren's sense of humor. "Okay. Let's go meet Mama. What time are you picking me up?"

"I'm actually outside right now in the parking lot with Mrs. Daniels."

Oh great. Drew winced. She'd hoped to not have to endure a cheering squad as she left with Wren. She looked across the table at her grandma who was watching her conversation with great interest. "Grandma, your girlfriend is here."

Grandma gasped and wagged her finger at her sass. "I'll go grab my bag."

"Wren is downstairs as well. Do NOT embarrass me any further than you already have."

Her grandma looked affronted. "As if I would."

"She most definitely would," Wren said in Drew's ear.

"I'll grab my backpack and we'll be right down." Drew hung up and hurried to get her pack with her overnight needs. She grabbed a couple of breakfast bars to go and a bottle of water and was waiting at the front door ready to help her grandma. Once Grandma was off her stairlift, Drew went to check on Noah who was in charge again. He gave Drew a thumbs-up and a wink. Drew rolled her eyes. *Is there no one Grandma hasn't told?*

Dakota ran over to her, gave her a swift hug, and whispered in her ear. "Remember, take precautions because you don't want to get her pregnant."

Drew pushed her away, shaking her head at Dakota's amusement. "One of these days I'm going to make it mandatory that you wear a proper store uniform," she said.

Dakota tapped her jaunty sailor hat with a grin. "Have fun, boss."

Drew was glad to get outside away from all-knowing eyes. She almost bumped into Mrs. Daniels who was helping Grandma get in her car.

"Good morning, Drew. You have a good day now."

Drew braced herself for the punch line. Mrs. Daniels just smiled at her sweetly.

"I'll look after your grandma, don't you worry. We have our own special night planned."

Drew raised her eyebrows at her grandma who was blushing up a storm.

"Canasta and one of Takira's special pies. I know all Mae's favorites to treat her right."

Drew nodded slowly, trying not to laugh at her grandma trying desperately to remain poker faced at Mrs. Daniels's innocent words. Wren hid her own laughter in a series of coughs and splutters. Concerned, Mrs. Daniels looked over at her.

"I hope you're not coming down with something, Chef Wren. It would be a pity to spoil your day off."

Wren waved a hand to show she was fine. Drew waved good-bye to them both as Mrs. Daniels drove off. Wren burst into peals of laughter once they'd gone.

"Oh my God, Mae's face!" Doubled over, Wren clutched at her stomach.

"It was worth enduring all her incessant teasing today to see her get that flustered." Drew waited for Wren to calm down. "So, you going to take me to meet your mama before you drag me to your bed to have your wicked way with me?"

"I had plans to spend the whole day in bed with you. Damn laptop and Mama being tech-phobic." Wren pouted in her disappointment but reached up to pull Drew down to her for a kiss. The shared kiss was soft and gentle and over way too soon. "Now that's the proper way to start the day."

Drew tossed her backpack into the back of the car and took the passenger's seat. "I was right," she said, eyeing the car's interior.

"About what?" Wren took her own seat.

"That back seat would have me twisted up like a pretzel."

"Good thing my bed is bigger then. Plenty of room for me to stretch *you* out."

Drew groaned at the seductive promise Wren made her and at the twinkle in her eyes.

Damned laptop indeed.

CHAPTER SIXTEEN

Music played from Wren's radio and Drew tapped along to the rhythm on her thigh.

Wren, concentrating on the busy road, spared her a glance. "I know you don't sing now, but you seem to still enjoy music. How does that work?"

"My love of music never stopped. I just don't sing publicly anymore."

Wren made an unhappy sound. "I think that's a damned shame. You shouldn't have to stifle what is obviously a God-given talent."

"It's not so much stifled as shelved." Drew stretched her arms out to relieve a kink in her shoulders. "My life took a different turn. There's not much call for me singing in the store."

"I seem to recall you singing when I found you waiting that time for Dakota and Aaron to pick you up. It was so faint though. I wasn't sure I was hearing it."

Drew shifted uncomfortably. "Just because I choose not to sing doesn't mean that sometimes, the *need* to sing doesn't escape me. It was such a big part of my life."

And still is but I'm so afraid to let that particular genie out of the bottle again.

"I'm not sure I understand your reluctance to sing even just for yourself, though."

"To be honest, Wren, I'm not sure I understand it either. The grief counselor I saw as a kid thought it stemmed from the bad memories I had of being forced to perform. Physical and mental abuse were always associated with my singing. So, to stop the memory of that, I apparently stopped singing out loud." Drew had only ever seen one counselor. Her grandparents had decided that they'd let Drew decide on her own way of dealing with things. They'd given her back her right to *choose*. "It's been so long ago. It's kind of like seeing a flame. You reach out to touch it and burn your hand on it. Your mind becomes programmed to warn you every time you see a flame not to touch it because it will hurt. I think, as a kid, my mind gave me the same warning. I never touched music again because, to me, it's associated with pain."

"Do you think you could take your voice back now? Being older and happier?"

Wren's face was so earnest and kind Drew could only marvel at her. No one had ever looked at her the way Wren did. It made her feel special. Special just for who she was, and not for what she could do. Drew took a moment to think about what Wren had said.

"I don't know. It's never been something I considered as my life is so different now. My career choices became mine alone and I chose to pursue what I loved most after my grandpa took me to my first comic book store."

"But, in quiet times, when your heart needs to, you sing to yourself. However quietly, you *sing*."

Wren's voice was so gentle. She'd never once accused Drew of being stupid for choosing not to sing again. Drew wondered if she should tell Wren that, sometimes, the need to play on her guitar gripped at her chest like a hunger. That her love for singing hadn't died as she'd thought. She'd tried burying it, six feet deep. It was supposed to lay alongside the bodies of her parents, in the cemetery in a state far away from where Drew was now.

But it hadn't remained buried. Drew was just too frightened to let it back into her life in case it became all-consuming again.

Wren pulled into the driveway in front of a large house. Drew was thankful the topic of conversation would have to change now to something less fraught with bad memories.

The large house and its flower-lined driveway stopped Drew's heart in her chest for a moment. It reminded her of the house she'd grown up in and she couldn't stop the fear that struck her as her memory played tricks on her and made her think she was home.

No, not home. Home is above the comic book store now.

"Wow, this is some place." Desperately trying to sound normal, Drew got out the car and looked around. The more she looked, the less it resembled the house she'd grown up in. Her heart rate steadied again as her nerves calmed down. She fancied she could see Wren as a child running around the fantastic lawns and picking the flowers. "Is this part of the gardens you had Monica's landscapers come sort out?"

"Yes, and believe me, this front area is nothing compared to the yard out the back. They worked minor miracles back there." Wren reached for Drew's hand.

Drew tugged nervously at her clothing as Wren led her to the front door. "I didn't exactly dress for meeting your family today. I was too frazzled trying to find a suitable T-shirt for our *personal* occasion."

Wren laughed. "Drew, you do know you don't always have to coordinate what you're wearing with what you're doing?" Wren's considering gaze took Drew in and she narrowed her eyes at her. "Hmm, I didn't realize how OCD you can be."

Drew huffed. "Tell me *you* didn't spend ages trying on stuff to see what felt best for today?"

Wren stood on her tiptoes and kissed Drew's pouting lips. "Sweetheart, I just chose the clothes I was least attached to in case you felt the need to rip them off me."

Stunned, Drew remained rooted to the spot by that admission. She grumbled under her breath at Wren. "You can't tell me something like that, moments away from you taking me inside to introduce me to your mama. You've planted a myriad of naughty ideas into my brain. How am I going to be able to think of anything other than busting the buttons off that shirt now?"

Wren's laughter filled the air. "Just hold that thought. We'll come back to it; I promise." She tugged Drew forward again, swinging their hands between them, happy and carefree.

"Do you think your mama will like me?" Drew asked quietly, smoothing her hand again down the front of her T-shirt. She was thankful she'd had her hair cut. First impressions were crucial. Not that she'd met any of the parents of the few women she'd attempted to date.

"I'm sure she will. I'll just warn you now, she's not going to expect me to do her laptop then have us leave immediately. You'll have to endure a coffee and cake inquisition first."

"Ahh, hence the cake I spied in the back seat."

Wren screeched to a halt and rushed back to the car. "Fuck! Thank you for reminding me!" She carefully carried the cake box back. "She'd be disappointed if I forgot this. I always have to bring her some of Takira's cake."

Drew smiled. "Then we have that in common at least. Neat. So, what have you told her about me that I should be worried about?"

Wren looked guilty. "I *might* have been keeping you all to myself for a while."

"So, I'm going in there with you and she has *no* idea we've been seeing each other?"

"No?" Wren cringed and tried to give Drew a reassuring smile. "It's no biggie. It's just my mama you're meeting. Think of her kind of like Mae—nosey, dramatic, only with a more Italian flair."

"You and I will talk more later about you leading me into a virtual lion's den."

Wren nodded, contrite. She side-eyed Drew. "I don't know why you're worried. You're wearing on your shirt the biggest, baddest, wand-swinging witch in the multi-verse. According to my niece, that is, who has taken to enlightening me of *every* single character in the MUC like I'm cramming for a test."

"MCU," Drew corrected automatically. "And Wanda doesn't use a wand. She has all the magic she needs right in the palms of her hands."

"So, you're telling me *you* didn't bring a wand either to keep all my mischief suitably managed?"

Drew shook her head and didn't miss when Wren's teasing changed to something way more sexual. Her eyes gave her away every time. They *smoldered*.

"Well, *I* have just the thing we can make magic with together when we get back home…" Wren said. She laced each word with an unmistakable sensual edge.

Drew pushed Wren toward the house. "That thought stops right there if you want us to even get to the front door." Resigned to Wren's unashamed laughter at her blushing's expense, Drew retaliated by tugging gently at a long lock of Wren's hair.

"I'll meet your mama first and *then* we can talk all you want about magical wands and even more magical hands."

Drew didn't miss the startled look Wren's mother wore when Wren walked into the living room with her in tow. The older woman quickly hid it and gave Drew a measured stare. Drew straightened her shoulders, a little intimidated at meeting the Banderas matriarch. She was short like Wren, had similar features around the nose and mouth, but her silver hair was short and expertly coiffed. Her whole look and demeanor radiated a rich elegance. Her sharp eyes quickly took Drew all in before she looked to Wren.

Wren introduced them. "Mama, this is Drew Dawes. She owns Dawes & Destiny Comics, the comic book store next door to Takira's. Drew, this is my mama, Renata."

Renata held out her hand to Drew. "A pleasure to meet you, Drew."

Drew shook her hand. "It's lovely to meet you too, Mrs. Banderas. I can see where Wren gets her beauty from."

Renata's smile grew. "Ooh, flattery. I'm liking you already. Florencia…?"

Wren smiled. "Yes, Mama. I'd like for you to meet my girlfriend."

Renata clapped her hands and reached for Drew. "Come, sit with me." She led Drew to a sofa in the elegant living room and patted the seat beside her. "Sit. We'll talk while Florencia puts on the coffee and does her thing in the kitchen." Renata dismissed Wren with a wave of her hand. "The large plates, dear."

Wren chuckled under her breath. "Drew, you need only give her your name, rank, and serial number."

Renata tutted after her. "My daughter, she thinks she's so funny."

Drew watched Wren as she headed to the kitchen. She turned her attention back to see Renata watching her closely.

Renata's eyes softened. "She's kept you hidden from me. Why is that?"

"We're still just getting to know each other and we're both very busy in our work. Sometimes there isn't enough time in the day for us to meet up properly, let alone spend time with others." Drew hoped that was a good enough excuse. Renata seemed suitably appeased by it.

"Mama, Drew comes to the restaurant every night when we close to make sure I get to my car safely." Wren came in from the kitchen carrying three plates. Renata's eyes sparkled when she saw the richly decorated red velvet cake.

Drew was hoping her stomach wouldn't embarrass her by growling pitifully because she'd missed breakfast. The cake looked amazing and Wren's smiling face made Drew's nerves calm down.

"You go *every* night to see to Florencia's safety?" Renata asked, taking her plate but not losing her line of questioning.

"Every night she works late, yes." Drew gratefully received her plate and wondered what the Banderas family etiquette was. Could she just start in on the cake now? She looked to Wren who sat beside her and took a mouthful. Drew sighed and did the same. She couldn't stifle to moan at the rich, velvety goodness. She made sure not to speak with her mouth full. "This is heavenly."

Wren's smile was proud. "It's one of my recipes Takira uses. I put more than a dash of paprika in. It adds a little kick." Wren took another bite. "Mama, Drew's just like you, she loves her cake."

"Have you cooked for her yet?"

"No, but I visit her store as much as I can in my lunch break and always take her a piece of cake."

"She looks after you?" Renata asked, eyeing Drew carefully.

Drew nodded. "She does."

Renata nodded at Wren approvingly then switched back to Drew. "Your mama and papa, what do they do?"

Drew's fork screeched against the plate and she grimaced as the sound made her teeth ache. She quickly regained her composure. "They're both dead, Mrs. Banderas. But I live with my grandma and she's the best family I am blessed with."

"You live with her?"

"We share the apartment above my store. Grandma has some mobility issues. I look after her but, really, we take care of each other."

Renata looked past Drew to Wren. "She looks after her family. I like that." Her attention turned back to Drew, her questioning not done. "How old are you?"

"Thirty-one."

"And you own your own store?"

"Yes, ma'am."

"You do good business there?"

Wren huffed. "Mama!"

Renata looked surprised. "What? I'm merely asking if your Drew has a successful business."

"I do," Drew said simply. "And I love my work so it's a joy to be there."

Satisfied with her answer, Renata took a bite from her cake and Drew took the opportunity to turn to Wren to make sure she was okay. Wren leaned in closer to her and Drew relaxed more.

"You make a beautiful couple," Renata said. "You complement each other. Yin and yang. Your light," Renata gestured to Drew's hair, "to her dark."

Wren ran her hand over Drew's short hair. "Look how blond she is, Mama. I've seen her baby pictures. Her hair was almost white!"

Renata sat up straight. "Baby pictures? Drew, would you like to see Florencia's baby pictures?" She got up before Drew could answer and wandered over to a shelf lined with albums.

Drew quickly swallowed her mouthful of cake, gave Wren a wicked grin, then answered Renata. "I'd love to see her baby pictures, please!"

Wren narrowed her eyes at her. "Mama, I did not bring Drew here so you could embarrass me with the 'chubby baby in the bath' photos."

Renata sat back down, paying Wren no mind. She scooted closer to Drew and put the large album across their laps. "Shush," she directed toward Wren. "Go sort out my laptop while I show your sweetie how cute you were in your little chef aprons."

Drew had to smile when Wren dutifully got up to go get the laptop but brought it right back to where she was sitting to keep an eye on them both. Drew leaned over to whisper in Wren's ear. "You're right, she's *just* like Grandma!"

The photo album was a delight. Drew knew that Wren would have been a cute baby, but the photos were so precious. Toddler Chef Wren was Drew's favorite. Especially the one with her holding up a wooden spoon dripping with cake batter, her little round cheeks covered in flour. Drew got to see Luca Banderas and a very dour faced teenaged Val. Ana barely resembled her at all. Drew listened intently to Renata as she told her Wren's story. She felt honored to have it shared with her.

Wren sorted out the laptop in seconds but, as warned, Renata was not ready to let them go. Wren sent Drew an apologetic look, but Drew was enjoying herself. Renata was a delight to be with and Drew was fascinated by all she was telling her about her own life and everyone in the Banderas family.

On their second cup of coffee, Renata reached out to touch Drew's tattoo. Drew felt Wren stiffen behind her.

"This is beautiful artistry," Renata said, tapping a finger along each star inked into Drew's flesh. "It's the Tardis, yes?"

"Oh my God! Am I literally the only person on the entire planet who didn't know this damn show?" Wren exploded behind her. Her exasperated face made Drew smile.

"I watch it sometimes," Renata admitted. "It gets lonely here, on my own. Sometimes the television is my only companion. I know of the Doctor and her traveling box. I like this new one. It was about time we had a female in the role."

Drew looked at Wren. "I really like your mama a lot." She turned back to speak to Renata. "Mrs. Banderas, one day you have to come to Takira's and meet my grandma. I think you two would get on famously too."

"The restaurant would never recover from such a meeting," Wren muttered.

"I would love that. I haven't visited for a long while, not since Wren first started there."

The sound of the front door slamming made them all jump. Drew was surprised to see Ana come running in.

"Auntie Wren!" Ana spotted Drew and her excitement grew. "Drew! Look! Look at the T-shirt my dad bought me." She proudly showed off her Avengers T-shirt.

"That's fantastic! You have the whole team on there," Drew said, distracted by the fact Wren let out a barely audible groan beside her. Drew had the feeling it wouldn't be Marco bringing Ana for a visit.

In Drew's mind, the woman who walked into the room could only be Wren's sister, Val. She stood a little taller than Wren, wasn't as strikingly attractive, and her whole demeanor was entirely different. She was straight-faced, her keen eyes didn't seem to miss a thing, and she stared first at Drew and then at Wren as if expecting an explanation for their being there.

"Valentina," Renata greeted her, a warning in her tone.

"What brings you here?" Val asked Wren, not unkindly, but still with an edge of accusation.

Drew had a feeling that was something Val employed as a lawyer to great success.

"I set up Mama's laptop with the internet for her."

Val turned to her mother. "I could have done that for you when I was here last. Why didn't you say?"

"I didn't want to bother you. I didn't realize I couldn't get online until after you'd left. I thought I could do it myself, but I couldn't. Wren came to introduce Drew to me and offered to help."

Drew knew that wasn't entirely true but kept her eyes on Val, waiting to see how long she'd go not speaking to her.

Val eyed Drew intently. "Drew? From the comic book store that Ana hasn't shut up about since she visited it?"

Drew nodded. "That's me. Drew Dawes." She stood to shake Val's hand. "It's nice to meet you. Your daughter was such a joy at the store. She had our youngest customers trailing after her like little ducklings."

"Little Baby Yoda and Spider-Man were so cute!" Ana said. "You wouldn't think kids their age would know about comic books and stuff but they knew more than I do!"

"There's cake in the kitchen if you want any," Wren said. "There's fresh coffee too."

Ana quickly raced off. Her sneakers squealed loudly on the kitchen tiles as she skidded to a halt.

"Ana!" Val chastised her, taking a more leisurely pace after her.

"Sorry, Mom!" Ana shouted back. "Oh my God, it's red velvet! Mom, get in here!"

Wren leaned across Drew to whisper to Renata. "Did you know she was coming today?"

Renata swiftly shook her head. "I wouldn't have had you drive all this way had I known. But then I wouldn't have gotten to meet this charming young lady." She patted Drew's knee. "So, I'm not in the least bit sorry."

Val wandered back in with a plate in hand and the smallest slither of cake Drew had ever seen.

"Why aren't you at the restaurant today, Wren?" Val asked, using her fork to cut off the tiniest morsel of cake. Ana sat beside her with a much bigger piece to eat and her fork loaded.

"I have the weekend off."

"Can they afford to not have you there? You're the head chef, after all."

"That doesn't mean I can't have time off. Takira is running the kitchen this weekend in my absence. It's not like she doesn't remember how to do it."

"Is it wise to let her fill in for you? She might decide she can manage the restaurant without you again."

Drew watched their exchange. She could see Val was calmly asking her questions but Wren was clenching her teeth so hard Drew was worried she'd hear them crack.

"Wren's indispensable there. Takira has too many other things she's juggling not to be grateful that Wren has taken the majority of it off her hands." Drew pulled Wren's hand into her lap and laced their fingers together. She saw Val's eyes widen as she realized just why Drew was there.

"You two are seeing each other?" Val asked.

Ana's head whipped up. "*Are you*? That would be great! Drew is so neat!"

Drew laughed at her enthusiasm. "Thank you, Ana."

Wren nodded. "Yes, we're seeing each other."

Ana fist-pumped the air before tucking into her cake again.

Val frowned a little. "Not to be rude…"

"That's never stopped you before," Wren muttered loud enough for everyone to hear.

Val hesitated but spoke anyway. "You're working so hard to reach your goal, Wren. Can you really devote time to a relationship as well when you're so close to achieving what Papa set out for you to do?"

"Val, that's the thing. I'm nowhere *near* what Papa dreamed up for me to work toward. And to be honest, I don't think I care anymore. I'm finally in a job that I work damned hard at but love every minute of. I love the people I work with and the customers are wonderful. I'm still getting a chance to experiment in the kitchen and contribute to the menu, all while I'm learning new things every day."

"But it's not the same as having your own restaurant, Wren. It's not your name over the door," Val said stubbornly.

"Neither is it *your* Banderas on the firm's letterhead. It will always be *Papa's*. But you still work hard to keep that company in business because you run it now and have a vested interest in it."

Drew saw that comment hit Val where it hurt. She felt Wren's fingers tighten around her own. She squeezed back in support.

"Just because you couldn't work all the hours God gave you and keep your marriage intact doesn't mean I have to be as lonely and single-minded as you are, Val."

Renata let out a gasp of surprise. "Florencia!" she said.

"It's true, Mama. Every time I see her, Val pushes and needles me about where I am on the path Papa laid out for me. That was something written up when I was a teenager, filled with lofty dreams in my head. But I don't think that's what I need to do now in order to be happy. I love Takira's and Takira has told me herself she'll do anything in her power to keep me there. My name might not be over the door, but that restaurant is *mine* because I'm investing my heart and soul into it."

"Are you sure it's not just because Drew lives next door in her little store?" Val asked.

Drew laughed and answered before Wren could. "My store is in no way *little*. It's almost the same size as Takira's and I *own* it, every damn inch." She had a feeling Val thought she was just a server there and was determined to put her straight on that matter. "It's *my* name over the door, too."

"My falling for Drew has nothing to do with my questioning the need for having my own restaurant. Papa never wanted me to be alone, Val. You've only seen the paperwork of his plans for me to run a business of my own. *His* timeline for it. I've come to realize it was never mine. You weren't in on our talks when he hoped I'd find a nice girl and settle down. It was never all about a restaurant being the pot of gold at the end of the rainbow for me, Val. It was about what would make me happy in my career. And I have found that happiness at Takira's *and* with Drew and I'm not letting go of either."

"I only want what's best for you, Wren," Val said.

"I know you do, and I thank you for it, but you have to let me live my own life. Not the one Papa thought I'd want or the one *you* think I need. I don't need you finding me investors for a nonexistent restaurant. I don't need you sending me emails of buildings going empty or land I could build on. Let me win or lose on my own terms, please. I'm a big girl now. I rise or fall on my own merits." Wren turned her gaze to Drew. "If there's anything I've learned from Drew it's that you don't let other people decide your dreams."

Val didn't look happy but she remained silent. Wren's relief was unmistakable. Drew looked at Ana who was licking her plate free of icing without a care in the world.

"I could really eat ice cream now," Ana said, oblivious to the laying down of swords that had just occurred.

"God, me too," Drew blurted out before checking herself.

Wren squeezed her hand again. "I don't know how you stay so damn skinny." She stood up. "There's a Dairy Queen just down the road. Val and I will go get something for everyone." She got out her phone to take their orders. "Mama, be sure to show Drew your garden while we're gone."

Ana bounced over to Drew and reached for her hand to help her up. "I have a tree of my own out there. I'll show it to you."

"Does it look like Groot?" Drew asked, making Ana giggle.

Wren reached over Ana's head to kiss Drew good-bye. "I'll be back in a bit. Don't let Mama try to encourage you to move in with her."

Renata deliberately hooked her arm through Drew's to lead her out to the garden. Drew followed her lead, listening to Ana's excitable chatter and Renata's descriptions of all her favorite flowers.

Drew knew something significant had happened in this family today. She hoped Wren finally got some peace from it.

CHAPTER SEVENTEEN

Wren's mood had her feeling higher than a kite as she drove Drew back to her apartment. The impromptu family afternoon had turned out way more fun than Wren had expected. Val had managed to interact like a real human being and Ana had been a joy as always. Her mother had clearly taken to Drew and was already dropping huge hints that she needed to visit and have lunch at Takira's to meet Mae.

"You totally charmed my mama," Wren said, looking over at Drew who was silently mouthing the words to the song playing. Wren wondered if she was even aware she did that. It broke her heart that Drew couldn't, or wouldn't, just sing along.

"It's one of my superpowers. I'm catnip to old ladies." Drew grinned at her. "Your mama is lovely. Val is…so not like you."

"Yeah, it's hard to believe we came from the same parents sometimes. She's always walked around like she has a stick up her ass."

Drew laughed. "I'm glad Ana seems more approachable, like her dad. I liked Marco. I might see him and Ana again soon."

"Really?"

"Ana told me she wants to come back and pick up some more comic books. Her mom, and I quote, 'wouldn't know a superhero from a supermodel' so I guess Marco gets to be the cool parent."

Wren chuckled. "He's always been that. I don't know why Val ever agreed to having a child. But I'm glad she did. Ana brought a much-needed spark of joy back into the family after Papa died."

"Your mama misses him dreadfully."

"I know she does. We all do." Wren was quiet for a moment, remembering him. "I think he'd have liked you."

"What's not to like? I have my name over the door of my own business. That seems to be a family requirement." Drew shifted in her seat to face Wren. "I'm proud of you and for what you did today. I'm guessing standing up to your sister hasn't always been an easy task."

"No, it hasn't. She's browbeaten me most of my life because she knows everything so much more than I do."

"I think she got the message today."

"I did tell her, while we were getting ice cream, that *if* I ever change my mind about owing a place, I'd be sure to run it by her first. That seemed to appease her. But it's a very big 'if' from where I am at this moment in my life."

Drew settled back in her seat. "So, any more adventures lined up for today or are you taking me home? To your home, I mean?"

"I'm done surprising you for today."

"Oh, *Florencia*," Drew drawled, "I'm sure that's not true at all."

Wren shivered as Drew's words touched her like a caress. The way Drew said her full name made her melt on the spot. "Do not use that sexy tone of voice with me when I'm driving."

"I have a sexy tone?" Drew sounded honestly surprised.

"My God, Drew, you really have no idea what power you have over me." Wren couldn't help but marvel at how innocent Drew could be. She supposed it stood to reason. Drew had admitted herself that she hadn't been with a lot of women. Wren really liked the idea of being a first in a great many things for Drew.

"I'll only ever use it for good, I promise." Drew's grin was anything but innocent.

Wren tried not to look in her direction and instead kept her eyes firmly on the road to get them back to her home in one piece. They were just a block away and Wren had never been happier to pull up outside of the apartment building.

Drew was unusually quiet as Wren led her up the stairs to where she lived.

"Please bear in mind I've only lived here a few months. It was the first thing I managed to rent when I took Takira's job offer." Wren pushed open her door and let Drew in first. They walked into an open plan living room and kitchen. Wren's bedroom and the bathroom branched off a small hallway. The whole apartment had stark white walls. It favored a minimalist or barely lived in look.

Wren only now realized how sparce it felt. She wished she'd at least brought some flowers to stick on the table so there was a bigger splash of color in the room. She spent so much time at the restaurant that this had become just a place to sleep. It wasn't a home by any stretch of the imagination. She had a few things scattered around to make it look a little less vacant. Haphazardly placed colored cushions lay on the sofa and a few photos of her family sat on otherwise bare shelves. Wren's favorite thing was a Build-A-Bear teddy dressed as a chef. It had been a gift from Ana on her getting the job at Takira's. The bear sat alongside Wren on the sofa every night.

Drew looked around, taking it all in. "It's like you."

Wren narrowed her eyes at her. "In what way?"

"It's tiny."

Wren playfully shoved Drew down onto her sofa. She then climbed into her lap to straddle her. "I may be small but I'm mighty."

"Yes, you are." Drew clutched Wren's hips to keep her in place. "But you really need to put up a picture or two. Anything to cut down the glaringly plain walls so you don't go completely white blind."

"Maybe I'll frame the ones of you and me that you gave me."

"That would be a nice start," Drew said. She grimaced as her stomach rumbled. "Sorry. I've had cake, ice cream, and shared a tiny pizza with you on our drive back, but I'm still hungry. Can I order something in for us?"

Wren shook her head. "No, I'm cooking for you tonight. I bought fresh stuff in especially."

"Wren, no," Drew said. "You don't have to do that. You work all week in a kitchen."

"Yes, but this is the first time I get to cook for *you*." Wren pressed a kiss to Drew's frowning forehead and reluctantly got off her. "The kitchen counter serves as a nice breakfast bar so we can eat from there."

"Can I watch you?" Drew was already getting up to follow after her.

"Sure. I love an audience while I create." Wren washed her hands thoroughly then began bustling around her kitchen. She reached for her apron. Drew made an unhappy noise.

"What?" Wren looked down at the plain functional apron, wondering what Drew was disappointed about.

"I need to get you one that says 'Kiss the Cook' on it."

Wren laughed at her, leaned over the counter, and kissed her. "You don't need an apron to tell you when you can do it. Kisses are free to you."

"I'm going to come to this kitchen diner more often if they're on the menu," Drew teased her.

"I'll have to bring some of my cooking gear over to your apartment so I can cook for you and Mae after work." Wren was already deciding which equipment would be best to take.

"You're not coming to us after work and cooking," Drew argued again.

"You forget, Drew, cooking for me has always been a form of relaxation. Cooking for you and Mae wouldn't be at all like what happens in the restaurant. Besides, I have to eat once my shift is over and I do not live on takeout."

"Yeah, well, it still sounds like you working too hard after a day at Takira's."

"Do you cook?" Wren asked, gathering everything she needed from her fridge.

"I can. Nothing too fancy though. Grandpa taught me when we were looking after Grandma once she came home from the hospital. I do a mean stew pot." Drew watched everything Wren did. "Of course, I only really need to cook for one seeing as Grandma gets catered to by Takira's most days."

Wren smiled. "She does seem a permanent fixture."

"I wish I could say it was the menu, but I think it's because she gets to meet up with Mrs. Daniels. It gets her out of the apartment and socializing. I can't argue with that. It makes her happy."

"And what makes you happy, Drew?" Wren paused for a moment in ripping apart a head of lettuce.

"You," Drew said, looking at her so earnestly that Wren wanted to rip her apron off and go satisfy a different hunger.

"I'm just fixing us a salad because you can't say sweet things like that and not expect me to want to skip the meal and take you straight to the bedroom." Wren gathered cherry tomatoes, walnuts, and mozzarella. "If you're hungry later, I'll call Takira's for takeout or Taco Bell." She gathered all her herbs and olive oil and quickly and efficiently whipped up a salad that had Drew moaning in appreciation at the first mouthful. Her enjoyment of food warmed Wren's heart. They ate in silence, sitting as close as they could be at the counter. Wren fed Drew from her plate when she found a delicious looking piece of mozzarella that she knew Drew would enjoy. For Wren, it was almost foreplay. They drank a flavored spring water that Wren had bought to complement the meal without it being alcoholic. She wanted them both to be clear-headed.

Wren quickly slipped the plates into the sink and reached for Drew's hand. Drew lifted it and pressed kisses along Wren's knuckles.

"Before we go into the bedroom, if at any time you want to stop, or there's something I do that you don't like? Just say the word."

"You mean like a safe word?" Drew asked.

Wren laughed. "That was meant as just a figure of speech, but if you'd like to have a safe word or employ red for stop, green for go, then I'm here for it. I don't want to do anything you're uncomfortable with." Wren knew how reserved Drew could be when it came to touching so she wanted to make sure she felt safe at all times.

"So, if I said Red Hood for stop and Hulk for go…"

Wren stopped leading Drew to her room. "*Red Hood?*"

"He's kind of an anti-hero Batman. And the Hulk is the big green guy who you wouldn't like to make angry. When you said green for go my head immediately went to the Hulk and you really need to just stop me now before I talk myself out of you ever wanting to kiss me—"

Wren pulled Drew's head down to her and silenced her with a kiss. "You are the geekiest woman I have ever met and whether you shout green or Hulk, I don't care as long as you let me touch you."

"Hulk, Green Hornet, Green Lantern, Green Arrow, Kermit." Drew peppered each green-related character with a kiss on Wren's lips. "And every totally bodacious green Teenage Mutant Ninja Turtle, dude." Drew grinned at her. "I'm saying yes so let's keep on walking."

Wren tugged Drew toward her room. The room wasn't huge but it was more colorful than the rest of the apartment. The bed linen was bright and cheerful, and the furniture was obviously old but well cared for.

"Now, this is more you," Drew said. She looked at the large bed that Wren had. "How the hell did they get that mattress up all those stairs?"

"Have you ever watched that episode of *Friends* with the couch?"

Drew shook her head. "I never found that show in the least bit funny. They could be mean and I don't do mean."

Wren smiled at her. Drew was something else and Wren totally adored her. She deliberately removed the quilt from the bed then looked up at Drew, taking in the woman she was about to make love to. The color of her eyes, the shape of her nose, the lips that tempted her to do more than just stare.

"As super cool as your *Scarlet Witch* T-shirt is, I really think it's time for it to come off." Wren deliberately ran her fingers underneath the cloth and brushed at Drew's taut stomach. Drew sucked in a breath when Wren began drawing a circle around her belly button. Without preamble, Drew yanked her T-shirt over her head.

"Grogu," she said, tossing the shirt to land on a chair.

Wren started to chuckle. "Good thing I know he's green," she said. "I bet I can lay more kisses on you than you can rattle off green characters."

Drew picked Wren up into her arms and held her tight. "I'll take that bet."

❖

Drew had never had a lover that took such delight in a slow and steady undressing. Drew had always felt rushed, that all a lover had needed from her was a quick fuck, and then it was all over and done with. Wren's tender exploring of every inch of Drew was way more exciting. Once she put Wren down beside the bed, they each removed their jeans. Drew threw hers out the bedroom door and into the hallway in her haste to be rid of them. Wren stared at Drew's feet as she threw her own jeans across a chair.

"Those are very bright socks."

Drew nodded, balancing on one foot at a time to peel them off. "They're my 'you're getting laid' socks. They were a gift from my grandma."

Wren burst into laughter. "Mae really is something else." She pulled her own plain white ones off and got on the bed, beckoning Drew to follow.

Drew knelt on the bed beside Wren and helped her take off her shirt. Drew couldn't help but run her hands over Wren's luxurious hair in the process. "Your hair is so beautiful." She loved how it flowed over Wren's shoulders in gentle waves. Wren reached up and brushed her fingertips along the shaved area of Drew's head.

"I love how the bristles tickle," Wren said. "You look fantastic dressed as the Doctor, but long hair just isn't you. *This* is you." She ran her fingers through the longer hair on top and took a handful playfully. "Oh good, there's still plenty for me to hold onto."

Drew knew she was blushing by the snicker of amusement Wren released.

Drew helped Wren unfasten her bra and swore her brain fritzed out at the sight of Wren's breasts.

"Drew?" Wren tossed her bra aside.

"Give me one second. I am committing this moment to memory before my brain explodes over how fucking beautiful you are."

Wren's smile made the sight before Drew a million times more amazing. She moved to take Wren in her arms but Wren put a hand up to stop her.

"Sharing is caring, Drew Dawes. Take your bra off too."

Drew did so. "There's not much point me wearing one, to be honest." She barely had time to throw the bra behind her before Wren pressed up against her. Drew melted at the warmth and the soft feel of Wren's naked body against her own. They both knelt on the bed, arms wrapped around each other in the best hug Drew had ever dreamed of. She let out a long breath. Drew had felt trapped in a long and lonely, dark existence for so many years. Wren's touch was like the sunlight finally waking Drew to a brand-new day. She pressed a kiss to the top of Wren's head, welcoming her into her arms, her body, and soul.

Wren's head laid against Drew's chest, but she cupped Drew's breast and began teasing her nipple.

"You're more than big enough to fill my hand," Wren said, shifting so she could suck Drew's nipple between her lips.

Drew jolted at the swift blast of heat that slammed into her as Wren's tongue swirled a mysterious pattern around her hardened nub. Drew didn't think taking things slow was going to be an option if Wren kept that up. Since when had she been so damn sensitive? Drew laced her fingers through Wren's hair and kept her in place, loving the feel of Wren's active tongue swirling, licking, and flicking over her nipple. Each tug sent a frisson of electricity straight down to her clit and Drew started to writhe. Wren shifted and took her other nipple between her teeth to give it the same attention and Drew didn't know how much longer she could remain on her knees. She let out a moan and felt Wren smile against her flesh. She reached between them and cupped Wren's breasts in her own hands. Drew matched every tug and suck Wren gave her with a matching brush of her thumbs over Wren's hard nipples. When Wren teased her more, Drew trapped Wren's nipples between her fingers and tweaked them. Wren's head fell back and the groan she released made Drew push her down onto the bed so they could lie face to face. She kissed Wren then, open-mouthed and desperate. She loved how Wren fit in her arms and how her body moved against Drew's as their kisses grew firmer, more sensuous. Wren pressed a leg between Drew's and they both broke for air.

"Take your shorts off," Wren demanded, pushing away just enough that she could wriggle out of her panties.

Drew didn't move a muscle as she watched Wren take off the last item of clothing and bare herself to her. She wanted to taste her so bad, but Wren stopped her, tugging roughly at the waist of her boxers.

"Off, before I rip them off with my teeth."

Drew liked the sound of that and filed it away for another time. She shoved the shorts off and didn't care where they landed. Like magnets, Drew and Wren's bodies moved back together as close as they could touch. They kissed once more before exploring.

Drew loved the silkiness of Wren's back and the curve of her tight buttocks. In Drew's large hand, she could almost cup a whole cheek. She squeezed and Wren squirmed a little. Drew ran her hand along Wren's leg then up onto her thigh before reluctantly moving so she could lay Wren on her back and take in her beauty. Drew brushed her fingers teasingly through the dark hair that framed the top of Wren's legs. Unable to wait any longer, she slipped a finger between Wren's lower lips and found her clit uncovered, straining for her touch. Drew brushed a soft fingertip over the head of Wren's clit, making her gasp, then dropped lower to circle around her opening and capture Wren's desire. Drew brought her finger to her lips and tasted her.

Wren, her eyes darkened with desire, pushed Drew over onto her back and kissed her. She trailed kisses down Drew's neck, biting softly there and making Drew moan. Wren traced patterns down Drew's chest and then sucked her nipples until Drew could no longer keep still. Wren flipped her hair back over her shoulder and held it there while she pressed open-mouthed kisses down Drew's stomach until she reached the soft trimmed hair that covered Drew's sex.

"How green are you, Drew?" Wren asked, settling in between Drew's legs, her intention clear.

"As green as the forests of Endor," Drew said, trying desperately not to grab Wren's head and push her where she needed her the most.

Wren needed no directing. She spread Drew's flesh and licked at her clit without pause. Drew's hands went to Wren's head and she clung to her while Wren's tongue tortured her aching clit with soft kisses and her tongue. Wren's fingers brushed through Drew's wetness and played with her entrance before pressing in slowly. Drew whined at the feeling of Wren's fingers slowly slipping in and out of her, testing her, teasing her, before delving farther in. She closed her eyes as the sensations overwhelmed her. Wren's fingers sped up and her talented tongue made Drew buck beneath her.

Wren managed to free a hand to reach up and squeeze Drew's breast. Her fingers trapped the nipple and every squeeze and tug sent more flashes of pleasure through Drew's whole body. She could feel herself readying, her movements out of her control now as Wren took her, remade her, and brought her to a climax that wrenched a cry from Drew's lips and had her whole body shuddering as it hit. Wren didn't stop until Drew's bowed body landed back on the bed with a bump. Drew weakly tugged Wren's head up from between her legs, too sensitive to take any more.

Spasms rolled through Drew's body until she finally could catch a breath. She just lay there, boneless. Totally ruined, utterly fucked.

"Wow," Drew said, opening her eyes and looking down to see Wren grinning up at her. Her fingers were still inside Drew, and Wren watched her intently as she slowly pulled them out of her. Drew moaned at the loss. "Fuck, Wren. And I thought you were a master chef in the kitchen. Is there nothing you can't turn those talented hands to?"

Wren crawled up to lie on top of Drew to kiss her. Drew couldn't miss the taste of herself on Wren's lips.

"God, you're sexy as hell, Drew." Wren slipped her hand down again to capture Drew's breast and squeeze. "I don't ever want to leave this bed again." She trailed her wet fingers down to cup Drew and to slowly brush up, down, and around her clit again.

"How about you let me touch you?" Drew said, trying not to jerk at the sensations Wren was working up again against her sensitive clit.

"How about you let me bring you off by just rubbing and sucking on you?" Wren's head dipped and she sucked Drew's breast into her mouth, lashing Drew's nipple with her tongue.

It didn't take long before Drew was coming again, clasping Wren to her, almost curling around her as Wren sent her over the edge with her fingers and tongue. She felt helpless to Wren's touch. Wren rolled off her and pulled Drew over with her. Drew cuddled in, her mind and body overwhelmed by the pleasure Wren had given her. It had been so long since Drew had made love with someone and it had never felt like this. She felt...Drew didn't know *what* she felt. But it was exciting, utterly mind-blowing, and just a little scary.

"Are you okay, Drew?" Wren whispered against Drew's head that lay pressed into Wren's neck.

"Are all my limbs still intact? I'm frightened to look."

"This gorgeous lanky body of yours is all in one piece, but I'm more than willing to go over it again, inch by inch, to make sure."

Drew chuckled. "Let me catch my breath a second. I want so desperately to touch you, but I need my brain to reboot first after you blew its circuits to smithereens."

"You feel so good in my arms, Drew."

Wren held her tighter, and Drew felt safe. She breathed in the delicious scent of Wren's skin. "I can't think of any other place I'd rather be."

CHAPTER EIGHTEEN

Wren straddling Drew's lap was Drew's new favorite thing. It was cute and romantic when they did it fully dressed. Naked was a whole new ball game. Drew sat up against the headboard while a very naked and aroused Wren squirmed under her ministrations. Drew had two fingers just inside Wren, gently teasing, moving in and out. In this position Drew could watch every emotion wrought on Wren's face. Wren stared back at Drew, her desire and need visible in the dark depths of her eyes. Wren was way more vocal during sex Drew had found. She liked to tell Drew what she was doing to her, and Drew loved every word, gasp, and moan that fell from Wren's lips.

Drew dipped her head to kiss and lick at Wren's breasts that were, delightfully, right in her face.

"Oh fuck, what are you doing with your tongue?" Wren moaned as she clutched Drew's head, brushing her fingertips back and forth over the shaved hair.

Drew hadn't realized that was an erogenous zone until Wren started rubbing there. It only made her double her efforts on running her tongue roughly around Wren's areola causing it to tighten and her nipple to swell. She pushed her fingers in deeper and Wren's hands fell to clutch Drew's shoulders. Wren was warm and wet and Drew's fingers slid in deeper still, catching a spot inside Wren that make her shudder and cry out. Wren started to fuck herself on Drew's fingers, her need too great to wait. Drew watched her take her own pleasure for a moment, loving the urgency in her movements, and the pleasure on her face.

"Oh God, yes, right there," Wren panted in Drew's ear as she fell forward, curling herself around Drew.

Drew kept up with Wren's desperate need. Surrounded by Wren, Drew was awash in her scent, her body, the whispers of encouragement that Wren was uttering. Wren pulled back and took Drew's face in her hands.

"Look what you do to me." Wren's eyes were blazing, her body writhing and straining at Drew's touch. "You're going to make me come so fucking hard."

Drew's arm was aching with the exertion but she didn't care. All she wanted to do was drive Wren over the edge. *Again.* They had made love for hours, making up for lost time, lost in the sheer pleasure of it all. Both unable to stop once they had touched.

Wren kissed Drew frantically amid the craziness, the want, and the need. It frightened Drew how easily she had opened her heart to Wren, had laid her body bare, and fell so deeply. All she wanted was to keep that look on Wren's face, the one that made Drew feel she was good enough for her.

Drew knew the moment Wren was going to break. Wren's soft walls around Drew's fingers squeezed them so tight Drew almost winced. Wren buried her head in Drew's neck and muffled her scream into her flesh. Drew held on to Wren tightly, letting her ride the climax out, safe in Drew's arms.

After a moment, Drew was surprised to feel what felt like tears on her skin. "Hey, are you okay?" Drew tried to turn her head to see but Wren kept her immobile.

"Happy tears, I promise," Wren said, sniffling. "Good God, Drew. I think I saw stars!"

Mollified, Drew just held on tighter until Wren finally began to shift. Drew slipped her fingers out of her, making Wren moan in her ear at the loss.

"Who needs a magic wand when you can do so many tricks with just one hand?" Wren said, nipping at the pulse in Drew's neck then soothing the bite with her tongue. Wren fell back to splay herself on the bed, looking up at Drew with a tired smile across her sated face. "That's it, I'm all orgasmed out. You've fucked me into oblivion."

Amused, Drew caught sight of the clock beside Wren's bed. "We've been going for hours," she marveled, reaching for a bottle of water from beside the bed and quickly chugging it down. When she'd finished, she lay down beside Wren.

Wren snuggled into Drew's side, spread a leg across her, and fit herself neatly into Drew's arms. Drew loved the feel of her there. She felt safe with Wren's arm across her chest, her small hand resting over Drew's heart.

Drew hadn't felt that closeness with anyone else. It was something new, exciting, overwhelming…and downright terrifying. She'd long feared she'd never be enough for anyone. Her parents had wanted her singing talent more than they wanted her. Falling in love with Wren left Drew feeling vulnerable. She'd finally admitted it to herself. This was more than just sex. Wren was beginning to be everything Drew wanted.

Drew was too tired to think about it for now. Instead, she lay listening to the steady sound of Wren's breathing and let it lull her to sleep.

Twelve-year-old Drew was deliberately dragging her feet. She didn't want to go out. She'd rather stay home and do her homework. But her mother stood fuming at the front door, car keys in hand, while her father was squirreling away a flask in his coat pocket.

"Drew, quit dawdling. We need to go *now*." Her mother flung open the door just as Grandma was about to knock on it. "What are *you* doing here?" Her mother snarled and grabbed at Drew to tug her behind her, trying to hide her from her grandma.

"Grandma!" Relief flooded through Drew at the sight of her. It had been two long weeks since she'd last seen her. The last time had been when her mother had thrown her and Grandpa out the house. Grandma had said she'd be back. Drew had been frightened she'd forgotten about her.

"I'm here to see Drew. You can't stop me from doing that," Grandma said, getting up into Drew's mother's face.

"We're going out. Phone next time and make an appointment." Drew's father pushed past them both and headed toward the car without a backward glance.

"Where are you going?" Grandma asked, not taking her eyes off Drew.

"Drew has a doctor's appointment." Her mother dragged Drew out and shoved her toward the car. "Get in the car."

Drew instead rushed into her grandma's arms. "I missed you so much," Drew said, clinging to her. She looked over her shoulder at her mother. "You didn't tell me about any appointment."

Her mother slammed the front door behind her. "Don't question me. Get. In. The. Car. *NOW!*" She tried to pull Drew away, but Drew wasn't letting go of her grandma anytime soon and Grandma held on just as tight.

"Get in the fucking car right this second, Drew, or there'll be hell to pay when we get home." Her mother wrenched Drew out of her grandma's grasp by hauling her back by the collar of her dress. The cloth cut into Drew's flesh. She lost her grip on Grandma while trying to grab at her collar to stop it from strangling her.

Grandma kept a tight grip on Drew and followed her to the car. When her mother opened the door to shove Drew in, Grandma quickly scrambled in right behind her and wouldn't budge.

"Get the hell out of my car, you stupid old bitch!" Her mother grabbed hold of Grandma's arm to try to drag her out. Grandma braced herself in the seat and smacked at Drew's mother's hands until she let go.

"I'm coming with you. You keep hurting me and I swear, I'll scream so loud your fancy neighbors will call the police out on you. Then we'll see how you'll talk your way out of that." Grandma reached for Drew's arm and pushed up the arm of her cardigan. A vivid bruise stood out on her pale skin. "Or *this.*"

Drew's teeth rattled with how hard her mother slammed the door of the car on them.

"Aren't you going to say something, Bradley?" Grandma asked, as he sat silent in the front seat.

Drew's father merely unscrewed the top off his flask and took a drink. "No. I've got nothing to say to you."

Grandma hastened to fasten her seat belt, fumbling with the buckle that just wouldn't click into place. She gestured for Drew to hurry and do the same. Without bothering to fasten her own, Drew's mother started the car and shot off the driveway, straight out onto the road, with such speed it threw Grandma and Drew back harshly against their seats.

"Slow down!" Grandma ordered.

"You're in my car, *Mommie Dearest*. Don't you dare tell me what to do in it." Drew's mother sped down the road, ignoring Grandma's shouts to be careful as she drove too close to parked cars.

Drew had other things on her mind. "Why am I going to a doctor, Mother?"

"It's just a checkup."

"But I just had a checkup. The school nurse saw me. She said I was anemic. That's why I keep falling asleep in class."

Her grandma gave up fighting with the seat belt and clutched at Drew's hand. "Are you eating enough? You look even thinner than when I last saw you."

"Mother says I need to lose my puppy fat," Drew said, knowing that she probably shouldn't say anything because it would only make things worse. But really, how worse could it get? Her mother was starving her to reach some perfect target weight she had in mind. Drew couldn't even beg for food off anyone at school because she had no friends to speak to. Drew couldn't remember the last time she'd had a piece of cake. She missed that the most. She wondered, if she ran away to live with her grandparents, would they let her have cake? Just one slice, maybe? At least on her birthday?

"Drew, you shut your stupid mouth right now." Her mother barely looked at the road as she drove them toward a less populated area of the city. It was more rural and there were road works signs announcing a new road nearby under construction. The city was expanding and nothing would stand in its wake.

"Where is this doctor?" Grandma asked, looking out the windows. "You're taking us out of the city."

"It's none of your goddamn business." Drew's mother slammed the car over the uneven temporary road without a mind for the vehicle's suspension or the passengers.

Grandma grabbed onto the passenger seat in front of her. "It is my business because I know what you're doing to this child and it has to stop. *I'm* stopping it. I have a lawyer who's going to help me get Drew away from you."

Drew stared at her grandma. *"Really?"* She started to silently cry in relief.

"You pathetic bitch. If you think you can take her away from us, you're crazier than I thought." Drew's mother looked over her shoulder at Grandma for a moment too long. Her inattention caused them to hit a large pothole. It shook the whole car and made everyone cry out in pain. Her mother quickly switched her attention back to the road. Her face was furious as she glared at Grandma through the rearview mirror. "She's going nowhere but to the top. She's going to make me a fortune."

Drew's father, his hand shaking, took another long drink from his flask and left them to it, losing himself in his own world.

"You're abusing her. That's a crime."

"She needs discipline," Drew's mother argued. "She's willful and needs proper guidance to be great."

"She's more than just her singing voice!" Grandma argued back. "She's collapsing on stage, for God's sake."

"How the fuck do you know that?" Her mother's hands tightened on the steering wheel.

Drew gripped her leather seat as her mother's driving became even more erratic.

"I read everything about my granddaughter in the press. You're making her ill, keep pushing her so hard. You wouldn't let her see a doctor unless it suited your purpose, Mary-Louise. The abuse you're inflicting on her would be plain for one to see. So where are you really taking her?"

"It's none of your fucking business."

"Mary-Louise, you tell me right NOW!" Grandma yelled, startling Drew with the anger in her tone. She'd never heard her grandma sound that furious in her life. It even made her father flinch. It also startled her mother into confessing.

"She's not growing up right. I'm fixing it," her mother ground out.

"Fixing it how?" Grandma demanded, holding Drew's hand tighter as the speed of the car increased.

"She started her periods but puberty hasn't touched her. She's still this scrawny thing with no breasts. How can she sing and be as famous as Dolly Parton if she has no breasts?"

"Dolly's aren't real," Grandma said.

"*Exactly.*" Drew's mother's voice and demeanor was suddenly smug.

Drew wasn't sure what that meant. "Grandma?"

Grandma wasn't listening to Drew. She was staring incredulously at Mary-Louise. "You're going to get a twelve-year-old *breast implants*? No doctor would perform that kind of surgery on one so young. She's still growing."

"Not fast enough," her mother said. "Luckily, I know a guy. He specializes in this kind of thing, earns a little extra cash on the side away from his clinic. He's going to examine her, see what he can do to speed up Mother Nature." Her mother looked in the rearview mirror, all her contempt focused directly at Drew. "God knows she screwed up in making her pretty. But I know a guy who can fix that for me too."

"She's beautiful as she is. Why the hell can't you see that?" Grandma cupped Drew's face with her hand. "She's perfect in every way."

The car rocked violently as Drew's mother carelessly drove them over one hole after another in the road. Grandma's seat belt broke apart as her body jerked against its restraint. Untethered, she grabbed desperately for something to hold onto. Another unforgiving bump in the road pitched Grandma forward. She barely managed to stop herself from becoming wedged between the two front seats.

"You stop this car right now and let us out. She's not going anywhere with you." Grandma struggled to right herself as the car, driven by a maniac, tossed her around like a rag doll.

"She looks too much like a boy," her father said out of nowhere, becoming more and more oblivious to the rough ride they were enduring with every deep drink from his flask.

"Well, maybe she's born to follow in the footsteps of k.d. lang more than she ever could Dolly's." Her grandma looked Drew straight in the eye, making a promise. "She can be whatever she wants to be."

"It's bad enough my daughter doesn't look right, you want to make her queer too?" Drew's mother took one hand off the steering wheel and quickly brought her arm up to deliberately elbow Grandma in the face. The blow connected with Grandma's cheekbone, rocking her head back, and making her cry out in agony. Without both of Mother's hands firmly on the steering wheel, the car perilously slid across the road. Her mother struggled to right it while Grandma went flying across the back of the car. Her head hit the window with a terrible crack, to both skull and glass. Drew struggled against the tightness of her seat belt, frantic to try to grab her grandma before she hit the window again.

"You're going to kill us all! Stop the car! Stop the car!" Grandma screamed as she tumbled across the seats to end up in the footwell by a nearly hysterical Drew. Drew grabbed hold of her and didn't let go.

Drew's mother swung the wheel sharply, overcompensating as the car spun recklessly out of her control. They careened straight into the path of a huge bulldozer. The bulldozer appeared out of nowhere, cresting the hill in front of them on the opposite side of the road. The side their car was now on.

"Move out of my fucking way!" her mother screamed, scrambling to keep control of the car as the bulldozer headed right for them.

The lumbering bulldozer couldn't move in time. Drew barely even saw the vehicle before they hit it with a deafening bang. The force from the collision threw the car airborne. Drew felt her stomach plummet as the car flipped. Her seat belt kept her pinned in place while she clung desperately to her grandma whose body slammed mercilessly around the car's interior. They tossed over and over until the car came to a devastating, metal shattering, stop. It landed upside down, crushed and crumpled, half buried in a freshly dug ditch.

Drew's ears rang from the sound of the crash. She slowly regained her senses and realized her grandma's body was now pinning her in place. Her grandma's arms wrapped around Drew like a vice, shielding her from seeing anything in the car. Drew could hear her breathing above her. It sounded rasping and labored.

"Grandma?" Drew's voice sounded loud in the otherwise silent car.

"Oh, thank God," Grandma whispered from somewhere above Drew's head. "Are you okay? Are you hurt?"

Drew's chest was screaming from the tightness of the seat belt pinning her in place, and her head ached, but she didn't think she'd broken anything. She tried to move. Grandma tightened her hold.

"Don't move, sweetheart. I need you to stay very still until someone comes to help us."

Drew heard the fear and pain in her grandma's voice. "Are *you* hurt, Grandma?"

"Just a little, but don't worry about that for now. I need you to just let me hold onto you, okay?"

"I think we're upside down." Drew coughed a little and whined as it hurt her chest.

"Can you breathe?" Grandma asked.

"Yes, but you're squishing me. You're holding me really tight."

"I'm sorry, my darling, but I can't move. I think a piece of metal's gotten stuck in my hip. I won't squish you for long, I promise. I can hear voices outside. Someone's coming for us."

Voices were audible in the distance. Men's voices, and the sound of more trucks.

Drew was quiet for a moment, worrying about her grandma, and how there was a horrible smell of wet soil and gasoline filling the car. The combination made Drew want to gag. She tried to calm herself and not breathe in too much until she realized something else. "Grandma?" she asked, barely above a whisper.

"Yes, sweetheart?"

"I can't hear Mother." Drew strained her ears, but she heard nothing at all coming from the front seats. "Can you see them?"

"No, Drew. I can't see them at all." That ominous reply went straight over Drew's young head. Her grandma's breath shook and Drew thought she sounded like she was crying but she wasn't sure. "But don't you worry. Your grandma's here." Grandma groaned out in pain as the car shifted. "I'll keep you safe, I promise." Her head slumped a little against Drew's.

"Grandma? I don't think you should go to sleep. You banged your head real hard on the window."

"You'd best keep me entertained then." Grandma's voice weakened. "Tell me about school."

"I hate it. I don't want to talk about that. I missed you."

"I missed you too, so much. But I came for you, and your grandpa is at the lawyer's today getting paperwork signed. We're going to fight for you."

"I like the sound of that." Drew held onto her and felt her grandma flinch in pain. "Grandma?"

"Distract me, Drew. Don't let me fall asleep."

Drew nodded against her. She had no idea what position her grandma was in above her. Drew cleared her throat and began to sing her grandma's favorite songs. She sang to keep her awake and to distract her from the pain she wasn't telling Drew about.

"You have a beautiful voice, Drew, and you're beautiful, inside, and out. Don't let anyone ever make you think otherwise." Her grandma sounded drowsy.

Drew sang. She sang through the firemen sawing through the twisted metal to get to them. The firemen told Drew to keep singing to drown out her grandma's agonizing screams as they worked to cut her free from the metal that impaled her. She sang to keep her grandma awake when the firemen carefully lifted her out of the wreckage and rushed her to the waiting ambulance. Then they had Drew close her eyes while they fought to free her from the car. Drew never saw the damage wrought. She never saw where the Dozer's front blades had sliced the car clean in two and killed her parents instantly. Drew had just sung as if her life depended on it. She feared her grandma's did. They bundled them together in an ambulance and Drew grew silent as the medics worked on stabilizing her grandma's terrifying injuries.

So many broken bones. So much blood. Drew didn't utter a word, not even when they tried to wipe the blood off her own face.

It wasn't hers.

Drew was silent, terrified to make a sound to drown out the noise of the monitor beeping out her grandma's heartbeat. She needed to hear it. She needed to know she was still alive. She knew her parents were gone. She couldn't lose her grandma too.

All the songs in Drew's head dried up and blew away like dust on a breeze. Instead, all Drew heard was the rhythm of the heart monitor and its erratic beep beep beep...

CHAPTER NINETEEN

...Beep beep beep.

B Drew startled at the sound of a car alarm going off outside. She lay shaking in bed, scrambling to get back to reality. She couldn't afford to stay in the memory of them trapped in that crushed car with how long it had taken the firefighters to remove them from the tangled mess. Nor did she want to remember the frantic ride to the hospital where they revealed the extent of her grandma's injuries. Drew tried to calm her breathing down before she hyperventilated. She blindly looked around the room for something familiar to ground herself to. In her room she had a figure of Princess Leia in a prime spot that she concentrated on.

But this wasn't her room.

Wren lay beside her, fast asleep. Drew desperately wanted to burrow herself into Wren's arms and gain comfort from her. But she didn't want Wren to see this side of her, the one haunted by nightmares of a crash that killed her parents, and permanently disabled her grandma. The crash that she walked out of relatively unscathed. Drew wished the accident had never happened but, from all that devastation, she'd found herself freed from her abusive environment. Drew knew all about survivor's guilt. She'd heard the placating words from councilors and read the leaflets they'd given her. Deep down, Drew knew it wasn't her fault. Her mother had been driving in her usual careless way and the anger in the car had just set off a terrible series of events that led to the accident.

Her mother had been *deliberately* taking Drew somewhere to have unthinkable surgeries performed on her. That alone had left Drew suffering from a dreadful body dysmorphia for most of her teenage years. She'd eventually grown comfortable with exactly who she was, and how she looked. Grandma had been right all along. There was nothing wrong with Drew. It had all been her mother's warped view that had made Drew feel she was a monster because she wasn't the height of femininity. Drew had finally found her own sense of identity and peace.

Unfortunately, the rare nightmares never failed to leave Drew trapped in her head, trapped in the car, trapped in that twelve-year-old body. A child beaten down so much she could barely function as an individual.

Drew couldn't stay in bed. She eased out from under the sheets, desperate not to disturb Wren who slept on, unaware. She looked so beautiful that Drew just had to watch her for a moment. She tried to fill her head with the memories of their lovemaking the previous night to dispel the nightmare that still occupied her mind. She couldn't shake the sound of the heart machine that echoed in her head. Drew needed music to distract her, like it always did. Her guilty passion, her secret need not to lose all touch with the musical world. Drew had deliberately silenced herself. To take back her life from her mother's stranglehold, to not perform on a stage any more, and to not hear the sound of her own voice trying to drown out the sound of her grandma's agonizing screams as the rescuers finally lifted her from the wreckage. They'd had Drew close her eyes so she wouldn't see what remained of her parents buried in the ditch. They'd told her to keep singing until she reached the safety of the ambulance.

After that, Drew never sang out loud again.

Until two little children told her to sing a crying baby to sleep and Drew couldn't hold the song back anymore.

Drew padded out of the bedroom and had to smile at the sight of her jeans crumpled almost into a ball in the hallway. She was after her phone. She shook her jeans out, dug her phone out of a pocket, and was thankful it still had some charge left. Drew's heart stopped when she saw the multitude of messages that covered her screen. She checked the time quickly. It was ten o'clock. The slew of messages began from eight o'clock that morning. Drew quickly opened the first one.

Drew, your grandma has had a fall. I've called for an ambulance and they're taking her to the MU Hospital.

Fear slammed into Drew's whole being and she rocked from the blow. She quickly scrolled through the rest of the messages, all from Mrs. Daniels trying to reach her to no avail.

This wouldn't have happened if I'd been with her, Drew thought. She ran back into the bedroom and began to hastily grab her clothes.

Wren woke up to find her, jeans half on, pulling up a sock.

"Hey, you in a hurry to leave or something? I recall promising you breakfast." Wren smiled at her but her face fell the second she saw Drew's. "What's wrong?"

"Grandma fell this morning. I have to go to the hospital." Drew zipped up her jeans and pulled on her T-shirt roughly.

"Give me a moment to dress." Wren got out of bed and began grabbing her own clothes.

"No, you don't have to. I just need to go." Drew wasn't waiting for anyone. She needed to go *now*.

"Drew, you don't have your car here. I drove you, remember?"

Drew's frantic race to get out stalled to a halt. "Fuck," she muttered under her breath. She watched as Wren quickly dressed, willing her to go faster.

"Have you called Mrs. Daniels back?" Wren asked, tying her wild bed hair back into a ponytail to keep it out of her face.

Drew swore again. "I didn't even think about that." Drew cursed her scattered brain. She punched in the number she needed. The phone just rang. "She's not answering."

"She might be somewhere there's poor reception." Wren grabbed them both a bottle of water and snatched up her car keys. "Do you know where she is?"

Drew showed her the text.

"Okay, then let's go." Wren got them out of the apartment, down the stairs, and into her car.

❖

Drew was running on autopilot. She'd had very little sleep. The nightmare had left her feeling disorientated and frightened. And knowing her grandma had fallen just pushed Drew right over the edge she'd woken up teetering on.

This wouldn't have happened if I'd been at home. Drew couldn't stop the thought repeating over and over in her head. *I should have been there. I promised Grandpa I'd always take care of her.*

Wren drove them the short trip to the nearby hospital. Before Drew opened the car door, Wren pulled her back.

"I need to get in there," Drew bit out, frustrated Wren was stopping her.

Wren handed her a hand and face wipe and took one out for herself. "We didn't have time to even use the bathroom before we left. Have a quick wipe down. You can't go see your grandma smelling of sex!"

Drew scrubbed at her face, arms, and hands. She balled up the wipe, shoved it in her jeans pocket, and quickly got out the car. She knew Wren was having to almost run to keep up with her, but Drew couldn't wait. She had to know her grandma was all right. Drew felt Wren's hand slip into her own. She was grateful Wren was with her, but Drew blamed herself for her grandma's accident *because* she'd been with Wren. Drew couldn't stop berating herself for going out and leaving her grandma in someone else's care. Grandma was her responsibility and she'd failed her.

The smell of the hospital spun Drew back to the weeks her grandma had remained under numerous doctors' care while they rebuilt her body. She'd had to stay in longer as there was complication after complication and she'd had an infection. Young Drew had feared her grandma would never come home. Hospitals never brought pleasant memories. Now, the smell, the sounds, all grated on Drew's already shredded nerves.

Mrs. Daniels was pacing up and down the hallway when Drew and Wren rushed in.

"Oh God, Drew, I'm so sorry." Mrs. Daniels looked distraught and that only made Drew's anxiety worse. "I tried calling you, but the phone kept going to your voice mail and I didn't have Wren's number." She started crying and Wren moved to comfort her.

Drew left them, cursing herself for not having the forethought to give her grandma Wren's number in case of emergency. She could clearly hear her grandma's voice from down the hall. Grandma wasn't being cooperative and Drew couldn't miss the sheer terror in her voice. She quickly found the room she was in. Drew almost cried at seeing her awake, alert, but obviously in distress.

"Drew! Thank God you're here. Tell them I'm not staying. Get me out of here, please. I want to go home." Grandma tried to get off the bed she lay on. The nurse tending to her had to physically stop her.

"I'm sorry, Grandma. I got here as soon as I found the damn texts. What happened?" Drew rushed to her side and Grandma clung to her hand. She was clearly frightened and agitated. Drew looked between her grandma and the nurse for an answer. "I'm her granddaughter. Please tell me what's wrong."

"Mrs. Dawes suffered a fall this morning. She came in with a laceration to her right arm which I've just sewn up."

Drew looked at her grandma's arm that was an angry mottled red. Bruises were already showing on her pale skin. A neat line of stitches ran the length of her arm. The nurse had obviously been trying to bandage it when Drew had come in.

"I hit my arm on that damned ugly set of drawers Mrs. Daniels has in her spare room. You know my skin is like tissue paper. They've thrown some stitches in there. It's done. I want to go home." Grandma watched the nurse wrap her arm, acting a little calmer now that Drew was beside her.

"She'd also fallen to the floor and the doctor wants to make sure she hasn't damaged or dislodged any of the plates inside her leg."

"I told you both, I didn't land on my bionic side. I fell on my good knee." Grandma looked up at Drew. "I'm not staying here. Don't let them keep me in here again."

"Does she have to stay?" Drew asked, not wanting to be in the hospital any longer than necessary herself.

"We're waiting on the results of the x-rays the doctor ordered. We want to make sure she hasn't broken her good knee. It's very swollen at the moment. The x-rays are our best chance to see what she's done to it." The nurse finished bandaging Grandma's arm. "Your grandmother is *very* determined to leave."

"Don't take it personally. We were in a bad car crash years ago. Neither of us really enjoy hospital visits." Drew knew all of Grandma's medical history was at the nurse's fingertips. If she wanted to know anything more, she could just look it up. Drew grabbed a chair and brought it to the side of the bed, all without her grandma letting go of her hand. Drew looked her over. Her grandma was trying so hard not to cry but was shaking like a leaf. She looked pitifully frail. Her pain, etched all over her face, broke Drew's heart. "I'm here now. I'm so sorry I didn't get here straight away."

"You were with Wren," Grandma said, more understanding about the situation than Drew was.

"Yeah, but I should have kept my phone close so I could have been here as soon as this happened."

If I'd just been at home, you would have been as well, and none of this would have happened in the first place. Drew couldn't shake that undeniable truth. Her grandma was lying in a hospital bed while Drew had been otherwise engaged. She'd been so busy with Wren that she'd forgotten everything and everyone else. Drew cursed the fact her grandma had gotten hurt while she was not around. "You're going to be okay, Grandma. Do you remember hitting your hip or bad leg?"

"I remember sleeping all night with Tigger sleeping on my chest, rumbling like a freight train, like he always does."

Drew knew Tigger was Mrs. Daniels's fat orange cat that her grandma absolutely adored.

"But that furry little goober wrapped himself around my ankles as I was coming back from the bathroom this morning and managed to trip me up." Grandma shot a look toward the open door and whispered. "Don't tell Mrs. Daniels, though. She's already feeling guilty."

Drew knew that feeling well.

"I caught my arm trying to grab hold of the drawers to keep me upright, but I couldn't grab it in time and cut myself on one of the handles. I lost my grip on my stick and went down like a ton of bricks, landing on the one good knee I have left."

"And she hit her face, which I'm about to apply some butterfly stitches to now, if she'll cooperate with me this time," the nurse said pointedly, gathering her equipment.

Drew gently eased her grandma's face around so she could see the damage. "Oh, Grandma." She mourned at the sight of dried blood streaking down her grandma's pale cheek.

"It's just a scratch. I didn't bang my head. I must have caught this on the drawers as well when I fell." Her grandma gave her a pointed look. "I've looked worse."

Drew's nightmare came back into sharp focus once more. She closed her eyes to fight against returning to the terror of being back inside that crumpled car again. The memories almost overwhelmed her, knowing only she and her grandma had survived.

The squeeze of Grandma's hand in her own brought Drew's eyes flying back open to see her concerned face looking at her.

"I dreamt about the accident this morning," Drew admitted quietly. She wondered if it had been a premonition.

"Did you wake Wren?"

"No, thank goodness. But I woke up with such a strange sense of foreboding." Drew smiled wryly at her. "Guess I was right in feeling a disturbance in the Force, eh?"

"I'm sorry. It was such a stupid accident. Usually, Tigger is such a good boy and doesn't get in the way of my feet, but today he was extra loving and has probably shed a week's worth of fur on my pajama pants. Which I'm still wearing because I couldn't get myself dressed in time before an ambulance rolled up to the door." Her grandma winced as the nurse started touching her face.

"Are you okay?" Drew asked, alert to every twitch and grimace.

"Hurts like a mother," Grandma gritted out, her eyes narrowed at the nurse in a death glare that the nurse studiously ignored.

"I won't take a minute," the nurse replied, continuing her task.

"Wren's out with Mrs. Daniels," Drew said, trying to keep her grandma otherwise occupied. She tried not to flinch out of sympathy at every hiss of pain Grandma let out.

"She came with you?"

"She had to. My car is still back at the store."

While the nurse attended to her grandma, a doctor came in with an x-ray in his hand. He fitted it against the light box and looked it over for a moment. Then he walked over to the bed, unceremoniously pulled back the sheet covering Grandma, and tugged up her pajama pant. Her grandma let out a cry and Drew clenched her fists.

The doctor took one look at Drew's furious face and gentled his hands. "Sorry," he said, easing the fabric up Grandma's leg much slower this time to reveal her knee.

Drew gasped at how bad the knee looked. "Is it broken?" she asked, fearing the worse.

"No, but it's dislocated. We're going to give her a sedative to relax her while we get it popped back into place then we can start her on some treatment to get that swelling down."

"You are not knocking me out," Grandma said, batting the doctor's hand away and trying, again, to get off the bed.

"I'll be with you the whole time, Grandma. The sooner you get this done, the quicker I can get you home so you can recover there." Drew deliberately blocked her grandma's escape path.

"I hate this so much," Grandma said, her voice pitiful and pained.

"I know." Drew looked up at the doctor. "How soon can you do it because if you don't do it fast, she *will* find a way to leave under her own steam, and neither you nor I will be able to stop her."

"You're going to have very limited mobility for a while," the doctor warned Grandma. "And with the damage you've already sustained on the opposite side you're going to have to be extremely careful."

"She's got a mobility scooter, wheelchair, and a walker at home," Drew told him. "And I care for her. I'll make sure she does everything she needs to in order to be mobile again, without rushing it and making it worse."

The doctor looked at Grandma who was staring him down. "I'll get this done as quickly as possible. You, stay in bed." He wagged his finger at her and gestured for the nurse to follow him outside for a quick consult.

"What is he? Twelve? He looks like he should still be in the sixth grade," Grandma said, her flash of bravado failing her as she started to shake again. Her eyes filled with tears. "I'm so sorry I fell."

"Grandma, these things happen." Drew stood up and carefully sat on the bed to hold her grandma in her arms without touching anywhere that could cause her pain. "I'm sorry I wasn't here straight away."

"Mrs. Daniels said she couldn't get through to you."

"My phone was in my jeans pocket. I never heard it ring." Drew agonized over that for the umpteenth time.

"Do I want to know which surface your jeans were hanging from?" Grandma chuckled weakly against her and hissed at the pain it caused.

"Stop sassing me," Drew grumbled, hating how small her grandma felt in her arms. "Or I'll ask for them to take your knee cap off so I can use it as a plant holder." Drew looked down at her. "Did they give you any medication yet?"

"No. Probably just in case I had to have something else, I guess."

"How bad are you hurting?" Drew could almost hear her grandma clenching her teeth against the pain she was obviously in.

"Bad enough."

"Grandma, what am I going to do with you?" Drew sighed and rested her head on top of her grandma's.

"Get me out of this damn place and take me home. The walls feel like they're closing in on me and I can't breathe in here. I hate these places."

"Soon," Drew said. "I promise we'll be home soon."

"Do you need to go tell Wren and Mrs. Daniels what's happening?"

Drew shook her head. "Not just yet. I'm not leaving you, Grandma. I'm right here."

Her grandma relaxed a little more. "You're a good girl, do you know that?"

"Remember that when I'm strapping a bag of peas around your knee to ice it."

Grandma ignored her. "You were always our good girl. Mine and your grandpa's. We should have taken you from them sooner. Your mother and my disappointment for a son didn't deserve you."

At that moment, Drew didn't feel anyone deserved her. She'd let down her grandma by making her wait over two hours before she got to her side. And Wren. Wren didn't deserve a lover who would never be able to fully commit to putting her and her needs first.

Drew didn't blame her grandma for any of this. It had been a silly accident. Drew had grown up putting her grandma's care before everything else. They'd only had each other and Drew took caring for her very seriously. Grandma was old and feisty, but illnesses or injuries left her heartbreakingly fragile. She *was* breakable, for all her tough exterior. Drew had looked after her, to the best of her ability, for years. Her grandpa had left her with that instruction and she'd done her best to fulfil his wishes.

Her grandma's accident had shaken Drew from the deliriously happy little bubble she'd been floating in with Wren. Her grandma had needed her, but Drew, wrapped up in pursuing her own selfish pleasures, hadn't been there. Drew wouldn't let her down again because when she'd needed rescuing, her grandma had fought for her. When they lay crumpled in the car wreck, it was Grandma's body that had shielded her from the crash. She'd raised Drew through the awful years that saw Drew struggling to start over anew.

Freed from abusive parents. No longer forced down roads she didn't want to take. Given choices instead of being told what to do.

Drew owed her everything. Even if that meant Drew had to forgo a personal life with Wren. No woman would or should allow herself to come second in any relationship. Wren deserved more than Drew could ever give her. Especially now, when her grandma would need all of Drew's attention while she healed.

Drew had had duty drummed into her from a young age. *To God, to family, to fame and fortune.* Drew had left the fame and fortune behind without regret. *To family* took on a whole new meaning once she lived with her loving grandparents.

Drew just couldn't move beyond her guilt at not answering the calls sooner. Still shaken by the nightmare that had haunted her for years, all Drew could hear was her mother's voice.

Friends are a distraction.

And lovers twice as much, Drew mourned.

Chapter Twenty

Wren knew there was something wrong the minute Drew came back to inform them what Mae had to have done. It felt like more than just worry for her grandma. She noticed Drew was very careful to make sure Mrs. Daniels knew that none of what had transpired was her fault. Mrs. Daniels still blamed herself though, arguing that she'd tried time and again to make sure Tigger didn't bother Mae so much. Tigger, however, never left her side on her visits and Mae doted on the animal too much for Mrs. Daniels to shoo him away from her. Drew confided that Mae was now fretting about the cat more than herself, worried in case she'd hurt him in her fall. Mrs. Daniels promised she'd check him over and let her know so she could calm Mae's fears.

Wren watched their interactions in silence. Drew was wringing her hands together in a nervous gesture until she caught Wren's gaze on her and shoved her hands deep into her jeans pockets.

"You both might as well go home," Drew said, finally including Wren in her conversation. "Grandma is sedated now and I don't know how long it will be after the procedure that they'll let me take her home."

"I'll take Mrs. Daniels home then come back to you." Wren noticed Drew looked surprised by her comment. Did Drew really think she was going to leave her here to deal with this all by herself?

Mrs. Daniels gathered up her handbag. "I'll just take a cab home, that way you can stay here and won't lose your parking space. Drew, you be sure to phone me when Mae is back home, okay?"

"Yes, ma'am."

Mrs. Daniels patted Drew's cheek and kissed Wren on hers. "We knew you two would make a perfect couple." With those last words delivered, accompanied by a sly wink, Mrs. Daniels walked away.

Wren deliberately didn't bombard Drew with questions or inane chatter. She hadn't grown up with a sister like Val not to notice when someone was brooding and needed only one push of the wrong button to explode. It was plain to see that Drew was desperate to get back to her grandma's side but was not happy about leaving Wren alone in the waiting room.

"Go. I'll be fine. I'll be waiting right here when you need me," Wren said.

The flash of pain in Drew's eyes and the closed off look that followed it was something Wren had never seen before on Drew's face. She understood Drew was stressed about Mae. But the Drew she had made love to last night was not this Drew who stood before her looking drawn, angry, and defeated.

"Drew..."

"I have to go. Grandma needs me and I've already let her down once today." Drew bit down hard on her bottom lip as if wishing the words unsaid.

But Wren heard them and understood them all too clearly. It was the same guilt Wren was feeling. If she hadn't suggested they have one night to themselves, away from the store, away from Mae, then they wouldn't be here. If they hadn't still been sleeping after a night of marvelous lovemaking, when the text messages started pinging through, Drew could have answered them and raced to Mae's side.

Wren knew exactly what was wearing at Drew. She felt the same. But it was too late to change things. Wren was ready to help both of them in any way she could to get Mae back on her feet again. She settled back down on the hard seat and got out her phone. The first thing she could do was make sure there was a meal ready when they returned to the apartment.

"Hi, Takira, I'm going to need your help."

❖

The ambulance brought Mae and Drew back to the store. Wren followed behind in her car and parked in the lot while the EMTs got Mae out of the vehicle and into a wheelchair. Once inside the building, they settled her on her stairlift to get her up to the apartment.

When she reached the top of the stairs, Drew lifted Mae off the seat and into her arms before the EMTs had a chance to react.

"I've done this before," Drew said simply and carried Mae into the apartment and straight through to her bedroom.

Wren thought how small and old Mae looked in Drew's arms. It nearly broke her heart to see someone she knew to be so feisty now looking tired and scared. The EMTs left within minutes of checking that Mae was comfortable. Wren stood alone in the living room, feeling a little lost. She had Takira's fixing them a light meal that they would deliver shortly. She knew Drew wouldn't have the time or thought to make something while she focused on getting Mae settled and calm now that she was finally home.

Drew wandered back into the living room and looked surprised that Wren was there. "She's fallen straight to sleep. I think the day has caught up with her."

"How are *you* doing, Drew? We've barely had a minute to talk."

"That's because I was too busy making sure my grandma was okay." Drew's voice was suddenly angry and biting. Wren blinked rapidly in surprise.

"That wasn't what I meant. I'm just asking if you're okay?" Wren knew Drew was shook by what had happened, that was plainly obvious. Her anger was something Wren hadn't seen before. And certainly not directed at *her*.

Drew's anger disappeared as quickly as it had flared. Her shoulders dropped and she looked embarrassed for having snapped at Wren. "I'm sorry. I just feel like this was something that should never have happened. If she'd have been here…"

"And *we'd* have been here instead of at my apartment for the night…" Wren knew that was niggling at Drew.

Drew nodded slowly. "This is why I don't leave her, Wren. She's independent and on her good days she can look after herself without a fuss. But it's times like this that I need to be there for. A fall for her is so dangerous. She tripped over a fucking cat and now she's immobile. She already has one side held together by pins and plates and now she's dislocated the knee on her good side. She can't walk and will need my help 24/7."

"She's lucky to have you." Wren believed that. She knew Drew would do everything in her power to keep Mae comfortable and to help her heal.

"But if I'd just been here, none of this would have happened." Drew ran her hands over her hair in despair. "If she'd have been home…"

"But she wasn't and you weren't. You were with me." Wren took a shaky breath. "It breaks my heart that everything beautiful about last night you're going to blame for what happened to Mae. Accidents happen, Drew. She's been at Mrs. Daniels's place before and nothing has happened. It's just unfortunate that the one night you spend with me, she falls."

"I should have heard the texts. I should have been waiting when they wheeled her into the hospital."

"But you weren't. But you were still there for her."

"I was late. Two fucking hours too late. She'd been there on her own while I lay in bed, fast asleep, totally oblivious." Drew sounded thoroughly disgusted with herself.

"Mrs. Daniels was with her," Wren reminded her. "She wasn't alone."

"Mrs. Daniels doesn't know what Grandma has been through. No one does. No one but me. Because I was *there*. Through it all, through everything, I have been there. And this time I wasn't."

"Because you were with me." Resigned, Wren straightened her shoulders, preparing herself for the final blow to strike. "Don't you think I feel guilty for asking you to spend one night away so we could be together without anything distracting us? Just one night was all I asked for. One night where the only thing that mattered was you and me and how we feel."

"Last night was everything I'd dreamed of with you," Drew said, her voice breaking.

"But it wasn't enough. Because today, you're blaming that one night for something that could have happened at any time, in any place." Wren sighed. "But it didn't, it just happened to be when you were with me."

"If we'd have been here..."

"But we weren't here, Drew, and I think that's the whole point of your argument. I asked you for something that turned out to be unfortunate given the circumstances we couldn't possibly have foreseen. But I've never asked you to choose me over your grandma. I'm just asking you to find a space for me too in your life."

"I don't think I can right now," Drew said, her voice low but audible.

The words cut through Wren with all the devastation of a flurry of double-edged blades. Each one cruelly sliced open her skin, exposing her to the bone, and leaving her bleeding out all over the floor. She closed her eyes for a moment, unable to see the agony on Drew's face any longer while she concentrated on steeling herself to answer back.

"You deserve more than this, Wren. I'm always going to be the one caring for my grandma. You deserve someone who can be there for you without them having someone else who comes first."

"But that's *been* you, Drew. You were there for me every time you came and stood at my car to see me before I went home. It was every time you left what you were doing in your store to spend an hour with me on my break. You've been there for *me*. Don't you dare try to break us up over someone who has never once come between us all this time."

"I'm sorry, Wren. I just can't deal with this right now. I have to do this alone." Drew's tired words were stark and final.

Wren knew Drew was worried about Mae. She knew there was something more to both their reactions in the hospital. She'd hoped Drew would tell her, explain it to her, open up to her. But apparently not. Wren felt her temper rise and though she knew this wasn't the most appropriate time, especially with Mae asleep in the next room, she had to speak. She'd kept her mouth shut all those trying years with Val assuming she could run her life for her. Drew had helped her see that wasn't how her life should be. Now Drew was breaking her heart into a million pieces and Wren was not walking out without speaking her mind.

"You're an idiot, Drew Dawes. You're going to let the best thing that has ever happened to you walk out that door, because of what? You want to spare me the 'trial' of helping you care for your grandma?" Wren was fuming. Drew's silence only made her angrier. "Goddammit, Drew, I'm *in love* with you." Wren watched Drew reel from her heartfelt confession. Drew's eyes glistened with tears, but her pain did nothing to soothe Wren's. "And I could love her too, because she's important to you. She'd never be a trial to look after; she'd be *family*."

Drew stifled a sob and Wren knew she needed to leave now or she'd never have the strength to. "I'm going to walk away now. This isn't the day for me to argue with you. You have enough to contend with. But this isn't over. So, when you come to your senses and realize you've just made the biggest mistake of your life, you know where I'll be."

Drew stared at her, visibly trembling, and the sight of Drew so broken tore Wren to shreds. She left before she pleaded with Drew to change her mind. Wren was stronger than that and had too much self-respect.

She stopped in the doorway, not turning around.

"When you find your voice, Drew, come find *me*."

CHAPTER TWENTY-ONE

The apartment was quiet. Her grandma was still fast asleep in her room and Drew was wallowing in her own misery in hers. Curled up in a ball on her bed, Drew lay exhausted by a lack of sleep from the previous night and drained by the new stresses piled on her in just a few short hours. She'd fretted over her grandma's new injury until she'd formed a tentative plan of how she'd manage. She'd cried until she had no more tears left over Wren. Drew knew she was stupid, but a part of her felt giving Wren an escape clause might have been the best thing in the end. It was just eating away at her inside, the look on Wren's face as she left. Drew rolled herself onto her back and stared at the ceiling.

I really suck at peopling.

She heard the doorbell ring and hoped whoever it was would just go away and leave her in peace. She didn't want to have to talk to anyone. She felt hollow and just not in the mood for conversation. A knock came on the door and Drew knew that was Noah. He was the only person in the shop with access to the apartment. She rubbed at her eyes and reluctantly got off the bed. She hoped he hadn't disturbed Grandma. She opened the door and there stood Noah, holding two large bags.

"Hey, Drew, I didn't think you guys were back home yet. Next door has just delivered these for," he checked the paper on the one bag, "Wren." He smiled at Drew. "That's your girl, isn't it?"

Drew couldn't answer and gave something close to a nod followed by a shake of the head.

"Looks like she's looking after you," Noah said, totally unaware. Drew didn't want to take the food. She guessed Wren had been the sweetheart Drew knew her to be and got them something for when they were ready to eat. Her insides rolled, reminding her she needed to eat to keep her strength up for her grandma.

"Drew, you look terrible. Is everything okay?" Noah shuffled his feet, obviously not wanting to intrude but aware Drew was not her normal self.

"Grandma had a fall this morning. We've been at the hospital for the last few hours. She's dislocated her good knee and hurt her arm so she's going to be pretty immobile for a while."

"Shit," Noah said, sympathizing. "If you need me to cover for you, you've got it. I'll even rope in those kids of yours so you don't have to worry about the store and just concentrate on Mae. We won't let you down, Drew."

Unlike me, Drew thought morosely. I let everyone down.

She liked Noah. He was short, bald-headed, and sported a full beard like the one worn by his gaming idol from the *God of War* series, *Kratos*. He also sported the most amazing *God of War*-themed tattoo sleeves that Drew never tired of watching him add to. He was intensely loyal and honest to a fault. Drew hated she'd have to rely on him so much because of Grandma's accident. She'd make it up to him. Noah, Dakota, and Owen, who were all going to have to fill in for her.

"I'll keep the keys for now if you want," Noah said. "That way I can open up and you can just wander down and check on the store when and if you can."

"Thanks, Noah. I don't know what I'd do without you."

Noah smiled. "You were there for me when Trevor left and took all my savings, the dog, and my entire Queen collection. You're an amazing boss. I've told you; I'll work in the store for you until I drop dead there." His charming grin finally made Drew smile.

"Please don't. Dakota would either try to sell you or keep you to use as a tailor's dummy," Drew said, not really joking.

Noah laughed out loud and rubbed at his belly. "With this poor excuse for a six-pack? I think not." He patted Drew's arm. "You need me? You know where I am." He headed back to the shop while Drew tried not to hear Wren's same words echo around in her head. The bags were full as always when Takira's delivered food. Drew pulled out thick sandwiches and salads accompanied by pasta and cheese. Wren had to have ordered these for all of them. There were three separate meals packed.

Of course, Wren had expected to stay.

Drew opened the second bag and found a box. She hesitated before opening it. Wren knew her so well and Drew didn't know if she had the guts to acknowledge that over something as simple as dessert. She opened the lid and found three slices of cake. Coconut for her grandma, one she'd been raving about for a week now. A rich fruit filled cake for Drew, and a second piece exactly the same. The piece that Wren would have pretended was for herself but would have left for Drew. Just like she did every break time they had shared together.

Drew closed the box and fought herself not to give in to more tears. She knew she'd done the right thing. She'd spared Wren being stuck with her. Someone who still fought the nightmare of an anger-fueled car crash. Someone who could never make her grandma an afterthought while Drew indulged in a shiny new life with a lover. Someone who couldn't sing, even though it had once meant the world to Drew. The same someone who hadn't had the guts to tell Wren that she loved her too before stupidly blaming her for an accident that Drew now knew, with a clearer mind, wasn't really *anybody's* fault.

Drew sat at the table with a thump, put her head in her hands, and cursed herself for not coming to that realization sooner. Before Wren walked out the door. Before Drew even began to be so stupid and lashed out at whoever was closest in her fear of losing her grandma.

But it was too late. The words spoken. The anger spilled. The silence deafening.

Drew desperately needed to do something, anything, to deal with the myriad of feelings churning inside her. She checked in on her grandma who was still sleeping with her leg and arm propped up on pillows. Drew pulled the door to a little more and then went straight to her room. She closed the door and flung open her closet. This time, with no hesitation, she pulled out her guitar case and grabbed the guitar. She didn't listen to any of the doubts in her head as to why she shouldn't put her fingers to the strings. Drew didn't want to think about anything but the need to play. The urgency to immerse herself in a melody like she used to. To lose herself in a song. To play once more, for no one but herself.

At first, she had no melody in mind, she just strummed, plucked, and felt the guitar vibrate with its own special heartbeat. Slowly, the music formed structure and transitioned into the beautifully haunting song, "Never Be Mine," from the magical mind of Kate Bush. The yearning lyrics, tinged with a heavy air of grief, tumbled from Drew's lips unbridled. She sang quietly at first, her voice only gaining volume as her confidence rose. She sang of the pursuit of a fantasy lover that would, sadly, never exist in reality. She knew this singer was Dante's favorite artist. She wondered if she could ever do the songs justice to Dante's ears. For now, she sang only for herself, immersed in the music that had once been her only safe haven, before becoming her road to hell. The guitar felt right in her hands, the strings a necessary vibration against her fingertips. This time as Drew sang, she finally felt some of the weight of the past slip from her shoulders. The music started a healing process on her soul. The more she played, running one song into another and then another, the more the joy of music returned to her heart. It retook its special place there.

This time, the weight of each melody wasn't a burden.

This time, the music was hers again and she welcomed it home with open arms.

It was hours later, when Drew was pulling out the meals from the fridge, that she finally heard sounds coming from her grandma's room. She knocked softly on the door and popped her head around it.

"You ready for something to eat?"

Grandma's face lit up. "Hell yes! I'm starving. I missed out on my breakfast and whatever it was that nurse brought me wasn't the most appetizing of things."

"Hospital food never is. I recommend we don't go there again." Drew easily scooped her grandma up into her arms and took her to the bathroom. Grandma didn't need any help in there. It already had all the aids she needed. Drew was soon helping her back into the living room and settling her on the sofa. Her grandma sat with her leg elevated and an ice pack in place to start bringing down the swelling on her knee.

"I'm getting too old for this shit," Grandma grumbled, trying to get comfortable.

"Me too, so don't do it again." Drew positioned her grandma's TV tray closer to her and set out her meal.

"Where'd all this come from?" Grandma rubbed her hands together, ready to dig in. "It looks like Takira's."

"I think Wren ordered it." Drew busied herself with her own meal, feeling all shades of guilty for eating what Wren had so kindly gotten for them.

"Where is she? I thought you'd both be inseparable after yesterday. Tell me you had sex. I don't need all the salacious details, but tell me you at least did more than Netflix and chill."

"Grandma!" Drew knew she was blushing.

"Judging by the color of your face I'd say you did and it was good!" Her grandma drawled the last word out, teasing her. "So, where'd she go? There's enough food here to feed the three of us."

"She...I..." Drew didn't know how to explain. It sounded so stupid after the fact.

Her grandma put her fork down and stared Drew down. "What did you do?"

Drew hated that she knew her so well. "I was angry at myself for not being at the hospital and the fact that, had we been *here*, none of this would have happened. You wouldn't have fallen."

Grandma stared at her. "So, let me guess, you were angry at yourself but blamed *her* for wanting some private time last night?"

The carefully controlled tone she used made Drew want to hang her head in shame. It worked better than a raised voice ever had.

"In my defense, I was working on very little sleep, was frightened out of my wits that you'd gotten hurt, and I hate damned hospitals as much as you do. If I hadn't been so distracted..."

"I wasn't dying. It was a dumb accident between me and that lard ass Tigger. It could have happened any time I have stayed at Mrs. Daniels's. In fact, it's not the first time he's tripped me. I just managed not to fall those other times."

"You've never mentioned that." Drew was horrified.

"Why would I? Do you think you'd stop me from staying there because of him? I think not, young lady. It's just what cats do and I'm usually more aware of him. This time the little varmint managed to trip me and I couldn't stop myself from falling. It's no different from me tripping here over the edge of a rug. It happens. It's just one of those things. It *wasn't* your fault. I didn't trip over the cat because you were out with your girlfriend, getting hot and steamy. You weren't *distracted*, Drew, you were living your life like you should be doing."

Drew couldn't look at her and her grandma let out a long sigh.

"I fucking hate your mother and the 'everyone and everything is a distraction' line she deliberately brainwashed you with to keep you friendless and alone. She did it so all you'd have was her role for you to fulfill. It was to *control* you. Just like that whole 'duty' roll you had to recite. Don't let her still control your life, Drew. Not from the grave." Her grandma waved her fork around angrily. "I swear, if she wasn't dead, I'd kill her. I'd kill her, bury her, dig her back up, and kill her again for what she did to you."

"I think dreaming of the crash then waking up to find you were back in the hospital just messed with my head. I was so angry. I didn't know what to do with how I felt. But I lashed out at the wrong person. It's unforgiveable."

Grandma started eating again. "You don't usually do anger. You could seriously out-zen Keanu Reeves in that regard."

"I think I was angry at myself, more than anything. I promised Grandpa I'd always look after you and I failed."

Her grandma shook her head. "You can be so damn literal at times. He didn't mean you were to look after me, and only me, to the detriment of your own happiness. You're allowed a life of your own. You're allowed to fall in love, Drew. You're allowed a night out to cut loose and be fancy-free." Her grandma twirled her fork in her pasta, chasing after the cheese. "Sometimes I can't help but wish you'd been more of a player with the ladies."

Drew frowned at her. "*Really?*"

"Yes. Maybe, if you had more experience with relationships. then you'd know what to do once you found the right one. And I think Wren is the right one for you, isn't she?"

Drew nodded. "She's everything. But it frightens me realizing how much I could lose myself to her."

"It's never a loss, Drew. You'd be gaining so much back. Don't you think you've spent long enough alone? And before you argue, *I* don't count."

"You'll always count, Grandma," Drew said.

"Well, I brought you up better than to treat someone so poorly for no reason. You need to apologize to Wren. You need to show her you're sorry for being such a dumbass and let her see how much you need her."

"She'll probably want nothing to do with me. I fucked up so bad." Drew poked at her salad, knowing she'd screwed up spectacularly and had no clue how to even begin to fix it.

"She works at a restaurant. Phone up for a booking. Tell her you're throwing a pity party. Table for one." Grandma chuckled at her own wit and just kept eating.

Drew huffed at her. "This isn't funny," she grumbled.

"No, it's not. This is your future we're talking about. A future with a woman who adores you. It's plain to see that. And one who still takes care of us, even when you've been a total jackass and broken up with her."

"Technically, I don't think we broke up. She kind of walked out before anything was made official." Drew hated that she sounded so pathetic. Wren was mad at her, now her grandma was mad at her, and Drew was mad at herself. This was not one of her better days.

"So, what now? You're on a *break*?" Her grandma looked at her incredulously. "How do you screw up breaking up with someone? Drew, what the hell did you *do*?"

Drew shrugged. "I have no idea. All I know is I felt so sure I was doing the right thing, but now all I feel is lost and empty."

"Fix it." Grandma brandished her fork at her. "Quit thinking you have to sacrifice everything for the sake of your own happiness. Go get that girl back. Your grandpa and I always told you, everything you ever want, love, or dream of, grab it and don't let go."

Drew played with her food a little. "How do I apologize to Wren, Grandma? I did an unforgivable thing. I hurt her and I don't ever want to do that again."

Her grandma pondered a moment. "See, if you just paid more attention to those romantic chick flicks you avoid like the plague, you might have a clue how to put things back together again."

"I'm not watching *Bridget Jones* with you again. I swear I lost brain cells that one time you made me watch it." Drew made a disgusted face at her. Rom-coms would never be her genre.

"You need a big, romantic gesture. Something that will knock her off her feet with how smooth you are."

"Smooth is the last thing I am."

"You need something like a huge bouquet of flowers or maybe you could inundate her with chocolates. You could even write her poetry. I know you have a way with words. You'd have been writing your own songs if you'd been left to your own devices."

Drew took all the suggestions gratefully and mulled them over. She eyed the cake box she had placed on her TV table. She felt torn. She knew she didn't deserve the treat. Grandma nudged her to shake her from her musings.

"I'm only going to say this once, Drew. Making poor Wren feel like she had no place in your life because of me? I don't like the sound of that at all. That's not fair to her or me." Her grandma's voice wasn't harsh but, instead, desperately disappointed.

That cut Drew right to her core.

In the moment that Drew had blamed Wren, responsibility and need had clashed. Neither had come out victorious. Drew had disappointed the two women she loved the most.

She had to fix this.

"Flowers and chocolates, you say?" Drew looked sheepishly at her grandma.

"Always worked with your grandpa and me."

"I don't remember you two ever arguing." Drew tried to remember an instance but couldn't.

"That's because I was always right and he knew it." Grandma's impish smirk made Drew laugh finally.

"So, Wren will always be right?"

Her grandma nodded. "Learn it early, my child. That way, you won't screw up again. Remember, the bigger the gesture, the more you show how sorry you are. A simple Hallmark card isn't enough to fix this mess you've created."

Wren had told Drew she loved her. Drew was going to have to fix it all, put everything right, and show Wren how much she loved her too.

When you find your voice, come find me.

Drew didn't think flowers or chocolates were enough to fix her mistake. But she had an idea.

She just didn't know if she had the guts to go through with it.

Chapter Twenty-two

Wren settled herself in her seat and opened an app on her phone. She kept a watchful eye out and quickly dialed a number. She smiled as Mae's face appeared on her screen.

"Hi, Mae. How are you feeling today?" Wren was grateful to see Mae looking a lot better than she had a few days ago. Wren had deliberately chosen not to go to see her at the apartment but she had phoned her every day and they FaceTimed.

"All the better for seeing you, Wren. How are you doing, sweetheart?"

"Oh, you know, working hard. Someone has to keep Takira's running to its owner's high standards."

"Good thing she's got you then." Mae squinted at the screen. "Where are you?"

"Sitting in my car out in the parking lot. I'm parked out front so I can make sure Drew is in the store so I can talk to you. I feel like I'm low-key stalking her." From her vantage point, Wren could see Drew talking to Dakota. Wren yearned to go in and see her. She made the most of what she could see now, knowing Drew would soon be back upstairs, tending to Mae.

"She knows you call. She has some weird sixth sense about it. Either that or I'm really bad at keeping secrets now. I think she guessed after the first call left me smiling like a fool. I told her it was just a friend checking up on me, but I know she saw straight through that. She just said she was glad I had a friend who made me smile like that."

"Your granddaughter is driving me certifiably crazy, Mae." Wren shook her head, exasperated by Drew not getting in touch with her yet. It had been four days with no contact and it was making Wren insane.

"I know. In her defense, she has been stuck by my side as we try to work out how I can navigate the apartment without her having to carry me around."

"I still can't believe she can do that." Wren had been very impressed that one time she got to witness it. Before Drew had been an asshole. Before Wren had walked out.

"She thinks I don't know why she started weight training years ago. It did give her that neat little six-pack she sports. I'm sure you've seen it." Mae grinned into the camera at her. "Seems that girl had been preparing ahead of time for when I got older and less mobile."

"She's always had your best interests at heart, Mae. And yes, I've seen it. It's very impressive." Wren recalled running her fingers over each and every line, feeling the muscles twitch beneath Drew's soft skin. *And I'd have liked to have seen more of it*, Wren groused to herself. The hours they'd spent together in each other's arms had made Wren hunger for more. She hoped Drew was feeling even a fraction of the separation anxiety Wren was experiencing. Coupled with the insatiable need she had to just storm into the comic book store to drag Drew off to yell at her, shake her until her teeth rattled, and then kiss her senseless. Wren knew Mae was watching all these emotions play across her face. Caught, Wren had to ask, "How is she?"

"Miserable. Sorry for what she did. Beating herself up about it. It was so unlike her, Wren. My Drew never gives in to the Dark Side."

Wren had to chuckle at her. "You spend way too much time with her. She's made you geeky."

"I've been there every step of the way as she embraced her geeky side. You pick up the lingo." Mae paused a moment. "She wasn't really angry at you, you know that, right?"

"I know she wasn't. She was furious and frightened and kicking *herself* for not being there for you."

Mae nodded. "We're all the family we've had for years. Her parents died. Arthur died a few years after that. We've looked after each other ever since. I should have gone into a nursing home, but Drew has always been adamant I would be with her."

"Because you mean the world to her. You've been there for her, especially after the accident."

"Arguing with Mary-Louise while she was driving like a maniac was not my most well thought out of plans. For my sins, I didn't walk away unscathed. In fact, for a long time, I didn't think I'd ever walk again." Mae got a distant look in her eye as she remembered. "The firemen made sure Drew never saw the wreckage. But I did. I saw what remained of them. But I couldn't grieve for them, not after what they'd done to Drew. And they were intending to do worse. They took her God-given talent for singing and whored that child out, grabbing what money she made, and making her life a misery every goddamn day." Mae was silent for a long moment, then shook herself, as if ridding herself of the memories. "You hang in there for her, Wren. She just needs to get her head on straight, but she's worth it."

"I know she is, Mae. I have to stop myself every day from coming into the store and taking my break with her. Or from storming up those stairs of yours and demanding she talk to me. It can't be me, Mae. This has to be *her* choice. I'd already made mine and she took it from me."

"She sat out on the balcony on Monday, you know, to make sure you got to your car after your shift. She came back in looking quite despondent."

Wren knew why. "My shift altered this week. I'm starting earlier and going home at a more reasonable hour."

"You've parked your car elsewhere too."

"I'm not going to make this easy for her, Mae. I'm allowed to be petty. She hurt me. I understand why, but she can't think I'm just going to sit on my hands and wait for her to be standing by my car as if nothing has changed."

Mae nodded in understanding. "God blessed me with just the one grandchild. She's been the light of my life since I first cradled her in my arms. Now she carries me in hers. I've loved that girl from the moment I set eyes on her. But I have enough love in my heart for two granddaughters, Wren. You've been a long time coming into our lives."

Wren felt herself start to tear up. "Drew told me early on that you two came as a packaged deal."

"Yeah, but truth be told? *I'm* the better part of the deal. I'm older, more experienced, and I have my own set of wheels. I'm a catch, I tell you." Mae winked at her.

Wren laughed at Mae's incorrigible ways. "I'll bear that in mind." She shook her head at Mae's own laughter. She was so glad to hear it after all Mae had been through.

"Drew says I should be able to come to Takira's next Friday to get me out of the apartment." Mae looked so excited. "She's had a word with Dante about seating me somewhere my leg is out of everyone's reach."

"Really? That's great. I'll have to make sure all your favorites are on the menu."

"I want your lasagna," Mae said without hesitation.

"You've got it," Wren said. "I'll make sure you get spoiled. We've missed you."

"I've missed coming in. I know it's silly. The restaurant is literally just next door, but it's become such a happy place for me to visit. I get excellent food, get to see you and the others there…"

"Sit and gaze adoringly at Mrs. Daniels…" Wren couldn't resist teasing her.

"Hey! One day she's going to look up across that table and realize I'm exactly what she's missing out on. We Dawes girls are quite the catch." Mae ran a hand through her hair, preening.

"Yes, you are." Wren caught movement in the store. She could see Drew leaving. "Looks like Drew is on her way back up to you. I'll speak to you tomorrow, Mae."

"Okay, sweetie. Don't you work too hard and don't give up on her. She's just hardheaded sometimes."

"Let me guess, she gets that from you?"

"She got all her best features from me. God only knows where she got her lanky string bean build though."

"Not eating enough lasagna," Wren said, enjoying Mae's laughter. "I hope you feel better, Mae."

"I always do after speaking to you, sweetheart. I love you, Wren."

Wren felt her lips quiver with the sudden rush of emotion that struck her. "I love you too, Mae."

The screen went off and Wren fought to compose herself before heading back into the restaurant. She found Dante helping out at the bar, preparing coffees.

"Hey, I hear we have a special visitor returning next week," Wren said to her.

Dante hesitated for a split second before smiling. "Yes, Mae's coming in. I'm setting up a special table for her so she can sit comfortably. Mrs. Daniels will be in attendance too, as always."

"Can't have one without the other," Wren agreed.

"It will be good to have Mae back. The restaurant needs customers like her."

"*Family*," Wren said, realizing that was at the heart of Takira's. The food was important, but it was the atmosphere and the people the restaurant drew back time and again that made it work.

Dante gave Wren a look. "Did you get to speak to Drew this time?"

"No, she's still MIA."

"She'll come round," Dante said. "She'd be an idiot to let you go. And I don't think she's that."

Wren smiled at Dante and patted her on the arm as she passed by her. "You're such a romantic, Dante."

"So my girlfriend tells me." Dante skillfully added milk to the round cup she was holding, making a pretty heart-shaped pattern on top of the coffee. She handed it to Wren. "You're not due back on yet. Go take five minutes for yourself. Takira is making a new dish, she'll want your opinion when you're back."

Wren carried her cup off to find a seat and just zone out for a moment before she threw herself back into the fray. She looked around the restaurant, watching the customers enjoying their food, seeing the staff go about their work. Wren knew the dream of her own restaurant was something her father, and then Val, had groomed her to achieve. But seated in Takira's, surrounded by the familiar sights, sounds, and smells, Wren didn't think anything could compare to the sense of home she felt there.

All she needed was the love of her life by her side. Drew was just a parking lot away but, at this precise moment, that felt like a million miles.

Wren took a sip from her coffee and watched as the milky heart changed shape with every sip until it disappeared. Wren drank the rest down quickly. No matter what, she had a restaurant to run. Mae was coming in next week. Wren wanted to check she had all the ingredients necessary to make her some rich and gooey fudge brownies to accompany her lasagna. If she couldn't spoil Drew at the moment like she wished, then she'd make sure her grandma ate like a queen. Wren had grown up learning at her mother's side that making food was as good as a declaration of love. Food was also a great comfort tool and making it gave Wren the peace of mind she craved.

Maybe she'd have Mae take one home specifically for Drew. Remind her what she was missing.

"Wren! Come try this!"

Takira called to her from across the kitchen. Wren quickly put a clean apron on and went to investigate, grateful to have her mind directed anywhere than on the comic book store owner next door.

Friday dawned and Drew took one final look at herself in the mirror. Her T-shirt, emblazoned with a rainbow-colored star field, had a tiny Tardis tumbling through it. Drew's insides felt like she was in that traveling box. She took a deep, calming breath, then let it out slowly to quiet the jangling of her nerves. Everything was set. Her guitar was waiting for her in the living room. Dante had come to escort her grandma next door to the restaurant. Grandma had looked surprised that Drew wasn't going with her, at least to get her settled in. Drew had other plans though and had let Dante look after her grandma for her. That had been half an hour ago and Drew was now psyching herself up to leave the apartment. For a moment, staring at the front door, Drew could almost see the heavy curtains that lined a stage's wings. She could hear the crowd waiting. Could feel the sharp dig of her mother's hands clamped onto her shoulders ready to shove her forward to perform. Drew took another breath.

"Not today, Mother. It's no longer about you."

Her mind set, Drew picked up her guitar. She'd already tuned it. The instrument was ready even if she wasn't one hundred percent sure she was. Drew diligently locked the apartment behind her and walked down the stairs. She was thankful none of her staff came to see her leave. She needed to focus. She needed to be able to walk to the restaurant without chickening out.

The sun was bright when she stepped out her back door. It blinded her, just like the stage lights always had. In a flash, she was back on a stage before an expectant audience, defenseless like a lamb to the slaughter. She blinked against the light and the memory was gone.

Drew made her way around her store to the parking lot of Takira's. Her heart began to race the closer Drew got to the entrance. She stood back to let customers enter first. With a quick look at her watch, Drew walked in behind them.

There's no turning back now.

Drew caught sight of Dante standing at the bar, waiting for her as they'd discussed. Drew would be forever grateful that Dante had given her the go-ahead for her crazy plan.

Drew looked around the restaurant and found her grandma. She picked her way through the tables to be nearer to her but not seen by her. Not yet. She hung her guitar around her neck and settled it in her hands. She already had drawn some attention from the customers, who were whispering among themselves, wondering what she was doing. Drew waited then heard the restaurant's background music fall silent as Dante turned it off. The room suddenly seemed too small and Drew had to close her eyes to stop herself from panicking. She gripped her guitar and held on to the fact that, somewhere in that kitchen, was Wren. She opened her eyes again and the room steadied. Drew looked over to Dante to let her know she was ready. She spotted Kae quickly take a spot beside Dante, her iPad held steady, and obviously set on record. Drew shot her a disgruntled look, but both Kae and Dante just grinned back at her.

The room was Drew's. She sidled up behind her grandma, leaned in, and kissed her on the cheek. Grandma startled then smiled up at her. She opened her mouth to say something but caught sight of the guitar in Drew's hands instead. Tears filled her eyes.

"Oh, sweetheart," she whispered, her voice choked.

Drew shut her mind to everything and everyone else in that huge room. She focused on Wren, put her fingers to the strings, and began to sing to her. Everyone in the restaurant stilled. All eyes were on Drew. She stayed beside her grandma for a moment, soaking in her support. Drew sang the first few lines of a Taylor Swift song that fit the occasion perfectly. "How You Get the Girl" was a step-by-step guide on telling someone who'd been at fault in a relationship how to get their girl back. Drew loved how it encompassed everything she wanted to say but had been too tongue-tied and stupid to utter.

She had her eyes fixed firmly on the kitchen as she sang. She could see the staff in there.

And then she saw Wren.

Drew began walking through the restaurant toward her, never missing a beat as she weaved her way around chairs and shopping bags. She poured her heart out in every line of the song, singing only for Wren who was staring at her through the kitchen pass through with the most beautiful stunned look on her face. This was Drew's heartfelt apology. This was Drew taking back the music and making it her own again. This was Drew showing everyone in that room that she was there for Wren. She was singing every word *to* her. To make her realize that Drew wanted her, would work hard to deserve her, and that she wanted her back.

By the time Drew got to the bar, Wren was waiting for her there. She looked beautiful in her apron, with her hair tied back. Her eyes were shiny with unshed tears because she had to know what it was taking for Drew to do this. To perform before a group of people, to be this exposed, to have her voice *heard*.

Drew stopped in front of her and sang the last lines of the song directly to her. She saw nothing but the beautiful face of the woman she loved and sang her heart out with the joy that feeling gave her. This was Wren. She was all that Drew needed to complete her life.

If she could find it in her heart to forgive her. If she'd take on all that came with being with Drew.

If she'd be hers.

With the last words sung, the restaurant erupted into cheers. Drew only had eyes for Wren.

"I found my voice," Drew said to her. "And I'm in with love you too."

Wren's gorgeous smile lit up her whole face and she threw herself at Drew, only for the guitar to get in the way. Drew quickly took it off and passed it to Dante without even looking. She welcomed Wren into her arms for a kiss that made her world right itself again in its orbit. They only parted when a loud whistle pierced the air.

Drew looked over at her grandma. She had her fingers in her mouth, whistling the loudest for them. Drew spotted other people with their phones raised. She didn't care. She had Wren back in her arms where she belonged.

"I've missed you," Drew said, holding Wren tight, frightened to let go.

"Well, it was worth twelve days of hell for that performance." Wren kissed her again, her eyes shining with pride. She peeked around Drew. "Dante, can we go hide in your office a minute while our lives are splashed all over YouTube?"

Dante waved them off, handing Drew her guitar back. Drew, her hand held tightly in Wren's, paid no attention to the customers calling for an encore. She'd done what she'd had to do.

She just hoped it was enough to get Wren back in her life.

Chapter Twenty-three

M indful that Wren had to go back to work, Drew left after so many kisses and just a few words. She wasn't going to talk with Wren about personal things in Dante's office. She'd gotten a promise from Wren that she'd come to the apartment after her shift finished. Drew had snuck out the back door of the restaurant. She knew that with so many phones recording her performance, sooner or later someone would work out who she was. Or, more likely, who she *had* been. There was a part of Drew that was frightened people would recognize her from the past. But the other part of her, the part that had deliberately walked into the restaurant ready to sing her heart out, didn't care. Young Drew Dawes had hung up her guitar and stepped off the stage. Older Drew ran her dream store and was only just finding her long buried talent again. If nothing else, it would bring publicity for Dawes & Destiny Comics.

Inside the blissfully quiet apartment, Drew sat on the sofa and laid her guitar beside her.

"Thanks, old friend," she said, running her hand over the guitar's still shiny wood and tracing her name on the body. "I won't leave it as long next time, I promise." Drew rested her head against the back of the sofa and tried to relax. Wren had kissed her. She hadn't had Drew kicked out of the restaurant. And Drew had actually sung in public, without passing out. Drew's mind was awhirl with all her chaotic thoughts. Sacked out on the sofa, Drew was surprised when she heard the unmistakable sound of the chair lift in use. Drew checked the clock. She'd sat for over half an hour, lost in her own world. She got up to help Dante bring her grandma home.

It wasn't Dante at her grandma's side. Wren used Grandma's key to open the door.

"Express delivery!" Wren said, moving into the apartment so Drew could help her grandma out of the chair.

Grandma reached for Drew and hugged her tightly once Drew had her in her arms. "You were fantastic! I always feared you'd keep that voice of yours hidden forever. But hearing it today..." Grandma's smile was full of pride. "I thought your voice was unmatched as a child, but this voice now? This voice is *magnificent*."

Drew smiled at her. "This voice will sell comic books and superheroes. I'm never going back, Grandma."

Her grandma nodded. "I know. And I'm glad, because that world nearly killed you. But will you at least sing 'Happy Birthday' to me at my birthday soon? You haven't done that since you were a child."

Drew nodded. "If I can remember the words..." She grinned as her grandma huffed at her. "Where do I need to put you?"

"I've just gotten spoiled rotten at Takira's. My 'welcome back' lunch was to die for. I need a nap to let it all settle. Also, Mrs. Daniels talked my ear off and wore me out." She peeked around Drew's shoulder. "Wren, you'll still be here when I wake up, yes?"

Wren nodded. "I'll be here, Mae."

"Good. It's where you belong." Her grandma looked up at Drew and whispered, "Don't screw this up again!"

Drew dutifully carried her into her bedroom, removed her shoes, and got her grandma comfy on her bed. Grandma smiled up at her.

"God, it was good to hear you sing today. I can die a happy woman having heard that."

"Grandma, you are not dying yet," Drew warned her.

"Of course not. Not when I have to be here to listen to you sing at your wedding." Her grandma's eyes sparkled. "I told you this was the woman who'd be perfect for you."

"There's nothing more annoying than an 'I told you so' person," Drew said, teasing her.

"Has Taylor got a song you can sing at it though?" Grandma said. "I know you've always listened to her music over the years. I saw how much it tore at your heart not to sing along."

Drew pondered a moment. "Lover" would be perfect. She'd just have to change the *him* to *her* in the lyrics. She frowned when she realized what her grandma was up to. "Stop putting ideas into my head. I've got to go apologize first before you can work out which belt buckle is suitable wedding attire."

"Oh, honey, I had that one picked out years ago when you were just a little girl." She snuggled into her pillow. "Go sort things out with that gorgeous woman of yours. She's waiting for you."

Drew placed a kiss on her grandma's forehead. "Sleep your food off. I'll wake you up later if there's champagne popping." Drew stopped at the door. "Oh wait, you're on painkillers. Just apple juice for you, then."

"You're not too big for me to ground you, Drew Dawes," Grandma said without any menace behind it.

Drew just laughed at her and closed the door behind her. She found Wren sitting at the kitchen table, nervously twirling a spoon.

"There's a big part of me that wants to just drag you into your bedroom and pick up where we left off from that Saturday but I know we need to talk first."

Drew swallowed hard. This was going to be more nerve-wracking than her picking up her guitar and singing had ever been.

❖

Drew deliberately sat down opposite her. She saw the surprise in Wren's eyes at her choice of seat.

"If I sit by you, I'll be tempted to hold your hands and I won't be able to stop there and I really need to apologize before we go any further." Drew tried to stop herself from reaching out across the table instead. "Did Dante kick you out of the restaurant?"

Wren smiled. "Pretty much. She said she knew we had to talk, and that they'd probably get very little work out of me today after your performance. So Takira took my apron off me, put it on herself, and shooed me out to help bring Mae back. Dante pushed her all the way home." Wren got a shy look on her face. "Mae held my hand all the way here, gushing about your singing. She was so happy and very proud of you."

"I'm just thankful I didn't give her a heart attack."

Wren's laughter was a beautiful sound, but she soon turned serious once more. "I wasn't expecting you to do that. Come into the restaurant, carrying a guitar, *singing* to me."

Drew nodded. She'd surprised herself. But it had been worth it. "I found my voice, like you told me to. What was the point of me telling you to follow *your* dreams when I couldn't even let myself sing anymore? I've been keeping that side of me pushed down and silenced for way too many years."

"Did you miss it?"

"Yes. Because singing was such a big part of who I was. It was my talent, my blessing, but my mother took it, like she took so much of my life, and twisted it until it became a nightmare to perform. I didn't have many good memories linked to my singing by the time I stopped doing it."

"How did you feel today?"

"Scared, at first. But then I focused on why I was there and what I was singing for. I was in a room, packed full of your customers, but I was singing for *you*. I was singing *because* of you."

"I love your voice. It's a shame the whole world doesn't get to hear it, but if you'd have followed that path in life we'd have never met." Wren reached across the table for Drew's hand. "And if I'd have followed my father's urging and gotten my own restaurant by now, we wouldn't have met either."

"Everything has a reason," Drew said. "That makes more sense now." She gripped Wren's hand in her own. "I'm sorry. I'm sorry for what I said and how I acted."

"You were frightened for your grandma, I understand that."

"Yes, but I could have dealt with it better. I shouldn't have taken it out on you." Drew still felt awful. She'd been so stupid and couldn't justify her actions.

"You're going to have to realize you can't control everything in your grandma's life, Drew. She's undeniably fragile at times, but she's fought so hard to keep her independence and to have an active social life outside of her disabilities. And you need to let yourself do the same. You can't hover over her 24/7, just waiting for the worst to happen. You'll never enjoy the time you have with her, otherwise. You've already had to give up so much in your life." Wren stared at her and smiled sadly. "I just didn't expect my place in your life would be another you'd choose to lose. Especially over an accident neither of us could have seen or avoided happening."

Drew nodded, feeling totally ashamed. "With hindsight, it's safe to say I was an utter fucking idiot. In blaming myself for not being there I also blamed you. I was just so frightened to hear she was in the hospital again. Back when the car accident happened, she was so broken. She suffered so many setbacks in her treatment it kept her in the hospital way longer than she should have been. Having all that happen while I was grieving the loss of my parents…" Drew took a breath and couldn't help but remember that time. "For all the abuse my parents put me through, they were still my parents. And I mourned for them, while at the same time, I felt a profound sense of relief they were no longer alive. That's a horrible feeling for a child to carry. As an adult I understand it, but twelve-year-old me thought I was a monster for being glad they were gone."

"You weren't, you were a child finally freed from an abusive family. I'm so glad you got to grow into the woman I see now because that woman is amazing."

"I'm constantly terrified my grandma will die," Drew said, finally giving voice to her worse fear. "It's just been the two of us for so long and I've cared for her since I was twelve. When my grandpa was dying, he asked me to look after her. I've done what he asked, but I'd have done it anyway. She's my grandma. She came for me when I needed her to get me away from my parents. She helped me through my schooling, and college, and through all the jobs I did until I had enough experience to get my own store and move us away from the past to start new." Drew hung her head. "But I'm so scared she's going to die. I'll have no family left at all then. I have no cousins, no siblings, just the memories of parents who sold out my childhood. I'm just thankful I had loving grandparents who showed me how family should be." She took a moment. "When I heard she was in the hospital, I felt I'd let her down. That I was too busy with you to have made sure she was safe."

"You can't control everything, Drew."

Drew loved the look of understanding in Wren's eyes. "There was a big part of me that felt I was selfish to want a life of my own. Rest assured, Grandma gave me her thoughts on that. But it doesn't erase the fact I hurt you by blaming you, blaming *us* for being together, when I should have realized that you were right by my side through it all. You never left until I made you. And that was unforgiveable of me. I didn't realize what I had until you were no longer there beside me."

"I'll always be there, Drew. I love Mae. She makes the place in my heart, that still mourns the loss of my own grandma, ache a little less now. If you'll let me, I'd love to look after the *both* of you. For one thing, you'll never go hungry. I'm told I'm quite the whiz in the kitchen." Wren playfully blew on her nails and buffed them up on her shirt.

"Can you forgive me for what I said and did?"

"I already did, Drew. When I walked away but didn't *leave*."

"You've been in daily contact with my grandma, haven't you?"

Wren nodded. "I was worried about her but didn't want to see you until you were ready to come to me of your own volition. You had to make the first move."

Drew couldn't believe how calm and understanding Wren was. She didn't deserve her. But she'd fight every day to prove she did, even if it took her a lifetime.

"I'm sorry I hurt you. I'm sorry I made you have to walk away because I was being so crazy. I'm sorry it took me so long to come to my senses, I shouldn't have left you waiting without a word."

"You had Mae to deal with. I understand. But if *either* of us screw up again, we'll talk about it there and then. No more walking away, no more keeping things bottled inside. You and me, our own little band of *Avengers*."

Drew laughed with her. Wren jumped as her phone rang. She took it out of her pocket and glared at the screen. "It's Zenya." Wren answered the call. "Hi? *Really*? I'll be sure to tell her, thank you." Wren ended the call and began searching for something on her phone. She held it out to Drew. "Apparently, someone recognized you and you're gaining traction on the internet."

Drew let out a sigh. "Yeah, I kinda figured that would happen when everyone in the damn restaurant had their cameras out. Including Kae. At Dante's request, no doubt."

"Yes, Kae very kindly sent me a copy for posterity. Yet you still did it, knowing your past could come to light once more?"

"I'd do it every day for eternity if it meant I got to show you how much I love you." Drew looked at the comments on the internet and shrugged them off. "If they think they have a comeback story then they're going to be very disappointed. What I did today was just me, playing love's refrain, for the woman I love. That's part of *our* story, not theirs."

Wren stood up and Drew stared up at her, not sure what was happening. Wren held out her hand and wiggled her fingers for Drew to take it.

"Well, are you going to show me your bedroom or not? I foresee I'm going to be spending a lot of time in there so I might as well start now."

"You'll move in with us?" Drew couldn't believe how lucky she was.

"Eventually, if there's room in your Batcave for me." Wren pulled Drew closer. "And we're going to have to talk about your kitchen. I might have to update it a little so I can work in it."

"You can do what you want to it," Drew said, letting Wren guide her to the opposite side of the apartment.

Wren waited expectantly at the door. Drew opened it and ushered her inside, making sure to close the door behind her even though her grandma was well out of earshot. She watched silently as Wren took in her room. It wasn't wall to wall heroes. Instead, there were gaming screenshots of sunsets and landscapes framed on the walls, and a large TV screen with her game consoles underneath.

However, it was the large glass case that held her most prized statues that Wren gave her full attention to.

"I'm seeing a theme here. Women in revealing clothing with whips," Wren said.

"Actually, Wonder Woman has the Lasso of Truth so, technically, not a whip," Drew said, looking over Wren's shoulder at all the statues of the Princess of Themyscira. They were Drew's prized possessions.

Wren pointed to a different set displayed on a lower shelf. "And this woman in the tight leather gear, high heels, and definitely a whip?"

"Catwoman," Drew dutifully explained but had a feeling Wren already knew.

"Just how many figures of her *do* you need?" Wren smirked at Drew over her shoulder.

"All of them," Drew said, grinning back.

"These have a special place in your bedroom."

"Yes, they do. Wonder Woman is my favorite superhero and Catwoman is my favorite anti-hero." Drew gathered Wren close in her arms. "But they've got nothing on you so you needn't feel threatened by the presence of Diana Prince or Selina Kyle in my room."

"Do you think that for Halloween Dakota could help me get into a suit like that?" Wren pointed to a Catwoman. Her smile was as seductive as the burning look in her eyes. Both ensnared Drew immediately.

"I'd think so," Drew said, pretending to consider it. "And believe me, I'd be more than happy to help you *out* of it."

Wren laughed and tugged Drew down to kiss her. Drew's mind wiped out any thought of Wren in a skintight catsuit. All she knew was Wren was in her arms again. Nothing else mattered. Time to release her tight hold on control and just *be*.

"How long do we have before Mae stirs?" Wren began pulling Drew's T-shirt up over her head.

"Two hours, maybe three because of the pain meds." Drew let her jeans drop to the floor in a heap before she began helping Wren out of her clothes.

"Let's make the most of that."

The feel of Wren's soft skin made Drew mourn the brief time they'd been apart. She never wanted that again. Drew began undoing Wren's hair from its confinement. "It's such a shame to have to tie all this beautiful hair back," she said, running her fingers through the length, playing with its softness.

"Kitchen regulations," Wren said. She reached up and brushed her fingers along the shaved sides of Drew's head. "I missed you, Drew."

Her words, laced with heartbreak, made Drew determined never to cause Wren pain again. "I missed you too. I'll do better this time, treat you better, take you on more dates."

"I don't need dates, Drew, I just need you."

"You've got me," Drew promised.

Wren smiled up at her, cupping Drew's face in her hands. "Taylor was right then."

Puzzled, Drew waited for Wren to explain. Wren's beautiful smile dazzled her as she reached up for another kiss.

"This is *exactly* how you get your girl," she murmured against Drew's lips before kissing her again.

CHAPTER TWENTY-FOUR

Takira's was a loud and happy place. Wren watched the party happening through the kitchen pass through and marveled at how many people were there celebrating Mae Dawes's seventy-fifth birthday. Wren couldn't believe it had been a month since Mae's accident. She was still healing and grumbling about the physio she knew she was going to have to start soon. This evening, however, Mae was holding court as the birthday girl. She was totally in her element as the center of attention.

Takira and Dante had arranged the party for her and Wren had been working on the menu in secret for a few weeks. The restaurant's designated party area was full of Mae's Old Biddy Brigade and their wider circle of friends. Mrs. Daniels was there, rarely leaving Mae's side. Wren's mother was there as a new edition to the brigade. As expected, Wren's mother and Mae got on like a house afire. Wren had a sneaking suspicion that sooner, rather than later, her mother would be looking for a smaller place to live and seemed very keen to make Columbia her new home. Every time she'd visited in the past month, she'd been more and more reluctant to go back to that big empty house alone. Wren had a feeling she'd soon be welcoming her to the restaurant every day too.

Wren picked up the tray of fudge brownies she'd had cooling nearby and headed back out toward the party. She wasn't supposed to be on kitchen duty that evening, but she couldn't help but make sure everything was just so for the guests. The rest of the customers seemed to be enjoying the atmosphere from the party too. They were about to be privy to free entertainment.

A karaoke machine was set up for the party. Drew had installed it herself.

Wren could see Drew talking to Trent and Juliet at their table. Harley and Finn had been at the party briefly. They'd sat with Mae and had some cake and ice cream with their honorary grandma until Juliet's sister, Kayleigh, who was their designated babysitter for the evening, had ushered them upstairs. Baby Natasha was with them too and Wren knew Dante had set up a little party of their own so they didn't feel left out. Wren noticed Ana was glued to Drew's side. She was so happy Ana had found a kindred spirit. Once the news had leaked about Drew being *that* Drew Dawes, and Ana had seen the footage of Drew's performance for Wren, Ana had shyly asked if Drew would show her how to play the guitar. She'd picked it up very quickly and Wren knew Mae was thrilled to sit in on their lessons and listen to them play and sing together.

Wren loved hearing Drew sing. She didn't do it all the time, but when she did, it was always special. Wren especially loved it when she was lying snuggled up in Drew's arms, slipping into slumber, and Drew softly sang her to sleep. Even if Drew never released her voice back out into the world, Wren knew Drew was at peace with it now.

"I can see why this place has such an appeal."

Wren turned to find Val at her side.

"Mama never shuts up about what a great place you are running." Val looked around the huge floor. "Do you think Takira would be interested in a buyout?"

Wren bristled. "Val…" she said. Val just grinned at her. Wren blinked in shock. Val rarely cracked a smile, let alone *grinned*.

"I'm joking. Lighten up, Florencia. It's a party." With a sly smirk that Wren was way more familiar with, Val wandered off to make her way around the tables.

Wren watched as Mae spotted Val and waved her over. For some totally bizarre reason, Mae and Val got on incredibly well. But then, Wren thought, she didn't know anyone who didn't fall in love with the Dawes women.

Her favorite one was walking her way and Wren couldn't help but smile. Drew was looking very handsome in her short-sleeved white shirt and *Doctor Who* bow tie. She'd left the cropped pants at home tonight and was just wearing black jeans that molded to her like a second skin and made Wren want to drag her from the room right that second. Drew couldn't have missed the intention radiating from Wren because she smiled and wagged a finger at her.

"Shame on you, Wren Banderas. This is a respectable party." Drew kissed her quickly. "No naughty thoughts are allowed amid cake and ice cream."

"I'd rather we had a party of our own," Wren said, straightening Drew's tie.

"Later, I promise. I'm sure I saw some Cool Whip around here somewhere we could take back with us." Drew grinned wickedly at her.

"Are you ready to give your speech?" Wren asked, knowing that was why Drew had come over to her. She could see how nervous Drew was.

Drew nodded. "Yeah, then we can have the cake brought out. I'm desperate to have a piece. It looks soooo good."

Wren wrapped her arms around Drew's waist. "I'm on cutting duty so I'll make sure you get an extra big piece as a treat for what you're about to do."

Drew took a deep breath in then let it out. "Okay, let's get this party started." She kissed Wren. "Wish me luck."

"You don't need it, you're Drew Dawes. Go make Mae's night."

Wren tried not to be too obvious about watching Drew's butt in those jeans as she walked away. Wren made her own way back to the main table and Mae reached out for her hand as soon as she came close.

"Hey, sweetheart. What's that granddaughter of mine up to?" Mae watched Drew pick up a microphone.

"She's doing the speech before your cake gets wheeled out," Wren said.

Drew's voice sounded out in the restaurant. "I'd like to thank everyone for coming tonight to celebrate the birthday of Mae Dawes, otherwise known as Grandma. We've lived here a few years now and we never dreamed we'd find such an amazing family of friends to welcome us home." Drew looked out at everyone then turned to her grandma. "Grandma, I'd hoped you'd be dancing at your seventy-fifth birthday, but we'll save that for another time. Thank you for always being there for me, and now for Wren. We love you very much. Happy birthday, Grandma!"

Music began to play and Drew kept a hold of the microphone for another reason. The heady mix of synthesizers and orchestra burst through the speakers and Drew began to sing. Mae let out a squeal as Drew began a spirited rendition of "Xanadu," especially for her. Wren watched in amazement as Drew bust out the moves that she knew Olivia Newton-John had performed in the movie. Mae had made Wren watch it with her one evening. Drew really had the voice and execution of the song down to a tee. Wren silently mourned the fact that Drew would never perform professionally again but, watching her here and seeing the adoration on Mae's face at what Drew was gifting her, it didn't matter. Drew used her singing to show her love now and that was more than enough for Wren. The whole room was watching her and dancing in their seats. As the song drew to its end, Wren couldn't help but be impressed by how high and how long Drew held that last note. The whole restaurant burst into applause. Drew turned a brilliant shade of red, but it was only her grandma's approval she looked for. Mae had her arms out wide for Drew to kneel down beside her and receive the biggest hug.

Takira wheeled out the cake. It was a three-piece creation, spelling out Mae in three different flavors of sponge and icing. Drew had already earmarked a piece from the cookies and cream letter E. Wren readied her knife to make sure Drew had the second slice. They had photos taken while everyone in the whole restaurant, including Drew, sang "Happy Birthday" to Mae. Then Wren started to cut the cake to feed everyone. The servers took slices from another cake to distribute to the other customers' tables so they wouldn't miss out in the celebration.

Drew made her way back to Wren's side again. "This is really good cake," she said, savoring each mouthful.

"There are three smaller versions of each cake so that Mae can have some from each one. Vanilla, chocolate, and cookies and cream. They're in the kitchen for us to take home later." Wren loved how Drew's eyes lit up at that.

"Grandma will love that. I will too." She looked over at the table where her grandma, Mrs. Daniels, and Wren's mother sat eating and chatting. "Your mama is staying with Mrs. Daniels tonight so she can spend tomorrow with us, apparently."

Wren shook her head. "We need to find her a home here before she starts sleeping on the sofa permanently."

"She's lonely, but when she's here she has so many new people to chat with. And Grandma loves her."

"Does Mrs. Daniels know?" Wren couldn't resist whispering that in Drew's ear.

Drew laughed. "Not like that!" She made a face. "That would make us what? Sisters? *Grand-sisters*? No, that's not happening!"

Ana came bouncing up to Drew, her face bright with excitement. Drew had put her empty plate down and was taking a long drink from her water bottle first. "Hey you. Are you ready to raise the roof?"

Ana nodded and gave Wren a squeeze. "This is the best party!"

"Guess I'll see you after the show," Wren said, loving the happy look on Drew's face.

"I'll save the last song for you," Drew said.

"You'd better. It's the only one I know." Wren tugged Drew down for one more kiss before she took to the stage once more.

Mae was in for a treat. Drew had gathered together all those who could hold a note, and a few who couldn't but nobody really cared, to hold a small karaoke party in Mae's honor. Ana and Drew were going to start the night off. Wren knew they'd been plotting and planning in secret, but Drew wouldn't tell her what they were going to do.

Ana was bouncing on her toes holding her microphone, eager to start. Drew messed with the machine and more eighties inspired music sounded out. This time it was Taylor Swift's "Welcome

To New York" playing. Wren had a feeling her niece would have chosen a Taylor song. Both she and Drew put on sunglasses and took up their stance. The pop song was very catchy and Wren noticed how everyone was bopping along in their seats. Drew sang and danced with Ana as if they'd always performed together. Their voices harmonized incredibly well. Wren would have to ask Drew how she'd managed to keep it secret that she could dance too. Ana was a revelation and Wren surreptitiously watched Val's jaw drop at her daughter holding her own with someone who had been a young musical talent. Someone who had been fielding calls and messages asking her to record again. Drew had refused them all. The old fans who remembered her had found her store but, while Drew had been welcoming, she'd made sure they left knowing that Dawes & Destiny Comics was the only future Drew had in mind.

Ana and Drew gave way to Elton and Monica, both dressed as impeccably as always in their signature gothic style. They sang Within Temptation's "Somewhere." Monica took the lead vocals, but they sang it as a duet. Wren had to admit, she'd never seen that coming. She saw Mae enjoying every minute. Mae loved music so much. It was ironic that her granddaughter had such a gift for it but would never reach for the fame she could have had within her grasp. Wren knew Mae just wanted Drew to be happy. And she was, with her comic book store.

And with Wren.

Drew came behind Wren and leaned down to rest her head on Wren's shoulder. She wrapped her arms around Wren's waist and swayed them both to the music. "You having fun?"

Wren nodded. "Who knew our friends could sing so well?" Wren marveled as Zenya gave a very spirited rendition of Tina Turner's "The Best" aimed at Mae. Kae was cheering for her from the bar. "Mae's loving it."

"She loves music. Always has. Things might have turned out different if her influence had been behind me as a child and not my mother's."

"I love you just the way you are. The geeks of the world need you more." She leaned her head back to rest it against Drew's.

Dakota stepped up to the mic next, wearing a short skirt, cowboy boots, and a long fringed white jacket covered in a multitude of rhinestones. They caught the lights and sparkled like a mirror ball. She wore a blond wig that was a riot of curls. The cleavage on show gave away who she was going to be before the music even started. Everyone began to rock out to her spirited "Jolene."

"Ten dollars says Grandma wrestles that jacket off Dakota before the song ends," Drew said in Wren's ear, making her laugh.

Mrs. Daniels looked up at them both and smiled. She leaned over to Mae. "Look at how cute they are together. There's just something so sweet about two women together, don't you think?"

Wren saw Mae nod very carefully as if not quite sure where this conversation was going.

"Maybe, after Mr. Daniels died, I was looking in the wrong direction. Perhaps I should have been looking for female company. I mean, look at us. We get along just fine!" Mrs. Daniels patted Mae's arm. The next singer came on and Mrs. Daniels's attention went right back to the podium.

Mae looked a little startled. In a daze, she looked up at Wren who just grinned back at her. Mae swallowed hard then slowly smiled back. *Best. Birthday. Ever,* she mouthed at Wren who giggled at Mae's renewed vigor.

"What are you laughing at?" Drew asked, totally oblivious to what had just happened.

"Life, Drew Dawes. Life with my favorite two girls. It's never going to be boring, is it?"

"No, and it's only going to get better when we pick up our kitten tomorrow." Drew squeezed Wren a little more. "Our first fur baby."

"And you won't change your mind on the name?" Wren knew Drew was adamant what their new pet's name would be.

Nope. The little critter is a stripey ginger cat. He can only have one name."

"Jonesy." Wren shook her head. While Mae had watched musicals with her, Drew had made her sit through *Alien* and *Aliens.* She knew exactly where the name had come from.

"It's classic," Drew said. "Comes with a guaranteed Ellen Ripley seal of approval."

"It's geeky," Wren shot back, deliberately teasing her.

"So am I." Drew nuzzled into Wren's neck, tickling her, and making her squirm. "But you love that about me."

"I do," Wren admitted. "Who knew that a Dawes would become *my* destiny?"

"We'll bring Jonesy home tomorrow, then once he's settled in, the builders can start on your new kitchen."

Wren couldn't wait. Some of the money she'd been saving for her own restaurant was going toward the modernization of the apartment's kitchen. She was buying them a dishwasher too, much to Drew's delight. Wren was already spending most of her time in the apartment over the store. She was just working out her lease and then she'd move in permanently. Drew had already cleared the spare room out for her to have a space of her own if she needed one to escape to or a place to work.

"What are you thinking about, my love?" Drew asked, still rocking Wren in her arms.

"Us, building a life together. All I can say is, thank God your grandma asked me out for you."

"Hey! I did my own asking too!"

Wren stole a kiss from Drew's pouting lips. "Yes, you did. So, in our time-honored tradition…" Wren reached into her pocket and handed Drew something.

Reluctantly, Drew released her hold on Wren and accepted the paper. She unfolded it, read it, then stared at Wren.

"I went with Disney Princesses on my invite for you. You can't expect superheroes all the time. And look, this one has Tiana on it. She's a chef too. Seemed appropriate."

Drew read the invitation over again. "You're inviting me to the food night held here at Takira's next week? The one you've all been working on?"

Wren nodded. "Mae's already got her name in and I know you said you'd come anyway, but I thought you'd like a formal invitation in a style that is kind of growing on me." She and Drew had taken to giving each other children's party invitations for the craziest of reasons. Date night, lunch breaks, TV marathon weekends. Invitations to the bedroom that seemed to be Drew's favorites. She knew Drew kept them all pristine, tucked away in a special folder. Drew had explained why to her one night. The next day Wren had gone out and brought three different packs and was going to use them at every opportunity she could find.

Wren was saving one for a marriage proposal.

Not yet, but one day she'd ask. Unless Drew beat her to it. But Wren wanted that kind of permanence with Drew. To make a family with her. An unusual family to be sure. Two women, a feisty grandma, and a cat named Jonesy.

Wren hadn't always been sure what she wanted for her future, but she knew one thing for certain. She wanted Drew there with her, every step along the path *they* chose to walk on, together.

The End

About the Author

Lesley Davis lives in the West Midlands of England. She is a die-hard science-fiction/ fantasy fan in all its forms and an extremely passionate gamer. When her games controller is out of her grasp, Lesley can be found seated at her laptop, writing. Her book *Dark Wings Descending* was a Lambda Literary award finalist for Best Lesbian Romance. Visit her online on Twitter @author_lesley

Books Available from Bold Strokes Books

A Haven for the Wanderer by Jenny Frame. When Griffin Harris comes to Rosebrook village, the love she finds with Bronte de Lacey creates a safe haven and she finally finds her place in the world. But will she run again when their love is tested? (978-1-63679-291-0)

A Spark in the Air by Dena Blake. Internet executive Crystal Tucker is sure Wi-Fi could really help small-town residents, even if it means putting an internet café out of business, but her instant attraction to the owner's daughter, Janie Elliott, makes moving ahead with her plans complicated. (978-1-63679-293-4)

Between Takes by CJ Birch. Simone Lavoie is convinced her new job as an intimacy coordinator will give her a fresh perspective. Instead, problems on set and her growing attraction to actress Evelyn Harper only add to her worries. (978-1-63679-309-2)

Camp Lost and Found by Georgia Beers. Nobody knows better than Cassidy and Frankie that life doesn't always give you what you want. But sometimes, if you're lucky, life gives you exactly what you need. (978-1-63679-263-7)

Felix Navidad by 'Nathan Burgoine. After the wedding of a good friend, instead of Felix's Hawaii Christmas treat to himself, ice rain strands him in Ontario with fellow wedding-guest—and handsome ex of said friend—Kevin in a small cabin for the holiday Felix definitely didn't plan on. (978-1-63679-411-2)

Fire, Water, and Rock by Alaina Erdell. As Jess and Clare reveal more about themselves, and their hot summer fling tips over into true love, they must confront their pasts before they can contemplate a future together. (978-1-63679-274-3)

Lines of Love by Brey Willows. When even the Muse of Love doesn't believe in forever, we're all in trouble. (978-1-63555-458-8)

Manny Porter and The Yuletide Murder by D.C. Robeline. Manny only has the holiday season to discover who killed prominent research scientist Phillip Nikolaidis before the judicial system condemns an innocent man to lethal injection. (978-1-63679-313-9)

Only This Summer by Radclyffe. A fling with Lily promises to be exactly what Chase is looking for—short-term, hot as a forest fire, and one Chase can extinguish whenever she wants. After all, it's only one summer. (978-1-63679-390-0)

Picture-Perfect Christmas by Charlotte Greene. Two former rivals compete to capture the essence of their small mountain town at Christmas, all the while fighting old and new feelings. (978-1-63679-311-5)

Playing Love's Refrain by Lesley Davis. Drew Dawes had shied away from the world of music until Wren Banderas gave her a reason to play their love's refrain. (978-1-63679-286-6)

Profile by Jackie D. The scales of justice are weighted against FBI agents Cassidy Wolf and Alex Derby. Loyalty and love may be the only advantage they have. (978-1-63679-282-8)

Almost Perfect by Tagan Shepard. A shared love of queer TV brings Olivia and Riley together, but can they keep their real-life love as picture perfect as their on-screen counterparts? (978-1-63679-322-1)

Corpus Calvin by David Swatling. Cloverkist Inn may be haunted, but a ghost materializes from Jason Dekker's past and Calvin's canine instinct kicks in to protect a young boy from mortal danger. (978-1-62639-428-5)

Craving Cassie by Skye Rowan. Siobhan Carney and Cassie Townsend share an instant attraction, but are they brave enough to give up everything they have ever known to be together? (978-1-63679-062-6)

Drifting by Lyn Hemphill. When Tess jumps into the ocean after Jet, she thinks she's saving her life. Of course, she can't possibly know Jet is actually a mermaid desperate to fix her mistake before she causes her clan's demise. (978-1-63679-242-2)

Enigma by Suzie Clarke. Polly has taken an oath to protect and serve her country, but when the spy she's tasked with hunting becomes the love of her life, will she be the one to betray her country? (978-1-63555-999-6)

Finding Fault by Annie McDonald. Can environmental activist Dr. Evie O'Halloran and government investigator Merritt Shepherd set aside their conflicting ideas about saving the planet and risk their hearts enough to save their love? (978-1-63679-257-6)

Hot Keys by R.E. Ward. In 1920s New York City, Betty May Dewitt and her best friend, Jack Norval, are determined to make their Tin Pan Alley dreams come true and discover they will have to fight—not only for their hearts and dreams, but for their lives. (978-1-63679-259-0)

Securing Ava by Anne Shade. Private investigator Paige Richards takes a case to locate and bring back runaway heiress Ava Prescott. But ignoring her attraction may prove impossible when their hearts and lives are at stake. (978-1-63679-297-2)

The Amaranthine Law by Gun Brooke. Tristan Kelly is being hunted for who she is and her incomprehensible past, and despite her overwhelming feelings for Olivia Bryce, she has to reject her to keep her safe. (978-1-63679-235-4)

The Forever Factor by Melissa Brayden. When Bethany and Reid confront their past, they give new meaning to letting go, forgiveness, and a future worth fighting for. (978-1-63679-357-3)

The Frenemy Zone by Yolanda Wallace. Ollie Smith-Nakamura thinks relocating from San Francisco to her dad's rural hometown is the worst idea in the world, but after she meets her new classmate Ariel Hall, she might have a change of heart. (978-1-63679-249-1)

A Cutting Deceit by Cathy Dunnell. Undercover cop Athena takes a job at Valeria's hair salon to gather evidence to prove her husband's connections to organized crime. What starts as a tentative friendship quickly turns into a dangerous affair. (978-1-63679-208-8)

As Seen on TV! by CF Frizzell. Despite their objections, TV hosts Ronnie Sharp, a laid-back chef; and paranormal investigator Peyton Stanford, have to work together. The public is watching. But joining forces is risky, contemptuous, unnerving, provocative—and ridiculously perfect. (978-1-63679-272-9)

Blood Memory by Sandra Barret. Can vampire Jade Murphy protect her friend from a human stalker and keep her dates with the gorgeous Beth Jenssen without revealing her secrets? (978-1-63679-307-8)

Foolproof by Leigh Hays. For Martine Roberts and Elliot Tillman, friends with benefits isn't a foolproof way to hide from the truth at the heart of an affair. (978-1-63679-184-5)

Glass and Stone by Renee Roman. Jordan must accept that she can't control everything that happens in life, and that includes her wayward heart. (978-1-63679-162-3)

Hard Pressed by Aurora Rey. When rivals Mira Lavigne and Dylan Miller are tapped to co-chair Finger Lakes Cider Week, competition gives way to compromise. But will their sexual chemistry lead to love? (978-1-63679-210-1)

The Laws of Magic by M. Ullrich. Nothing is ever what it seems, especially not in the small town of Bender, Massachusetts, where a witch lives to save lives and avoid love. (978-1-63679-222-4)

The Lonely Hearts Rescue by Morgan Lee Miller, Nell Stark, Missouri Vaun. In this novella collection, a hurricane hits the Gulf Coast, and the animals at the Lonely Hearts Rescue Shelter need love, and so do the humans who adopt them. (978-1-63679-231-6)

The Mage and the Monster by Barbara Ann Wright. Two powerful mages, one committed to magic and one controlled by it, strive to free each other and be together while the countries they serve descend into war. (978-1-63679-190-6)

Truly Wanted by J.J. Hale. Sam must decide if she's willing to risk losing her found family to find her happily ever after. (978-1-63679-333-7)

A Good Chance by Ali Vali. Harry, Desi, and Desi's sister Rachel are so close to getting everything they've ever wanted, but Desi's ex-husband is coming back to get his revenge and rip apart their chance at happiness. (978-1-63679-023-7)

A Perfect Fifth by Jaycie Morrison. Streetwise pianist Zara Keller and Lady Jillian Stansfield couldn't be more different; yet their connection brings a new awareness of who they are and what they truly want in their lives—including each other. (978-1-63679-132-6)

Catching Feelings by Ana Hartnett Reichardt. Andrea Foster expected to catch a lot of pitches from the Alder Lion's star pitcher, Maya, but she didn't expect to catch feelings. (978-1-63679-227-9)

Defiant Hearts by Lee Lynch. In these stories, you'll find your lovers, friends, and lesbians you wish you knew—maybe even yourself. (978-1-63679-237-8)

Love and Duty by Catherine Young. All Princess Roseli wants is to marry her three lovers, but with war looming, she must instead marry Princess Lucia to establish a military alliance between their planets. (978-1-63679-256-9)

Murder at Union Station by David S. Pederson. Private Detective Mason Adler struggles to determine who killed a woman found in a trunk without getting himself killed in the process. (978-1-63679-269-9)

Serendipity by Kris Bryant. Serendipity brings jingle writer Annie Foster and celebrity pop star Bristol Baines together, and their undeniable attraction keeps them close, but will their different paths drive them apart? (978-1-63679-224-8)

The Haunted Heart by Jane Kolven. A ghost, a ring, and a quest to find a missing psychic—it's a spell for love. (978-1-63679-245-3)

The Rules of Forever by Nan Campbell. After reconnecting at their high school reunion, Cara and Lauren agree to embark on a textbook definition friends-with-benefits relationship, but trying to keep it uncomplicated is harder than it seems. (978-1-63679-248-4)

Vision of Virtue by Brey Willows. When virtue and desire come together, be prepared for sparks in this next installment of the Memory's Muses series. (978-1-63679-118-0)

Cherry on Top by Georgia Beers. A chance meeting leaves Cherry and Ellis longing for a different life, but when Ellis's search for truth crashes into Cherry's insta-filter world, do they have any hope at all of a happily ever after? (978-1-63679-158-6)

Love and Other Rare Birds by Angie Williams. Ornithologist Dr. Jamie Martin and park ranger Rowan Fleming are searching the Alaskan wilderness for a bird thought to be extinct and they're about to discover opposites really do attract. (978-1-63679-108-1)

Parallel Paradise by Mayapee Chowdhury. When their love affair is put to the test by the homophobia of their family, community, and culture, Bindi and Rimli will need to fight for a chance at love. (978-1-63679-204-0)

Perfectly Matched by Toni Logan. A beautiful Cupid named Hannah, a runaway arrow, and just seventy-two hours to fix a mishap that could be the best mistake she has ever made. (978-1-63679-120-3)

Royal Exposé by Jenny Frame. When they're grouped together for a class assignment, Poppy's enthusiasm for life and love may just save Casey's soul, but will she ever forgive Casey for using her to expose royal secrets? (978-1-63679-165-4)

Slow Burn by Missouri Vaun. A wounded wildland firefighter from California and a struggling artist find solace and love in a small southern town. (978-1-63679-098-5)

The Artist by Sheri Lewis Wohl. Detective Casey Wilson and reclusive artist Tula Crane are drawn together in a web of passion, intrigue, and art that might just hold the key to stopping a killer. (978-1-63679-150-0)

The Inconvenient Heiress by Jane Walsh. An unlikely heiress and a spinster evade the Marriage Mart only to discover true love together. (978-1-63679-173-9)